Roger Keen is a writer, filmmaker and film critic with a special
interest in surrealism, counter-
contributed to many award-winn
and Channel 4, and his short sto
reviews have appeared in numero
lit memoir, *The Mad Artist: Psych*
published in 2010.

C000000806

Praise for *The Mad Artist*:

'…a significant addition to the canon of psychedelic literature.' —
Leaf Fielding, author of *To Live Outside the Law*

'The whole story is a delight from beginning to end.' — William J
Booker, author of *Trippers*

'I highly recommend this book to anyone with an interest in
psychedelics, good writing and the human condition.' — Rob
Dickins, Editor-in-Chief The Psychedelic Press UK

'…one of the best UK drug memoirs, highly recommended.' —
Professor Harry Sumnall, Liverpool John Moores University

'…a dazzling, intelligent and ambitious quest to cut through
conventional ways of looking at the world that ultimately yields
impresssive and potentially life-changing results.' — Noel
Megahey, *Digital Fix* reviewer

Also by Roger Keen

THE MAD ARTIST:
Psychonautic Adventures
in the 1970s

LITERARY STALKER

Roger Keen

Darkness Visible

First published in Great Britain in 2017
by Darkness Visible Publishing

www.dv-publishing.com

ISBN 978-1-9998516-2-0

For Jacqueline

What is done out of love always happens beyond good and evil.

Friedrich Nietzsche, *Beyond Good and Evil: Prelude to a Philosophy of the Future*

Author's Note

The version of the British horror- and fantasy-writing community presented here is a fictionalised one. The genre conventions Horripilation and Medusacon are my inventions, as are the magazines *The British SF & Fantasy Review*, *Miskanthropic* and *Tamaghis*; and also the Decahedron Press and the Blue Nebula bookshop. Where real-life authors, such as Neil Gaiman, make brief cameo appearances, the settings and action are entirely fictitious and bear no relation to actual events. All the other characters are fictitious and any resemblance to actual persons, living or dead, is purely coincidental. The town of Tormartley and the country villages of Coombe Monkdown and Dillisbury, and their environs, are also invented and have no real-life counterparts.

R.K. 2017

1. Theatre of Blood

This book is a work of fiction – but what does that mean anyway? Who can say where the boundary between the real and the invented exactly lies? All novels have chunks of real life in them, some more than others. Well this one will have rather a lot more than others! Any resemblance between the characters depicted here and real people is *not* coincidental. And since everything is preordained anyway, there is no such thing as coincidence!

I stop typing and read back what I've written from the screen. Not too bad…has a certain pithiness to it. For an opening paragraph it appears to have legs, but I've began many metafictional novels in this kind of way before and they've not stayed the course, so will this latest effort – *The Facebook Murders* – be any different?

I like the title certainly – it's catchy, it attracts attention, it makes you want to know more. Those three words on the shiny spine of a pristine paperback in Waterstones would seduce you into taking it off the shelf and giving it a skim, don't you think? Similarly on Amazon, that'd be a book you'd check out once its title and a suitably ghoulish cover had popped up in a list or as a thumbnail. Yes, I can see it now…

THE FACEBOOK MURDERS

Nicholas Chatterton

And the content too will be arrestingly macabre. The central premise of the novel is taken from one of my favourite hoary old Hammer horror films: *Theatre of Blood*, staring Vincent Price as the deeply wronged, crazed and vengeful Shakespearian actor Edward Lionheart. Having survived a suicide attempt, Lionheart makes up a hit list of the critics who've given him disparaging reviews and he bumps them off one by one, each in a different stylised theatrical setting taken from a Shakespeare play. So, for example, critic Snipe is speared and his corpse dragged behind a horse, depicting Hector's fate in *Troilus and Cressida*; and critic Larding is drowned in a butt of wine at a tasting, evoking the unfortunate end of George, Duke of Clarence in *Richard III*.

Similarly in *The Facebook Murders* psycho-nutter author Jago Farrar draws up a list of his fellow writers, editors, critics and so on who've annoyed him on Facebook or disrespected his person or his work in some other way. Therefore Jago revenges himself on those who, say, made inflammatory or disparaging comments on his wall, unfriended him, refused to 'like' his author page, rejected his stories or otherwise undermined him as a writer, either online or in the pages of magazines – that kind of thing. It'll become clearer what the offences are exactly as I do more work.

And I know these are very trivial 'offences' indeed, but Jago is such a disordered headcase, a complete obsessive with all his screws loose, an utterly unhinged lunatic, no less, that he broods and broods over such things till they build to monumental proportions and he feels compelled to act out to diffuse the tension and gain release. Moreover, in that wicked little cesspit of a mind of his, he knows that the very triviality of these slights will make for the ideal cover in any murder investigation. When searching for a suspect and a motive, the police are hardly going to consider a Facebook unfriend as sufficient grounds, are they? It's brilliant, ha, ha, ha, don't you think?

What's more, Jago is using the ongoing murders as material for a new novel he's putting together. As a writer, he's so lacking in imagination that he can't make stuff up, and so he has to live everything out in reality before committing it to paper. When it's published, this book will be the making of him, he thinks. Like Edward Lionheart, he's on a quest to prove that he's right and everyone else is wrong, and when it comes to asserting his might there will be absolutely no holds barred!

Having made a few pages of notes and written a paragraph, I'm really enjoying myself and I feel a rush of positivity about how it's all panning out. Yes, without doubt *The Facebook Murders* is going to be a winner!

Anyway, I must now break off from my creative reveries and consider the more pressing issues of housework. Robin, my partner, will be home from work in an hour and he'll expect the dishes to be done and the floors to be vacuumed. I don't see why these duties should always fall to me just because I work from home as a writer. We contribute more or less equally to the costs of our shared Bristol flat, but Robin has a 'breadwinner complex' and seeks to position me in the counterbalancing role of domestic servant. Oh well, I don't want another row about it all, not today when I'm in a good mood due to starting the new novel.

I stack the dishwasher and put it on, then wipe down the kitchen surfaces ready for tonight's meal preparation. I'm just finishing off skimming the floors with the Hoover when I hear the nauseating grate of Robin's key in the front door lock. He comes flouncing into the hallway, drops his shoulder bag by the umbrella stand and brushes back the long trailing end of his carefully streaked fringe with a careless toss of his right hand – his signature gesture. Robin is an ostentatiously camp hairdresser, almost a cliché really, and as if to hammer that point home, his body language sometimes borders on Louis Spence levels of excess. When I complain he has the effrontery to call me too butch! I suppose I am by comparison to him, but not by any other standard.

'Hiya Nick!' he says over animatedly, putting a hand on my arm and giving me a quick peck that somehow misses my lips.

'Hello Robin.'

'Had a good day, have *yoouuu*...? Whatya been doing? Facebookering? Twittering? Catching up with all your mates online, eh...?'

Robin sashays into the lounge, and I have to follow him to make my reply.

'No, not much of that – I don't like to waste my time in that way, contrary to popular belief. Actually I've been planning a new novel, and I think this one is going to gel. It's called *The Facebook Murders*. Good title, eh?'

As he throws himself onto the plush leather sofa that he bought, Robin bursts into a prolonged peel of high pitched cackling, as I knew with absolute certainty that he would.

'*Another* new novel? Ha, ha, ha. *The Facebook Murders*? Yeah… great title! And this one is going to gel, is it? Make you into a multi-millionaire and win you the Nobel Prize as well, no doubt?'

'You never know…'

'No, you never know. Make us a cuppa tea, love. I'm going to watch *Pointless*.'

He pulls off his Cuban-heeled snakeskin-effect boots, stretches out his spidery skinny-jeaned legs and reaches for the remote control of the 48 inch full HD television that he bought. He constantly reminds me of such events of purchasing history.

Robin has the confidence of a man whom most people regard as a success – especially himself. He works freelance, renting a chair at a posh Clifton salon, and he's built up an enviable client list of mostly well-heeled fashionable women wanting the elaborate layering, streaking and foil painting colour work that has become his trademark. He charges top dollar and many of his former clientele can no longer afford him, and when it comes to less lucrative male hairdressing he only retains a few of the old guard, mainly gay friends. Lately he has been passing on cutting my hair on the grounds of being too busy, fobbing me off onto junior colleagues. With a constant stream of superlative feedback on his artistic merits, his ego has grown bloated and his sense of superiority over me has become tyrannical, or so it feels from where I am.

We've been a couple for around two years now, and living together in this Clifton flat for just over a year. And it's not going well. I should have learned from experience – home sharing with previous partners has always come unstuck, and I vowed not to fall into the same trap again. But every relationship is a kind of rebirth and each new partner seems initially unique and special, and some strange delusional imperative of the mind persuades one that it will be okay this time around.

Moreover, when we took the flat we both had good cash flow,

Robin from his work and me from my lesser-paid job as a bookshop assistant manager, but bolstered by the inheritance I'd recently received after my mum passed away. We almost considered buying a place, but felt that too much of a stretch for somewhere in expensive swanky Clifton, so we rented rather than fan out to Bedminster or Montpelier, which we wouldn't have liked. Now I'm really glad we didn't tie ourselves into joint ownership – and I bet Robin is even more glad of that.

The problem with Robin is that like all my previous partners he's a total control freak. Everything has got to be his way – his taste in decoration, ornaments and furniture; his choice in what meals we have, what we watch on TV, and so on. I know this is very boring, and I promise I won't go on about it for too long. But how many vegetarian stir fries can a person of reasonable appetites be expected to eat in a week? And how can anyone keep pretending to like rubbish like *Made in Chelsea* and *The Real Housewives of Beverley Hills* for any length of time?

When I want to watch something that I like – a good sci fi or horror film, for example – Robin goes all sulky and disengaged. He just refuses point blank to try and follow what's going on. I've explained the rationale behind the *Matrix* films to him a dozen times, but he doesn't get it – he won't even acknowledge that Hugo Weaving as Agent Smith is really sexy in a commanding psychopathic kind of way, but he did go a bundle on Hugh Jackman in the X-Men series, and I can't disagree with him there!

I return with two cups of tea and make Robin budge up so I can watch *Pointless* too – one programme we both enjoy. The second round question involves naming any novel by either Jane Austen, Charlotte Bronte, Wilkie Collins, George Elliot or Elizabeth Gaskell. I always get the best answers on literature or film questions, and I smile as I challenge Robin to do his best.

'Er...*Sense and Sensibility*,' he says after a few seconds. '*Jane Eyre*,' he adds as a backup.

'*Daniel Deronda*,' I offer. '*Wives and Daughters. Hide and Seek.*'

Sense and Sensibility scores sixteen, a middling answer. But all three of mine prove to be pointless, and I give Robin a victorious dig in the ribs.

'With a brain like yours you ought to be achieving more,' he says slowly, and my sense of victory quickly deflates. 'Done any job hunting lately?'

This is one of his standard inflammatory questions, and I allow a couple of beats to pass so he doesn't get a rise out of me. It's true that I haven't worked for nearly a year, since the independent bookshop that I effectively ran had to close due to substantial losses. In that time I've applied for similar positions in Waterstones, Blackwells and Foyles, but the bookshop business is in decline thanks to Amazon, and competition for any job is ferocious. I didn't fancy tossing burgers or waiting at tables at my time of life, so I let things drift, admittedly enjoying having more free time in which to write. But my Jobseeker's Allowance ran out after six months and I'm eating more and more into my savings, which of course isn't good.

I know what Robin is thinking: if this goes on for much longer there will come a point where I won't be able to afford my half of the rent and other bills, and then he will have to carry me...or break up the band. But he won't see my side and understand that it isn't easy for a thirty-eight-year-old long-term unemployed man to reinvent himself in today's austere climate. Instead I just get self-righteous uptight huffiness from him, accompanied by name-calling. Lazy. Unmotivated. Up my own ass. In cloud cuckoo land. The way he constantly repeats these criticisms, as if saying them for the first time every time, sometimes drives me close to insanity. But today I'll play his game for the sake of keeping the peace.

'Yes, I look at all the jobs sites daily. But as usual there's nothing even close to being suitable.'

I know what's coming next.

'But...you've got to try harder, Nick. Get out there, meet people, take some voluntary work if needs be. Circulate yourself. Get off Facebook and Twitter!'

'Are you doing a stir fry tonight?'

The change of subject stops him cold, fortunately, and his face becomes furrowed and quizzical. He sits up and puts his feet on the carpet.

'Oh, I know it's my turn to cook but I'm going out early, so I'll just have a quick sandwich instead.'

'You didn't say you're going out…?'

'Didn't I? I meant to mention it. You know I usually go out on a Wednesday – it's one of the evenings I don't work late.'

'You don't always…Anyway, who're you going out with?'

'Oh, just the usual work crowd – Jules, Anastasia, Kevin, Royston.'

'Meeting up in the Tavern, are you?'

'Yeah…'

'Can I come along? Could do with getting out of the house and having a drink.'

'Oh, you'll be bored…It'll be all shop-talking and goss. We'll go out drinking together at the weekend. This is your chance to put on one of your gory horror DVDs and watch it in peace without me waving my finger…'

'Mmmn…'

'Be a love and fix us a tomato and cheese sarny with a bit of side salad, eh Nick. I'm going to change.' Robin stands and saunters towards the door. 'Thinly slice the tomatoes.'

'I'll thinly slice your nuts if you keep giving me orders.'

But he pretends not to hear as he makes his exit.

And so I dutifully go and make him a sandwich, and I grill some bacon for one for myself. I even use the big Sabatier chef knife to ensure the tomatoes are sliced almost as thin as paper, just as Robin wishes. Why am I so compliant? I ask myself – especially as I'm convinced he's seeing someone else. I've thought that before many a time about Robin and previous partners, and I know it's usually just paranoia. Even in open relationships where such a thing is within the rules, the paranoia still fulminates, carving out a version of reality all of its own. But my relationship with Robin isn't supposed to be open, and we agreed at the start that we'd tell each other if either one wanted to change that – no going behind each other's backs.

Robin and I have a usual pattern of falling out and making up, and even though the downsides can be severe indeed, they are soon forgotten and the positive re-accentuated. What's changed is that he's been subtly different, more aloof, in particular more physically aloof. We haven't shagged or done anything else for nearly two months now, which is a record, notwithstanding a measurable decline in passion over the past year or so.

We have a bedroom each, and we've always tended to sleep apart for some of the time, because we're both restless at night and keep waking one another up by moving around or snoring or going for a piss. But then at other times we hook up in bed with sleep the last thing on our minds, usually at the weekends. Recently though Robin has passed on all that, coming up with a tired litany of made-to-measure excuses. Sometimes I feel that we're no more than a pair of flat sharers, together for convenience. Are Robin and I coming close to the end? I've been putting off thinking about it – I can't go through that confrontation-and-breaking-up routine again, not at my time of life!

Robin reappears, dressed in a red silk shirt, black skin-tight jeans and a black leather blouson. I have to admit he does look very pretty as he gobbles down the sandwich whilst watching the news and simultaneously phoning for a taxi. Whatever delights his evening is going to hold, I won't be a party to them. When the doorbell rings, he gives me another quick peck on the cheek and flies away like some wispy black-and-red moth. The clunk of the front door closing and the ensuing silence resonate strongly for some reason, reminding me of prison movies like *Escape from Alcatraz* or *The Shawshank Redemption*.

I will take up Robin's suggestion, I decide. There are several bottles of Westons Vintage cider, 8.2% alcohol content, in the fridge – bought from Tesco on a three-for-five-pound deal, offering extremely good value but traditional intoxication. I shall sit down presently and slowly work my way through them, whilst vegging out with a gory horror DVD. And I know just which DVD I'll choose. This will be a working night for me, for I need to re-watch this masterpiece once again in order to generate some ideas for the new book. I go to the shelf unit and pick up the case, showing the manic-eyed, twirly-moustached face of Vincent Price, holding a skull in his hand. 'It's Curtains For His Critics!' says the tag line. I'm going to forget Robin and enjoy myself with this.

2. People Who Need to be Killed

D ating from 1973, *Theatre of Blood* contains a fine ensemble
of actors I remember vaguely from the film and TV of my
childhood – Jack Hawkins, Arthur Lowe, Dennis Price,
Robert Morley and Ian Hendry, who sports a pair of classic over-
luxuriant '70s sideboards. It also features Milo O'Shea and Eric
Sykes as the bumbling slow-on-the-uptake cops on the case, clearly
establishing the comic credentials underlying the horror and gore.
Diana Rigg as Lionheart's doting daughter and accomplice in crime
is also marvellous. It's really a very silly movie, but Vincent Price, in
what he said was his favourite role, turns it into a tour de force by
virtue of his ironically layered hammy, campy performance – a good
actor playing a dubious actor as only a true master can.

He gets to dress up as Mark Antony, Achilles, a gravedigger, a
surgeon, Shylock and Richard III – with putty noses and Pan-Cake
makeup – and as gay hairdresser 'Butch' with a ridiculous Afro wig.
And he gets to murder some of Shakespeare's most famous lines
whilst taunting the hapless critics in their death throes. The actual
murders are satisfyingly gruesome and nicely orchestrated, though
not realistic enough to evoke proper visceral horror. Arthur Lowe
gets drugged up and decapitated, with wife Joan Hickson waking to
find him, as Imogen does in *Cymbeline*. Coral Browne is
electrocuted with hair curlers by 'Butch', evoking the burning of
Joan of Arc in *Henry VI, Part 1*. Robert Morley, playing a
stereotypically effeminate gay, is tricked into eating his treasured pet
poodles baked in a pie, in the manner of Queen Tamora in *Titus
Andronicus*, before being force-fed to death. And Ian Hendry almost
gets his eyes put out by red-hot daggers on a trolley moving on rails,
an idea adapted from *King Lear*, of course. Six gallons of Kensington
Gore fake blood were used in staging the murders, quite impressive
if a little too bright to be totally convincing!

Watching the movie yet again, I still feel a tug of nostalgia for the
period and a joy at the sight of the London locations – I lived there

as a child back in the 1980s. The set-piece slayings are again so amusing to watch, and I particularly like the way Lionheart throws back the critics' disparagements of him as he dispatches them – 'My Shylock was inadequate – that is the adjective you used, I believe: inadequate?' – I'll have to adopt that technique in my novel.

The script is cannily crafted, pivoting on a flashback scene that takes place in Jeffrey Archer's Thames-side penthouse flat with its terrific views across the river to Westminster. Here Lionheart confronts the members of the Critics Circle and castigates them for giving their prestigious award to another. They deliberately withheld it from him, he says, and humiliated him before press, public and peers – the culmination of their determined denial of his genius! All the pent-up bile of years of under appreciation for an artist whose ego far overtrumps his talent is unleashed in a peerless performance from Price – yes, Jago Farrar will need an ego to match Lionheart's – and with over-the-top incandescence he does Hamlet's soliloquy whilst clutching the denied award, before jumping from the balcony into the waters below. Great stuff!

What works especially well is the way we're made to understand and sympathise with Lionheart's distress, so that the dreadful punishments he inflicts for only moderate offences seem totally justified; and we're utterly on Lionheart's side as the critics get their just desserts. The whole thing is a camp comedy, a pantomime, the light heartedness of which draws the sting from the graphic violence and makes it acceptable, not horrible and disproportionate. That will be my method in *The Facebook Murders*.

I'm well into my fourth bottle of Westons as the movie reaches its *King Lear*-inspired pyrotechnic climax, and I've forgotten all about Robin and now possess the satisfied glow that comes from making creative progress. As the credits roll over plaintive music, I reflect on the murders themselves and how they contribute to the pantomime sense by having baroque stylised pre-ordained templates, designed by no less a person that Shakespeare himself. So the murderer doesn't have to invent scenarios from scratch, but merely to adapt and stage manage them, following directions…

I like it tremendously, but how can I imitate it and modify it to meet my own needs? I can't use Shakespeare – too old hat for an edgy horror-crime novel of today. But hey, Shakespeare for all his classical aplomb and literary greatness was a right horror buff – all that stuff such as gouged out eyes, children baked in a pie, speared corpses dragged behind horses. Jesus, if he were around today he'd make a horror scriptwriter par excellence...

And yes...wow...I see it now, as if I've known it all along but it's only just entered my full awareness. My method has revealed itself! Instead of Shakespeare, I'll use scenarios from celebrated horror and crime movies as the blueprints for my murder set-ups. I'll collate all my favourite nasty bits!

Yes! I drain my glass and get up quickly in search of a pen and notepad. Ideas are popping into my head right now, so fast I can barely hang on to the tail of the last one before another comes along. I must get as much down as I can, so as I don't miss anything in my drunken ebullience. *Ha, ha, ha...*And only a couple of hours ago I was having doubts about the whole enterprise, brought down to earth as I was by the drag of Robin's negative energy. But that's all gone now.

The Facebook Murders is on a roll! *Eureka!*

I've just turned off my light when I hear Robin come home at around a quarter to three. I wonder what he got up to in the seven hours or more he was at large – but do I really care? He paces around a bit and then quickly goes to his room, making almost no noise, and shuts the door. I fall asleep and I'm woken just before eight by clunking and hissing coming from the bathroom. Robin is taking a shower, not unusual in itself – but it's rare he has one first thing in the morning. Is there some residue on his person that he wishes to wash away at the earliest opportunity? I won't get up and ask him – I'll let him go to work and we'll leave that one till later. Anyway a mild hangover is squatting on my brain and I need more sleep to let it lift.

I doze off and I'm briefly reawakened by the front door thudding shut, and then I wake up properly at quarter past ten, recalling a dream about arguing with Robin in a dungeon-like setting reminiscent of the basement of the Putney Hippodrome where Lionheart conducted several of his murders.

After a cup of coffee and a slice of toast, I tentatively enter Robin's room, feeling like a spy, some clandestine intruder, possibly under surveillance. I look at his sheets and smell them – nothing unusual there – and then I examine his most recently discarded underwear in the laundry basket and find no more than a faint pee stain on his pants. What am I expecting to discover, I ask myself – dried semen coupled with a miasma of Kevin's aftershave that would establish he gave Robin a blowjob last night beyond any reasonable doubt? That would be good! But knowing Kevin's thoroughness and tidiness, he most probably swallowed the evidence down to the last glob!

I laugh at this idea as I sit down at the desk in the corner of my room and boot up the computer ready for the day's work. As the mostly spam emails download, I have a quick look on Facebook, though I'm determined not to get detoured into extended chatting sessions today – I've got a novel to plan out! With nearly two thousand friends, the vast majority of whom I don't know from Adam – mostly writers or people associated with writing who've added me, or I've added them over the years – I get a lot of half-arsed requests and notifications. They're a bit of an annoyance, to be honest.

Jonathan Jamieson wants me to 'like' his author page. He does, does he? Who the fuck is Jonathan Jamieson? Has he ever liked anything of mine? I know for a fact he hasn't liked *my* author page, so he can go and stick a banana up where the sun don't shine! Dan Dalrymple has invited me to attend the launching of his new horror novel at a bookshop in Brisbane. Fantastic – I'll book a flight right away! I click on the news feed and top of the shop is the tragic, heartbreaking story of how Pasty Pettigrew's beloved cocker spaniel Alfie has passed away in his fourteenth year. Sixty-one likes and thirty-seven messages of condolence. Her profile picture depicts the loveable doleful-eyed, floppy-eared fella in his prime. I can't handle this…my eyes are watering…I'll have to go get a box of tissues…

Ha, ha, ha…

My *real* Facebook friends aren't doing much and I don't want to post myself, so I minimise the browser and open yesterday's Word document – Chapter 1 of *The Facebook Murders* – and read back what I wrote. It still seems okay, no sickening undertow, and quickly I commence a second paragraph, setting up my narrator Jago Farrar, the spurned and vengeful author who has now flipped and is out for revenge.

Yes, Jago has had enough – he's just like the Peter Finch character in *Network*, who projects his rage over the airwaves to become a messiah of anger, telling everyone to shout out: *I'm as mad as hell, and I'm not going to take this anymore!* I'm typing away and it's all going very smoothly, fluently, and in three pithy paragraphs Jago has come to life, and he's a force to be taken seriously!

Now what about his personal details and appearance? I ought to make him distinctly unlike myself in some regards, so people won't think he's me. As I've got a full head of lush, longish hair, I'll make Jago balding, with his hair short and stubbly, and I'll give him a designer-stubble beard into the bargain. He will be the same age as me, thirty-eight, in order to have that late-thirties mindset and interface correctly with the other characters. Shall I make him straight as I'm gay? Mmmn…I don't want to make a big deal out of his sexuality, but he needs to be gay in order for one his obsessions to work. We'll see how that pans out.

So now down to business. Jago has declared his intention to take revenge, but who exactly are his victims and what have they done to deserve retribution? Well, naturally they will be based on the people who've wronged me, disguised of course and with made-up names. But for the purposes of a first draft, I'll just stick to real names and real incidents and modify it all later. The important thing is to get my – I mean Jago's – authentic emotions into the mix, and the peripheral stuff can take a back seat. I need to put together my hit list and make it solid and plausible, like Lionheart's in *Theatre of Blood*. So I save my document and turn to notepad and pen for some quick random jottings.

The first question is how many victims to include on the list? It's got to be a minimum of five, I would say, perhaps six, seven or eight, but then again not too many. There are nine critics on Lionheart's list in *Theatre of Blood*, which result in seven murders fulfilled by Lionheart and his crew, plus the *Othello* scenario – where Jack Hawkins kills wife Diana Dors in a fit of jealously and goes to jail – and the two unfulfilled Ian Hendry scenes – the duel from *Romeo and Juliet* and the *King Lear* finale. That feels like plenty, more than enough, in fact too much for *The Facebook Murders* – I'd struggle to find nine candidates and make them all good ones.

That's the problem – the more you include, the more potential for weaknesses in the story. Undoubtedly the least successful episode in *Theatre of Blood* is the *Othello*. That the Jack Hawkins critic should fall so easily for Lionheart's sham masseur act and strangle his wife so quickly and deftly – a typical film killing – stretches suspension of disbelief even by the film's panto standards. It doesn't matter much because the other killings are so good, but it serves as a warning not to overstuff the suitcase. Bearing this in mind, I spend a quarter of an hour writing down names and offences in rough order of preference, weighing up the definites against the maybes and putting lines through a few. I come up with a final list of five that are rock-solid certainties, and decide to go with those. Perhaps I'll add more later, or perhaps they will suffice.

So, where shall we start? How about with Darren Winterbottom, writer of urban fantasy, best known for his *Sunset Street* series of novels, where psychic detective Josiah Stone tackles occult-related crime in a futuristic Gotham City-like English northern metropolis – a classic fusion of Chandleresque neo-noir with the tropes of the paranormal. Perhaps you've heard of Darren – his books do grace the shelves of Waterstones and Foyles, but he's not a household name. He does, however, have a firm and growing fan base in an eminently bankable area of genre fiction, and with this comes a good income stream and inevitably the syndrome of perpetual inflation in the ego department.

The thing is Darren used to be a good mate, especially back in the old days – the early 2000s – when we were all a lot younger and developing our writing careers. We drank and chewed the fat in The Graven Image, the East London pub that was the headquarters of the genre-writing crowd back then, and we would rub shoulders at conventions in cities across Britain and North America. At that time, Darren wrote fairly extreme horror novels and short stories, which appeared in genre magazines, and I had ambitions to do the same. As he was seven or eight years older than me and far more experienced, he set himself up as mentor figure, guiding me and giving me tips. When I eventually had stories published myself, he took some of the credit as a coach.

Darren remained a steady friend into the Facebook era, and when my story collection, *Dark Undertows*, was published five years ago, he was supportive, unlike many others. But more recently he over-reacted to a trivial event and turned funny, cold shouldering me on Facebook and one time in the flesh. Events came to a head at the time of Margaret Thatcher's funeral in 2013, but I won't go into all that now. The important thing is that Darren went from friend to enemy.

And who's the next candidate on the list? Has to be Eustace Crimp, another writer of a few years older than me, who moves in the genre convention circuit, and whom I've known for roughly the same time as Darren. Back in the early 2000s, Crimpy penned clever cyberpunkish stories that used elements of advanced physics, mainly quantum theory, to create weird convolutions and unexpected twists. He is a physics graduate, so he knows his stuff. Eustace was published in the better sci-fi magazines, such as *Asimov's* and *Analog*, and he soon got an agent and a book deal, churning out four-hundred-page hard sci-fi epics at the rate of one every two years. Over the past decade, he has become a solid part of the current British sci-fi scene, another success story.

So, do I resent Crimpy because of his success? Of course not. I resent him because of his high-handed, snobby and dismissive attitude toward me and my work. He was never really a mate, but we always remained frostily polite whenever we met at conventions and conversed about writing and other stuff. With an IQ of around two hundred and an overly pedantic approach to any intellectual matter, Crimpy was always picking you up on any slight inaccuracy or fault of logic in whatever you said, which got to be irritating after a time. It was the same in the Facebook era, where his corrections would be indelibly preserved as text, to be seen and revisited by the many in a cyberspace void of privacy. It was Facebook privacy issues that made for the final straw with old Eustace, but more of that later.

Onwards to Simon Ongar, the one and only critic on my list – the true heir to Peregrine Devlin and the others of *Theatre of Blood*. Simon was a fiction writer too in his early days, but he got a reputation as a star in the letters pages of magazines, and also internet message forums, where we aired our thoughts about relevant matters, often currently published magazine stories. Simon composed long, detailed missives analysing the pieces one by one and offered praise and disparagement in equal measure. He soon graduated to reviewing story magazines and also books for bigger more mainstream publications. After that he started his own magazine, *The British SF & Fantasy Review*, and steadily became a powerhouse editor and critic.

It's easy to guess what I've got against Ongarface – he just never liked my work and was always somewhat scathing when putting my stories under the microscope. Negative criticism is something an author has to take in his stride, but when the same things are said in a relentless fashion, you begin to feel the critic has got it in for you, and he's just waiting for your next piece to appear so he can pull that to pieces too. When I sent my collection of stories, *Dark Undertows*, to *The British SF & Fantasy Review*, I hoped he wouldn't be too savage, and it's true that Simon has mellowed somewhat over time. What he actually did was *worse* than a hatchet job in many ways; he damned with faint praise, taking an ironical turn and then delivered a killer verdict on my whole oeuvre. I'll never forget what he said.

Number four on the list is Neil Hornblower, editor of the horror story anthology *Tamaghis*, which as you probably know is one of the cities in the William Burroughs novel *Cities of the Red Night*. If you want a cool name go to Burroughs, as Steely Dan and Soft Machine will attest. I struck up a good rapport with Neil when he first entered the scene, and he published two of my stories. Then as *Tamaghis* began to grow in reputation and influence, Neil became a bit too big for his boots. A third story of mine entered a limbo world within the *Tamaghis* universe, and in my attempts to find out what had happened and extricate it, I fell into a dispute with Neil that escalated surprisingly in bitterness. Like with the Simon Ongar case, Neil said things about me that stuck in my mind and repeated over and over and over, requiring further action to put things to rights.

So with these four, I've almost completed my hit list, and only one other remains. But this one other is a bit special. My list, you see, is not proportionate, and Darren Winterbottom, Eustace Crimp, Simon Ongar and Neil Hornblower are merely venial sinners, bit-part players there to support the star of the show, who stands on a pinnacle light years above them. This main player far outstrips the others, both in terms of his exalted status within the writing world and in the magnitude of his nefarious deeds done against me. If not for him, I wouldn't be writing *The Facebook Murders* in the first place – the idea would not have formed, let alone have attained critical mass.

You most probably won't have heard of any of the others, but you'll definitely have heard of him. One of Britain's top genre writers, on par with J.K. Rowling, Neil Gaiman, Clive Barker, Philip Pullman and the late Terry Pratchett, he is a shining superstar of horror, once called 'the future of horror' – he is, of course, none other than Hugh Canford-Eversleigh.

3. Inking In the Bad Things

I t was over a decade ago that I glimpsed the poster in the window of Blackwell's bookshop at the top of Park Street, and the chain of events that would forge me into a literary stalker inexorably commenced. Such a light and innocent start to the proceedings really – I could never have envisaged the weird series of convolutions that would lead me to this point: committing murder by novel.

The poster was advertising a reading by Hugh Canford-Eversleigh from his newly published novel, *The Major Arcana*, in the middle of the following week. It would take place over the lunch hour, so it would be a simple matter for me to attend, as I was at that time working in the University library, a ten-minute walk away. As the moment got nearer, the prospect of seeing Hugh in the flesh began to fill me with a disproportionate joy. Here was someone who wasn't just a favoured author, he was practically a living god – and he was dishy into the bargain. So from a small seed a really strong frisson built up, giving me exactly the kind of feeling one would get anticipating a hot date.

The frisson became even stronger when I entered the bookshop and saw him standing at a raised table with a couple of helpers, making final preparations, a column of sunlight sharpening his image. As though he could sense me behind him, he turned his head right around and looked straight at me, meeting my gaze. That in itself was a major experience, and I became conscious of the feverish pumping of my heart. Then, after I'd sauntered away to browse at a table, and was pretending to read a copy of *Never Let Me Go*, he glanced pointedly in my direction, twice or three times. He was as attentive to me as I was to him. This early in our liaison I felt he'd decided I was some kind of a 'character'.

Naturally I'd seen plenty of photographs of Hugh, from moody monochrome book jacket headshots to colourful spreads in magazines, and I'd seen him on TV, interviewed in arts programmes; but the physical presence of the man was so many more orders of magnitude higher as to constitute some delicious new magic potion or elixir, one taste of which and you are hooked for life, forever bound to its unremitting output of ecstasy. Could it be possible, as in the old cliché of a thousand romantic novels – love at first sight?

In the same way as pop singers look like pop singers and boxers look like boxers, Hugh Canford-Eversleigh appeared the absolute epitome of the successful on-trend author. He had something of that handsome, strong-jawed quality of 1940s Hollywood film stars such as Ray Milland and Tyrone Power – classy and refined, yet a little bit rugged at the edges and carrying a hint of danger – and of course his father had been a screen actor. Hugh's luminous pale blue eyes and the tanned skin made for a dazzling combination, furthering that impression of innocence blended with depravity. His lush chestnut brown hair was combed across from a side parting, but it flopped over his brows somewhat, giving him the eternally boyish look of Hugh Grant. His body was in very good shape, with that classic triangular formation of square shoulders and full chest tapering down to narrow waist and hips, with a flat stomach and lithe, sparely muscled legs like a dancer's. Hugh looked a lot younger than his actual age, which was approaching forty, and at twelve years my senior he very much matched my ideal – I was into older men at that point in my erotic life.

Hugh's outfit too was carefully put together to strike all the right notes. He wore an open-necked collarless shirt that was obviously very expensive, subtly pinstriped and double cuffed, complimented by chunky gold cufflinks that occasionally shone and glittered in counterpoint with his loose gold Rolex and many finger rings – including, unfortunately, a wedding ring. A brown houndstooth tweed waistcoat lent Hugh a 'country gent' air, but it was all change at his slim waist, where a wide pirate-like designer belt, studded with skull motifs, was threaded into tight-fitting faded Versace jeans. Hand-tooled black and red cowboy boots, similarly bearing a skull-and-crossbones pattern, pointed their toes quizzically at me when Hugh was sat down with crossed legs. This was my kind of guy – top half Jekyll, bottom half Hyde!

And this couldn't have been a more opportune moment to meet such a person. I was newly single and looking for love, or the nearest approximation to love that I could find. The relationship with my last main boyfriend, Jason, had attenuated down to the vanishing point, and I had sensibly cut my losses and was moving on. I thought it funny now that when I'd first encountered Jason, a little over three years previously, I'd thought he was the one – the main man of my life, and would be forever. It's the kind of naïve idea you get when you're twenty-four.

Jason was then thirty-six or thirty-seven, so the twelve-year age gap was similarly in force. I bumped into him in the Somerset House pub in Clifton Village, and we got on superbly, talking about sci-fi and weird films, a favourite subject. Jason too was boyishly good looking with blond curly hair, but I thought he was straight, so I didn't get my hopes up too high. Then at closing time when we were both well sloshed, he leaned in close so no one around could hear and whispered, 'Tell me something…Are you gay…?' I could hardly believe it. 'Yes,' I said with slow deliberation, and he invited me back to his flat, a bohemian basement in Cornwallis Crescent, just down the road. We walked there lightly holding hands and giggling like schoolgirls as the stars twinkled over the bowl of Bristol.

I had the best sex of my life that night with Jason, in a bed with red silk sheets reflected in a floor-to-ceiling mirror on one side and posters for films such as *Eraserhead* and *Blow Up* on the other. We repeated the exercise over several more nights, and I thought I'd found nirvana, but naturally there was a catch. Jason hardly ever answered his phone and didn't return messages, so we only met up if he phoned me. Becoming suspicious, I took to cruising the flat at various times of the day and night and found it continually empty. After many remonstrations with Jason, where he remained evasive, the truth eventually emerged.

The basement flat was not, so it turned out, his main residence. That was a seven-bedroomed mansion over in posh Sneyd Park on the other side of the Downs, where Jason lived – you've guessed it – with his perfect, attractive and equally blonde wife – I nicknamed her 'the Stepford Wife'. Jason was a part-time gay, a double lifer, a classic compartmentaliser. He was wealthy and very successful, a partner and creative director in a rapidly expanding Bristol advertising agency, and he presented himself to the world as an urbane heterosexual, one of the lads. Jason mixed with all sorts of important people: bigwigs at the BBC, local entrepreneurs who'd become millionaires in the Blair boom, aspiring politicians in their well-cut suits – Labour, of course. He cultivated a cool, trendy left-wing window display as he amassed more and more wealth and power.

And behind that façade he operated as a careful and discreet bisexual cruiser, walking on Bristol's wild side and canoodling with mostly younger pickups. I could see it was a tremendous relief to him when he confessed, and then I was faced with sharing him not only with the wife but also with others of both sexes that he might meet in pubs or clubs and get to place between those red sheets. However our affair did involve genuinely reciprocated love and affection, and was of a different order to Jason's usual one- or two-night stands. We carried on seeing one another intermittently, but things were doomed by my possessiveness and jealously, which just served to accelerate a conclusion that was inevitable anyway. I continued to bump into him for years afterwards and we remained convivial. The wife stayed with him and is HIV free, as far as I know. There are no children.

So, I'd successfully washed Jason out of my hair when I encountered another who was just like him, my type – older but very attractive, intelligent, rich, sophisticated and even more exalted in status – famous, in fact. And even less gay. No hint of bisexuality existed; all of Hugh's many lovers, short-term conquests, longer-term partners, and indeed his wife, the supermodel Melody Longfellow, were all of the exclusively female variety. He was an important and glamorous enough figure to get written about in newspaper gossip columns and magazines, so his form was well known. What, then, was I doing? If I'd had the tiniest scrap of sense, I would have made an about turn and marched out of Blackwell's before I went any further down the road to the underworld. But of course that's not my style.

Instead I took a seat at the front of the small audience area and observed Hugh as he commenced his talk and reading. By now the bookshop was packed and many interested parties were standing around in the nearby spaces, blocking the free movement of the regular browsers. Hugh's charisma and celebrity radiance was palpably felt by the whole room. He started by making some pithy observations about being a horror writer, saying it had been seventeen years since his first short story was published in a magazine and he crossed that 'dreaded threshold'. He used the phrase humorously and got approving ripples of laughter from the gathered throngs. Then Hugh moved swiftly to the point of the speech, which was that whatever a horror writer can dream up in the wildest recesses of imagination, it will always be overtrumped by reality.

Next he mentioned the then recent 7/7 London bombings, the Dunblane and Hungerford massacres, and the activities of serial killers, such as Harold Shipman and Fred West, pointing his finger northwards in the direction of Gloucester as he touched on the horrors of Cromwell Street. With just the right measure of disgust, Hugh ruminated over the toxic brew of psychopathology, sadism and sexual deviancy that brought about these events, and concluded that such things reminded him of the heavy task and responsibility of the horror writer in plumbing the full capacity of human – and inhuman – evil.

What a performance! Everybody, not only myself, was by now completely in thrall, warmed up and ready for the main act. Hugh made for an enchanting spectacle, sat majestically on the raised platform, with crossed legs and expressively gesticulating arms. He was as alert, watchful and calculating as a bird of prey, and his movements had an alacrity that created an impression of graceful flashiness. Hugh's voice too added tremendously to the overall effect. His accent had a quality of sonorous fruitiness within its oracular upper crust Englishness, its tones marinated in the stonework of public schools for century upon century. Several more times we made eye contact as he spoke, and every word, every syllable seemed coated in the promise of future delights that only he and I would share when no one else was around.

Hugh went on to introduce *The Major Arcana*, which was then his seventh novel and around his tenth published book – his first was of course the explosive story collection *The Chronicles of Mayhem*, which I'd read as a sixth former and was one of the books that first hooked me on horror. He explained the significance of the Tarot theme, and then outlined some pertinent aspects of the plot. Like much of his previous work, it was highbrow, thinking-man's horror, not short on graphic violence but with fairly subtle supernatural elements, so the envelope of realism wasn't stretched too far.

It concerns Carl, a forty-something ex-army officer, now weapons consultant, whose twenty-year-old daughter Lucy is inducted into a satanic cult and brainwashed. In his attempts to extricate her, he receives more and more threats, and eventually he comes up against demonic presences. The cleverness of the writing ensures the reader is never completely sure whether these presences are real or merely the products of suggestion. But of course Carl won't be put off, and whilst retaining some degree of scepticism he enlists the help of a white magician – and he uses fisticuffs and firearms as well when things inevitably get ugly.

Hugh had carved out his own niche writing this kind of fiction, where plausible horror meshes with literary seriousness and channels into the mainstream thriller market. He appealed not only to gore-hounds and genre fans, but also to a wider spectrum of readers of all ages, and his sales were enormous. Any new novel of Hugh's was a major event, guaranteed to hit the bestseller lists. He had brought a measure of respectability to a genre that critics often considered dubious, and no one could deny his writing pedigree was peerless.

He obtained a First in English at Oxford, and then went on to complete a PhD in nineteenth and early twentieth century super-natural literature, so he was an expert in the field and had everything covered, including the history of spiritualism, involving figures such as Madame Blavatsky and Sir Arthur Conan Doyle. On the fiction front, Hugh knew his Poe, his M. R. James, his Arthur Machen, his Algernon Blackwood and of course his Lovecraft. He also knew his Dennis Wheatley, his Robert Bloch and his Stephen King, so he was well qualified to carry the torch onwards and become the new British horror *enfant terrible* of the early 1990s, picking up the torch from Clive Barker, who had that accolade a decade previously.

Like Barker with his legendary *Books of Blood*, Hugh's stories and early novels were replete with the macabre, the gory and the demonic. Common themes included murder, torture, sadomasochism, psychotic breakdown, multiple personality disorder, possession, haunting and more generalised 'evil forces' – just about every nasty thing in the horror cannon. More recently though he'd mellowed and broadened out his scope to include other content beyond the macabre excesses – and *The Major Arcana* was a continuance of that trend. Still, I loved Hugh for the daringness of his early stuff, read at a formative age, when I'd concluded we were kindred spirits, and if ever I were to write myself I wanted to write like him.

So now, with that historical freight in place, I came to witness the climax of today's show, which was a reading from the novel, delivered with Hugh's natural consummate aplomb. The passage he chose depicted a chase and fight sequence that took place on the platforms, escalators and trains of the London Underground, where Carl was trying to apprehend a cult member whom he knew had crucial information on the whereabouts of his daughter Lucy. It was ideal for two reasons: firstly it described a self-contained incident, fully comprehensible without knowledge of what came before in the text, and secondly it made an ideal showcase for the virtuosity of Hugh's writing.

As Hugh read, clearly, confidently and unwaveringly, the events came alive much more so than if one was reading it for oneself off the page. The sense of being inside Carl's head as he decides to try and capture his quarry, plus the ramping up of adrenalin and the stressed staccato quality of his calculations, were all so palpably authentic. Then as the chase progresses and the man runs – with the two of them scurrying along corridors, leaping in and out of trains and jumping across staircases – the observations of heightened perception created a mesmeric slow-motion effect. Add to that the surprise of unexpected retaliation leading to pain, loss of poise and the overlaid effect of dealing with nonplussed uncomprehending bystanders, who conclude Carl is the bad guy, and a scenario quite familiar from many action novels and movies became completely reminted by the vivid genius of Hugh's writing.

After he'd finished and received a round of rapturous applause, the punters lined up to buy the book from large stacks on adjacent tables and have him sign their copies. I selected an untouched hardback, joined the queue and prepared to pay with my credit card. It was weighty and substantial in my hand, over three hundred pages and priced at £17.99 – ouch! The jacket had a blue-black night scene field containing a montage of Tarot imagery, swirling as though in a dust storm – the Star, the Moon, the Fool, the High Priestess – with the title and Hugh's name rendered in the golden capitals of an elaborate Gothic font. Keying in my PIN number, I saw once again the canniness of such promotional readings, whipping up sales in an almost religious frenzy, with the author's signature sealing the specialness of the occasion.

When I handed over my copy to Hugh, I beamed a big smile and complimented him on the excellence of the chase sequence reading and asked if it was drawn from any actual experience. No, he replied, it was a complete fabrication. I then mentioned a chase I'd once witnessed, saying it was really fast and frenetic, just like his account. 'Tell me more,' Hugh said, and I did so, speaking at length but quite fluidly and without breathlessness. I was quite impressed with myself.

My chase took place on the Clifton Downs about two years previously. A woman was walking alone when a grungy-looking man dashed up, snatched her handbag off her shoulder and ran away. He was seen by two male joggers who gave pursuit, and when the man caught sight of them he panicked, zigzagging through the bushes and lashing out when the joggers cornered him. In the end he gave up the bag and managed to escape as one bystander got on her mobile, presumably to call the police.

Hugh was interested and he asked me how I'd felt watching the action and if I'd considered tackling the man myself. It was a good point and I replied that I'd felt a strong aversion to getting involved, if I could possibly help it. We then moved on to a quick-fire discussion of how experiencing bad things in reality is so different to how we conceive them based on movies and books. It was hard to keep up – Hugh's mind moved twice as fast as most people's, and he was possessed of a clinical intelligence, seizing upon a subject and instantly dissecting it to get to the heart. As human beings go, he was clearly not in the average range.

As we talked, I stood to one side and Hugh continued signing away, effortlessly multitasking. I noticed that several of the punters had copies of his older books requiring a signature, including one guy who had pristine hardback first editions of *The Chronicles of Mayhem* and Hugh's first two novels – *Thomas's Playroom* and *Chorus of Dead Souls* – which would be even more valuable having been given the author's imprimatur. Watching the Mont Blanc pen inscribe the long name with many flowery strokes and curlicues, I felt at home and that I'd arrived at a key juncture in my life.

Next I broached the subject of the nasty things that happen in Hugh's books, of which there were many, and I complimented him again on the stark lucidity with which he conveyed them. Almost magically, so it seemed, Hugh then confided to me the entire rationale behind this aspect of his work. He said that when writing he summons up personal ghosts and demons – his phobias, anxieties and other dark thoughts – and plays out the worst possibilities in his imagination.

'Have you noticed that the bad things you anticipate happening never actually happen?' he added. 'It's always different bad things that do happen.'

'Yes, that's very true, now you come to mention it.'

Hugh went on to say that thinking up terrible things therefore acted as a kind of insurance: the more you think up, the less there are at large to take you by surprise! His work was thus a progressive inking in of these bad scenarios and at the same time a process of catharsis and therapy.

I nodded away, highly impressed, and I felt really privileged to have heard these ideas – a fascinating insight into an extraordinary talent. There was that undeniable feeling of brushing up against a great man, a significant figure, an exceptional individual – quite apart from his attractiveness! I felt pumped-up and delirious, no doubt awash with adrenalin, endorphins and pheromones from the close contact. The earlier frisson, which had been steadily doubling and redoubling, now shot to the moon, and I heard melodies in my head that were based on snatches of old Irving Berlin-style love songs...

My conversation with Hugh reached a natural conclusion, and we said goodbye and I strolled out of Blackwell's, blinking at the glare of the afternoon sun. I casually glanced at my watch and saw that I'd massively overrun my lunch break and needed to get back to the library quickly, though the idea of work and indeed the idea of my future life containing any such mundane duties and practices, was all momentarily at a very distant remove.

4. The 'Literary Stalker' Letter

Looking back on that first encounter with Hugh, I find the most remarkable thing is how I experienced myself as a 'character' right from the outset. And another similarly speedy development coming out of our meeting of minds was the 'Literary Stalker' novel idea, the basics of which were fully formed a mere one week later. I know this for certain because I wrote a dated letter to Hugh detailing the idea, and I have a copy of that letter on my desk now, freshly printed out from my computer archives.

That week between the encounter and the formulation of the letter was a long one for me, as you can well comprehend. Leaving the bookshop behind, I cut across the busy Queen's Road, dodging traffic, and power walked through the crowds in front of the Museum, on my way back to the library in Tyndall Avenue. I was now firmly in the throes of the first of many phases in a seven-day emotional ride of my life. The uplift from the bookshop meeting continued to surge, and I felt bathed in the wonder of having inter-acted with a truly important writer – something I wished to be myself – a living embodiment of that ideal, an aspiration made flesh. Perhaps now that I'd met Hugh I was closer to becoming him. Somehow I was utterly transformed, and I knew that destiny would ensure that everything would go right from now on.

Getting back to work half an hour late and receiving a dressing down from Big George, my supervisor, cooled me off somewhat, but not for long. Whilst going through the motions of answering queries and looking out books from the shelves, I kept running the film of Hugh and I through my mind, pimping it up a little with each pass. I recalled vividly those initial stages when I was hovering and looking at him, and he was looking at me looking at him. We must have made proper eye contact on at least four or five occasions. He had singled me out, or so it felt, and later when we met and talked, he confided to me the 'secret' of his writing synthesis! It was a clear validation of what I'd felt – that an epoch-making connection had taken place.

So where do we go from here? When will I see him again…? A momentum had built up and it seemed entirely natural that following this significant breaking of the ice, things would roll on and the relationship would build…*But how exactly…?*

After perhaps an hour, this first phase of starry-eyed bedazzlement began to break down as those questions hovered, pressing themselves upon me, requiring answers. I ran the movie again, and it was different this time.

I fixated, slow-moed and freeze-framed on that first look Hugh had given me – that smouldering wanton stare – and he'd kept on looking, not trying to conceal or even tone down his interest. If we were in a gay bar, that look would have been absolutely unequivocal. When you *look* at another guy like that, it means what it means! But we weren't in a gay bar, we were in a bookshop – and Hugh is straight anyway – so I didn't attach the full weight of significance to the look. Now though I was seeing another angle, and in doing so I was uncovering the massive miscalculation I'd made.

Suppose Hugh were like Jason, he swung both ways but he kept the gay side firmly under wraps? With that look he was imparting a signal that wouldn't mean much unless the recipient was gay. It was a coded message. And I responded, I initiated a chat at the signing, and he reciprocated, keeping up the tennis match for all it was worth, even though there was a huge queue of people wanting their books signed. He didn't try to get rid of me, he didn't cut it short, despite the fact I was well overdue an average allotted span of chat time. He carried on signing and talking to me, keeping all the balls in the air. It seemed obvious now that he was doing his very best to come on to me within the restricted space of opportunity that existed. And it was *me* that pulled the plug…not Hugh…

The more I thought about it, the more I realised how stupid I'd been in my assumption that Hugh was completely heterosexual based on what was written about him in the press. He was undoubtedly another Jason type. No one knew Jason had a gay side apart from the gay men he approached; as far as everyone else was concerned he was straight – and a ladies' man into the bargain. Just like Hugh. And back in the bookshop Hugh had communicated his willingness, his availability to me, by means of those blatantly forward looks – and I doubted the whole deal! I started well and went through the motions correctly, and then what did I do? I fell at the final fence! All because I needed to get back to bloody work!

Blimey! Screw work! I could have phoned in later and said I'd been taken ill or had an accident or something. What I should have done was hang around till Hugh was completely finished and then casually ask if he wanted to get a coffee. And if I was wrong about him being up for some hanky panky, some afternoon delight, I'd have found out there and then. I'd have tested the situation. Now I'd never know what might have happened had I not been such an idiot. A putative interlude of ecstasy, perhaps in some convenient hotel – there are plenty in nearby St. Paul's Road – had evanesced into the ether of unfulfilled possibility all because of the fact I didn't stop and think for a couple of seconds before marching out of Blackwell's, eager instead to get back to the highly important work of searching out textbooks for a horde of ratty students!

My whole life might have pivoted on that one single moment, and I'd chosen empty daydreaming over a reality that was pregnant with promise! *How could I have been so stupid?*

That question reverberated around in my head throughout this current phase of self-recrimination, which was to last for the best part of a couple of days – well into the weekend. After that the whirlwind exhausted itself, I accepted I'd blown it, and then I moved on to the next phase, involving filling the void with fantasy, occupying the territory of what might have been. Actually this new phase started earlier in truth, overlapping with the other, but it was after a couple of days that I surrendered to it completely.

After Hugh had signed the final book, stood up on the dais, stretched his legs and arched his back, delineated nicely by the tobacco-coloured rear silk panel of his waistcoat, he bade his farewells and shook hands with the bookshop staff, and then turned in my direction. Catching sight of me again, he smiled very naturally, sauntered forward and in that honey-like upper class accent, he spoke the word, 'Hello…' stretching it out indefinitely like streaks of mozzarella cheese.

We got a taxi to the Regency Hotel and booked a room. Hugh went up first and I followed a couple of minutes later. Once the door had been shut with a muted thud, we looked at one another candidly and then slowly, carefully began kissing, gently at first and then with breathless probing intensity. Hugh's face was still virtually smooth from his morning close shave and there was none of that unpleasant raspiness of stubble in the contact. Next thing we moved on to undressing one another, joyously peeling off and tossing aside layers of outer garments, underwear, boots and shoes. Then we sank together into the bright white sheets of the bed surface and merged into a oneness, a yin/yang symbol made flesh, spinning away into the cosmos, deifying everything in its path…

Yeah, yeah, yeah…

And so it went, fantasy after fantasy, each one propagating further excesses in the next, the movie running unflaggingly, looping into itself and spiralling all around my brain for hour after hour after hour, till I was trussed up completely in its endless ribbons. In the earlier stages it was wonderful, a total escape into the limitless possibilities of invention; but as in a marathon run, stamina begins to sag eventually and a sense of fatigue sets in as you doggedly soldier on. Progressively the content became more and more clichéd and the movie started to resemble a tatty old TV Bank Holiday classic such as *Brief Encounter*, complete with a Noël Coward screenplay and spoken aloud in a febrile Celia Johnson voice.

I stared out of the grim casement window of my bedsitting room at the flecks of white cloud in the mackerel sky, and suddenly I was looking at those same clouds from above, out of the window of a 747 with the Atlantic shimmering far below like a silvery curtain. I turned in my comfortably reclined first class seat and saw Hugh sat next to me, smiling contentedly as he took my hand, both of us knowing that everything would be fine from now on, as Melody had disappeared from the picture, Hugh had taken the decisive step of publicly coming out, and we were off to New York where he'd sign books with me at his side, and then we'd attend lavish publishing parties and writers' conferences as a golden glitterati couple.

I saw us under a mushroom-like umbrella on the beach in Saint-Tropez, sipping huge fruit-laden cocktails as we leant over to kiss, being careful not to clash sunglasses. And later we had a lobster dinner with Krug and Chablis on board an eighty-metre motor yacht with a group of select friends, cruising slowly around the bay to the accompaniment of laughter and jokes as we watched the sun turn apricot and sink into the horizon. Then we were sat in the plush ivory leather seats of Hugh's open-top Aston Martin Virage Volante, the wind whipping over our heads and the engine growling like a big cat as we accelerated up to almost twice the speed limit. And next we were skiing in Verbier, riding the fresh powder as we swooped down the mountain, pumped up by adrenalin, watching the sunlight bounce off the snow in a trillion diamond points. But then the sun went behind a cloud and the piste turned into the grubby grey carpet of my lonely rented box, and all the silly dreams melted away to nothingness.

Every so often I returned to something like normal, amazed at how high the balloon of unreality had risen, but not really caring anymore. The notion that Hugh was a secret friend of Dorothy had now passed from theory into fact and was of course structurally hardwired into the script of the fantasies. I found it all quite titillating at first, but after another couple of days, despondency reared its head again, as I knew that despite the magnitude of my internal ramblings I was making no progress in the real world. I was no further forward than I'd been on the pavement outside Blackwell's, having taken the fateful step of not waiting for Hugh to finish. How could I pick up the thread from that point?

By around the fifth day my imagination started to change tack, moving away from the slushy Mills and Boon nonsense and back, really, to the beginning, to the spark that had initially ignited Hugh and I, independently of the fact I fancied him like crazy. That bookshop meeting now appeared to me as a kind of crucible where many varied elements were cooked up to the extremes of temperature and reforged into myriad new forms. My nascent love for Hugh was but one of the resultant products. Another was the shared literary perspective, the recognition of a congruence of mind, the parallel views over similar territory coming into a coalescence.

Naturally I was already familiar with Hugh's preoccupations through his work, and I was but a stranger to him; but from the moment we began to talk he correctly gauged that here was a fan who was right on his wavelength. That was why he confided the rationale behind his horror writing to me – as lovers do share secrets, making them emblems of the bond they both feel. The revelation about Hugh inking in the bad possibilities in his work, as an inoculation against them happening in reality, was deeply fascinating, and it yielded more and more with further inquiry.

Hugh and Melody's daughter, Ariadne, was a mere five years old, so doubtless back in her baby or toddlerhood Hugh had formed the fear of something bad happening to her later in life and had come up with the scenario of *The Major Arcana* – which incidentally I'd been reading and immensely enjoying during this fugue – an impressionable young adult girl seduced by Satanists. When I considered his earlier novels and the stories in *The Chronicles of Mayhem* using the prism of the rationale, the same thread could be discerned running throughout – nasty things happening to the unwary, the stuff of worst nightmares.

So, it was upon this literary synthesis, this foundation stone that Hugh had laid, that I based my next move. Returning to the bookshop scene for the umpteenth hundredth time, I now started to process it as actual material for a story, rather than as unfocussed fantasy fuel. And of course it would have to be a sinister Hugh-type narrative and not something mushy by Barbara Cartland – that simply wouldn't do! By the sixth day I was in constructive mode, working away with my notepad and pen in my spare time at work or back at home. The florid madness of earlier in the cycle had subsided, or else had transmogrified into something else altogether.

I sketched out a large and prestigious bookshop, together with a famous author back on the reading circuit having completed another novel. The author is exhilarated by this phase of activity; his senses have an unusual acuity and he's very aware of what's happening around him. In particular he's looking out for the offbeat, the exotic, something he can perhaps take hold of and mould, for having finished one novel he knows he will soon need to be starting another.

Amongst the throngs of nondescript customers in the shop, he spies an interesting-looking guy, a bit of a geezer, an undoubted character. Quite tall, almost six feet in height, he is dressed entirely in black – black jeans, a slimline black shirt with top buttons undone and a black leather decorative blouson jacket. He has twin gold hoops in one ear, a chunky gold chain around his neck and assorted coordinating rings on most of his long fingers. With his wild spiky dark brown hair, darker iron-filings beard shadow adorning a pale, gaunt hollow-cheeked face and very dark piercing eyes, he is a little menacing – but somehow his deportment suggests this is all a front and really he's quite warm and equitable. In other words, he's me as I was then at the age of twenty-seven – and I haven't changed much in ten or eleven years. People say I look like Ronnie Wood in his heyday. Anyhow, the author registers the guy as a bit borderline goth/freaky, undoubtedly not your average citizen, and he wonders exactly what kind of a character he'll develop into.

At the book signing the guy makes a conversational gambit with the author, who readily reciprocates as this is just what he hoped for – that the guy would voluntarily flesh himself out. As the guy talks, he becomes clearly revealed as a fan, an ardent fan, perhaps even an obsessive fan. He dotes on everything the author says, an enthusiastic yes man, his face lighting up like a Christmas display as the author interacts with him more and more, playing bigger cards to draw him out, until finally the author puts down his ace of trumps – the secret that lies at the heart of his writing.

After the guy has departed, the author experiences slight mis-givings, feeling that perhaps he went too far in showing himself to the guy – overplayed his hand a tad. For as the great philosopher once said, 'If you gaze for long into an abyss, the abyss gazes also into you.' Indeed the guy is a stranger to the author, and the author realises he doesn't know what weirdnesses may lurk in the nether regions of that stranger's psyche. Suppose the guy is some kind of a nutter – an obsessive, a psychopath, a psychotic, a pervert, or a mixture of these ingredients? And conjecture in addition that the author's fulsome empathising with him has maybe given out the wrong signal, unwittingly establishing a primal bond that was unsought? What might this lead to? The creation of a monster? A literary stalker, no less!

I was really pleased with my creative efforts, and in the evening after work on the seventh day I consolidated my notes into a full draft on the computer. It seemed only natural then to attempt some form of proper communication to Hugh, using the expressive momentum I'd generated. Naturally I'd checked the contact page of his author website, and there was no email address or form to fill, only the physical addresses of his publicist, publisher and agent. And the age of Facebook and Twitter hadn't yet blossomed – that was just around the corner. So it would have to be a good old fashioned letter.

Dear Hugh, I typed, and then I went on to say I was writing to continue the process that had commenced in Blackwell's. I reiterated my pleasure in talking to him and hearing the inking-in rationale behind his writing; then I told him how much I'd enjoyed *The Major Arcana*, saying I was irritated by certain reviews in the papers because they contained spoilers. It was a very chatty letter, a bit longwinded.

Further along, I said it was a pity our conversation had been cut short and there was more that we could have explored. I was careful not to put anything silly or lovey-dovey into a letter that might be read by others before reaching Hugh's eyes. When he had the information – my name, email and phone number – he could then follow it up. So I kept it on a business-like footing – literary business. I described my intuition that he had viewed me as a character, and the idea for a story that had come out of this. Then I took the actual draft of the story fragment I'd just composed and pasted it into the letter, editing and précising it down so it wasn't *War and Peace*.

Finally I asked Hugh for his opinion and invited him to continue the story or instead give his version of the same events. Now came the really clever part, as I said I was doing his job for him – inking in a bad scenario – as a famous author such as himself must surely have considered the possibility of obsessive fans stalking him, and he hadn't touched on that yet. I felt I approached this with just the right amount of irony and detachment, and I was sure he'd get where I was coming from and respond accordingly. Nudge, wink, and all that.

I printed the letter – ten A4 pages at one-and-a-half line space – and got to bed at close to three o'clock in the morning, and I was dead tired when the alarm clock went off at seven-thirty to summon me to the workday. During my lunch hour I slowly reread it and thought it quite brilliant in some parts and a bit gushing in others, but fundamentally it would do the job. With some trepidation I sealed it in the envelope, addressed to Hugh at his publishers, and let it fall into a post box, getting a wild uplift in my stomach as my fingers parted and the point of no return was crossed.

It was a Friday again, exactly a week on from the Blackwell's reading, a period that now seemed to constitute a major developmental phase in my life. I would go out pubbing and clubbing for the whole weekend, buoyed up by the knowledge that I'd done my best in difficult circumstances and rescued a critical situation that could so easily have floundered. Would Hugh reply? Of that I had absolutely no doubt. He would recognise the situation for what it was – an unfortunate truncation of something that was meant to go on and on – and he would applaud my efforts to get it back on track. I knew it might take a while for the letter to filter through and for him to respond, but I was prepared for the wait. I wasn't going to lose my head.

5. The Sun Sets On Sunset Street

Darren Winterbottom lives in a four-bedroom, two-reception half-timbered detached house in a quiet part of Chertsey, fairly near the River Thames, which is ideal for my purposes. I found his address on 192.com, from an old electoral roll entry, and then I had a look using Google Street View. Nice place – Zoopla value it at just north of seven hundred thousand pounds, but that seems low to me. From Darren's old Facebook posts, I know that he lives there alone, having broken up with his wife about two years back and bought her out – another plus from my point of view. She has the kids during the week and he gets them at weekends. Darren likes the Chertsey area because of the combination of its wide open spaces and the fact it's an easy commute to central London, a journey that he undertakes fairly frequently.

Darren is always boasting on Facebook about the power meetings and champagne lunches he has with publishers, agents and film executives. He's seems perpetually on the point of securing some major screen deal that never quite materialises – the next *Game of Thrones*, *Twilight* or *Vampire Diaries* – and he avoids being dogmatic when it comes to the details. Nonetheless his loyal inner circle on Facebook actively 'like' and make admiring comments on these posts, some of them outright sycophantic and cringe-making to read. Correspondingly Darren always 'likes' the most belly-crawling of these comments, throwing bones of reward to the gaggle of arse-lickers. I used to comment on his posts when I had something meaningful to say, but not anymore, not since we fell out and he unfriended me. I can still see his timeline because his privacy settings are set to a mixture of 'public' and 'friends of friends', so my monitoring propensities remain undiminished by his effrontery.

I check Darren's Facebook page and find that his recent posts are the usual mixture of links to stories with a paranormal theme, coupled with soft right-wing stuff, a lot of it from the *Daily Mail* –

criticisms of EU bureaucracy, immigration policy, political correctness, the activities of Bob Geldof and Russell Brand. Most writers have a left-wing inclination and abhor *Daily Mail*-style rhetoric, but Darren's followers always cut him some slack here, even sometimes admitting there can be another side to the arguments. Darren rarely goes as far as posting anything blatantly far-right on his wall, but if you go to the sidebar and burrow down into his many page 'likes', you will find the telltale yellow badge with purple script of UKIP, and when I first discovered this he was the only one of my seventeen hundred-odd friends to 'like' that particular page.

Darren's wall together with his Twitter feed make for the ideal means by which to track him, sometimes on an hour-by-hour if not minute-by-minute basis. When he's not announcing his movements around London and the contents of his lunch table by means of his iPhone, he's telling the world about his feats in penning three thousand words non-stop in a morning and then going out for a six-mile run and a workout in the gym. Give the man a gold star! And later in the day, it's incisive criticism of the films and TV shows he's watching, and how he intends to get up at six o'clock tomorrow and break the back of the next long chapter in Josiah Stone's intrepid quest to clear the streets of werewolves, or some other such puerile claptrap.

Normally all this is most yawn-inducing to me, but in my current mode it's a delight and I marvel at how technology has revolutionised the world of the stalker. I learn that in my target week Darren is going to be mainly at home, working on polishing up the second draft of his latest Josiah Stone novel. Perfect! I devise my plan of action, assemble together the equipment I will require and make enquires regarding ancillary contingencies that need to be covered. As the week gets underway, I'm watching Darren's every post like a hawk hovering in the sky, and I decide that I'll strike on the Wednesday.

I first met Darren at the 2002 Horripilation Convention, held around Halloween at a large hotel in Reading. It was one of those pyrotechnic events where my life went into a higher gear and I became part of a new select community, involving not only Darren but also many others in genre writing who were to become friends, and then in some cases mutate into being enemies – notably Eustace Crimp and Simon Ongar. Those whom I met over the Horripilation weekend who remain friends include Otto Monkman, Stanley Grainger, Darius Foley and Grant Crosby – a great bunch of guys; I wouldn't want to create the impression that I fall out with everybody!

At this point in my life, I had tried my hand at writing horror short stories, and sent two or three out to small press magazines, but wasn't yet producing work of publishable quality. I'd found out about the wonderful world of genre-writing conventions and hoped that first-hand contact with like-minded fans and actual writers would boost my creativity, and I was dead right. At Horripilation I could actually put faces to the names I'd been hearing about in the magazines, newsletters and message forums, and one of the first was Darren. Knowing who he was from his nametag, I said I'd liked his last story in *Miskanthropic* magazine, and he was immediately very friendly in an easy blokeish way, asking me about my writing and how I was liking the convention.

Propping up the main function room bar, we downed pints of 6X at a reckless pace, with Darren soon giving me the benefit of his advice, which was to keep writing day and night, and to send stuff out constantly, and to ignore rejection – good advice, actually. He had a broad Yorkshire twang in his voice and was very well built, with a prematurely bald bullet head, the hair at the sides pared down to stubble. Nose and ear piercings and sleeves of goth tattoos on his arms lent a tribal edge to his working class hard-man image. Even back then, I remember him ridiculing Tony Blair and mentioning Margaret Thatcher in tones of reverence, which I thought was distinctly out of phase with the community's general view.

Having broken the ice with Darren and also with Otto, Stan and others in similar encounters, I was naturally included in the larger gatherings that clustered around book signings, speeches and panels;

and when the time came to go for a massive blowout at a local curry house, I was invited along to that too, accepted as one of the boys. As someone who looked a bit goth and liked black and black leather, I fitted right into the subculture, and indeed I noticed that many of the convention attendees displayed notable elements of the archetypes of horror and fantasy fiction.

Some had dishevelled hair with matching eyebrows and sideboards, so that they carried a lycanthropic air. Others with pallid drawn faces, framed by jet black hair and similarly all-black attire, could easily pass for vampires. Yet another type had the flavour of Tolkien creatures – Hobbits, Trolls or variations of Gollum – some with shaven heads and perpetually deranged expressions on their faces. Of course women were present too, some overtly goth and others a bit witchy, punky or hippyish, though males predominated at a ratio of around sixty-forty. It was a whole other secret world of belonging, a bit like gay subculture, but with an altogether different set of references. No one looked completely 'normal' – that is bank clerk or estate agent normal.

Through the people I met at Horripilation, I got to know much more about the workings of the genre fiction business, and although this convention was styled around 'horror', the genres of horror, fantasy and sci-fi are really very intertwined, eliding into one another. As in any business it's important to make useful contacts, in this case amongst editors, publishers and agents, as well as other writers, so that when you contact people to try and place your stuff they know who you are. So I tapped into that network and kept up my involvement by attending the Open Nights that were held periodically in a spacious back room of The Graven Image pub in Whitechapel. Darren was always there, as he lived in London at the time, whilst others, including myself, came from further afield and either stayed over or travelled back late.

Back in those days, Darren's fiction could be classified as 'traditional horror', involving apocalyptic scenarios where zombies and other mutant creatures would wreck havoc on a displaced and terrified populace; or else power-crazy tyrants would make pacts with alien or supernatural forces in the pursuit of world domination. That kind of stuff. I did quite like the rumbustious nature of his early work, though I was constantly aware that Darren – unlike Hugh – was not the greatest of wordsmiths. His prose had a lumpen quality and he always overwrote; for example he would never describe someone dying in three or four sentences when he could take six pages instead. I would speed read on autopilot through his extemporised accounts of gore, bloodshed and terror, which had the same pointlessness as endless car chases in films, a kind of pornography of violence. Again unlike Hugh, Darren had seemingly never leant the lesson that in these matters less is often more.

But whatever Darren lacked as a literary artist, he made up for by possessing that core virtue of the upwardly mobile: being a very hard and tenacious worker. He churned out short stories by the dozen, and he managed a three- or four-hundred page novel a year, creating a strong presence and a firm fan base, much to the satisfaction of his publishers, who were more interested in the bottom line than the Nobel Prize. However, as the 2000s progressed the market for that kind of written horror went into a decline, perhaps because its predominantly young male readership had been seduced away by violent videogames and DVDs – changing times and changing media. Consequently commercial publishers weren't so interested in such traditional fare, and some previously successful horror scribes failed to get new book deals.

But Darren, ever the pragmatist, wasn't about to give up or accept a demotion to the indie press, with its small print runs and microscopic royalty cheques. Instead he started to shift his parameters towards the more favourable market of urban fantasy, in particular that strand of the genre, made popular by Laurell K. Hamilton, where horror and fantasy elements are embedded into a pulp thriller format, with a detective/enforcer character centre stage – part Philip Marlowe, part Van Helsing. Also the concept of a long-running series of books with a common lawman protagonist is attractive on the marketing front, and from Sherlock Holmes to Inspectors Morse, Rebus and Wallander this is well-proven territory.

So Josiah Stone was born and injected into a gritty dystopian semi-futuristic version of Leeds, where the undead, vampires, shapeshifters, incubuses – you name it – got up to all kinds of naughty stuff and had to be slapped down. *Sunset Street* wasn't that radical a departure from Darren's earlier stuff, but the focus was refined and a new editor trimmed back the excesses. It was, however, immensely popular as a series, catapulting Darren up to new heights of author success. I remember the launch party for the first book, *Janus-Faced*, in 2005, and the huge look of cheer on Darren's wide stubbly face as he signed copy after copy. From my previous experience of Darren's work, together with the garish comic book-styled jacket of the latest, I felt I wasn't going to much enjoy the exploits of Josiah Stone, but I acted otherwise as I handed over my copy for signature, and of course I said, 'Looking forward to this!' as I met his eye.

What can I say about *Sunset Street* and similar urban fantasy – or indeed its cousin, that other dumbed-down-for-the-youth-of-today genre, paranormal romance – that doesn't make me sound like a highbrow, snooty and out of touch kind of critic? Not a lot really – maybe it is me. I am a genuine fan of *intelligent* horror and other genre fiction, but all this stuff that comes across like children's fiction for grownups, involving wizards, fairies, assorted weird creatures and bands of quasi-medieval folklorist types who overcome problems by using bits of magic and hocus-pocus that have a make-it-up-on-the-hoof quality…I just can't be doing with it. I can't suspend disbelief and accept the veracity of invented worlds where the parameters are so sloppy, but apparently other people can, so good luck to them.

But when you have an author friend who writes in this mode and who takes it as a given that you will like his stuff, and who in addition wants evidence of that in the form of praise, it presents special difficulties. Over the years I managed to keep Darren happy with generalised epigrammatic positive comments whenever I bumped into him at conventions and other meet-ups. And when the age of Facebook got into full swing, and I was required to show my appreciation there, I could pick up information online about his books and what other people thought of them and thereby simulate the front of an interested fan.

But at a certain point I got complacent, lost the plot and made what turned out to be a grave error. It was around five years ago at the time of the new *Sunset Street* release, *The Colliderscope*. Darren had publicity links up on his personal Facebook wall, his author page and the *Sunset Street* page, and fans were busy 'liking' and making effusive comments. I checked out the posts, dutifully added my 'likes' and perused a few of the comment threads. One fan, Wendy something, had written: 'Loving the new book! Brill story, but things feel a little quiet in Sunset Street without Thanatos. I do miss him!'

Wendy was referring to the fact that Dr. Thanatos – evil genius, necromancer and Josiah Stone's arch nemesis – had been killed off several books ago in *Reichenbach Reloaded*, in an epic superhero re-imagining of the Holmes-Moriaty fight-to-the-finish in that same Swiss setting. Now came the stupid part. In a thoughtless flash of inspiration, I added my two cents worth to the thread. I said: 'Hey Darren, you ought to bring Thanatos back from the dead in the next instalment. That'd be tasty!'

Two sentences that took me no more than forty seconds to think up, write and post; but once that 'post' button had been pressed, that was it – no taking it back, no covering it over. In the unforgiving everything-set-in-stone digital world, emails of that comment were winging towards Darren, Wendy and any other contributors to the thread, so even if I deleted it I couldn't have erased my tracks.

In fact it was twenty minutes later, after I'd completely forgotten about my post in a melee of other online activity, that I received an email informing me of another comment by Wendy. Smiling I clicked it open, perhaps anticipating approval and agreement on her part, but instead it initiated what young folk call a classic OMG! moment. Wendy said: 'Er…Thanatos did come back from the dead. He was reanimated half way through The Quatrain Games???'

I felt suddenly cold and all at sea in the head. Quickly I Googled *The Quatrain Games*, the previous *Sunset Street* book, and I read the detailed Wikipedia synopsis. My brain generated self-rebuking swear words as I uncovered the full dimensions of my carelessness and idiocy. Now feeling hollowed out as well as cold, I saw that Wendy was of course correct, Thanatos had indeed been reanimated, and what she'd meant in her comment was *not* that she missed Thanatos because he'd been off the scene since being killed at Reichenbach, but he was with us again and she missed him because he simply didn't appear in *The Colliderscope*. Oh my God…

I clicked back to the Facebook tab and saw that Wendy's new comment had generated five 'likes' already, including one from Darren. It was now obvious to him and others that at the very least I hadn't read *The Quatrain Games* and I didn't have a clue about its contents, and most probably my ignorance of the whole *Sunset Street* oeuvre spread much further. In fact the truth was I hadn't read anything beyond page fifty of the first book, *Janus-Faced*, many years previously. The few bits of knowledge I had garnered by reading snippets online were unfortunately full of holes, and I was now unmasked as an unreliable fan.

But my discomfort soon wore off, as it wasn't that big a thing, not to me at least. I tried to patch it up with Darren by making my usual light-hearted comments on his posts, but he ignored them all, neither 'liking' nor replying. Shortly afterwards I noticed that my Facebook author page was down by one 'like', and when I scrolled through the list of 'people who like', Darren's name was absent. He also left the group I'd set up to promote *Dark Undertows*, my story collection. Things went quiet for a time, but when I next encountered him in the flesh, at the World Horror Convention in Salt Lake City, he just grunted when I said hello and cut me dead for the whole weekend. The sight of me must have served to renew his bitterness, for when I next checked he'd unfollowed me on Twitter.

Earlier I'd shrugged off Darren's huffiness as just another little mishap, but now I started to get angry myself at this massive and ridiculous show of protest. Believe me, writers have the largest egos out of practically any subspecies of mankind, but Darren's display of chronic hurt and pique was as overcooked as one of his plots. He'd decreed that my lackadaisical attitude toward *Sunset Street* constituted a lack of respect for him. The man and the work were one, indivisible. Could he not see that my indifference with regard to that type of fiction wasn't personal? No, he couldn't. I was beginning to regard him as a bit of a twat.

Then it all came to a head in that cruel month of April in the year 2013. The death of Margaret Thatcher was an occasion for rejoicing and revelry across the entire spectrum of everyone I knew, offline and online, including most every close friend on Facebook – that is with one significant exception. A right-wing agenda had always been evident in Darren's online postings and in his conversation, especially after he'd had a few beers. Sometimes he'd start to sound like an old fart from Thatcher's own generation, whingeing about the unions and successive Labour governments, and several of us exchanged quizzical looks around him when he was off on one of these rants. But when Thatcher died he excelled himself, going into emotional overdrive on Facebook, and you'd think it was his own mother that had departed!

Darren posted links to supportive news stories, obituaries and video clips, and the comments he added were unabashed hagiography, daring anyone to disagree with him at this time of great loss. No one did disagree, but also no one 'liked' or commented either – Darren was left alone in his grief. Most of my other British friends and myself did the opposite, posting links to critical and derogatory pieces and videos, and 'liking' and agreeing with each other's actions for all we were worth! The best of these featured the rising popularity of the song 'Ding-Dong! The Witch Is Dead' – from *The Wizard of Oz* – as a Thatcher funeral anthem, complete with the original track and video remixes. I shared them on my wall, with suitable approving comments, and I got loads of 'likes'…and I also heard from Darren for the first time in well over a year.

He commented: 'Have some respect for the dead, you left-wing putz!' And he unfriended me.

Putz...? I Googled it, as I wanted to be sure of its exact specifications as an insult. Putz is the Yiddish word for penis, used pejoratively so it has similar connotations to 'dickhead'. More generally it means an ignorant person who isn't sensitive to what goes on around him and makes stupid remarks.

I responded calmly and in a dignified manner on the Facebook thread: 'Thanks for the insult, Darren, and the unfriend. When I last checked free speech was allowed in this country and it hadn't yet become a fascist regime. I expect this will be the last exchange we shall have so goodbye! By the way I think Sunset Street is a load of pigs' testicles!'

No, I didn't put that last sentence, but I was strongly tempted – in fact I wrote it out but erased it before I posted. Maybe I should have posted it and been damned rather than endure the alternative, which was fuming, bubbling ever-percolating anger.

Putz! I was a putz for posting something that everybody else agreed with on my own Facebook wall? That was the limit, the end.

6. Clichéd Ways of Obtaining a Gun

In debates about gun crime and gun control, one old chestnut comment keeps cropping up: *It's not guns that kill people, it's people that kill people.* What an idiotic thing to say! When you have a gun in your hand, you know full well it's the gun that's going to do the killing and you're just a passenger. How would 'you', minus the gun, go about killing someone? Grab them by the throat and try to strangle them? Pound them to death with your fists? Kick them to death? Use the Five Point Palm Exploding Heart Technique? Or use a lesser weapon, such as a knife or baseball bat?

All are possibilities to be sure, but none are exactly easy and inevitably involve some level of physical prowess, fighting knowledge and skills. What's more, once you embark on such an attack, your victim is going to take evasive action, retaliate and perhaps over-power you. Taking all this into account, it's highly likely that 'you' wouldn't consider it advisable to undertake the killing attempt at all. But if you possess a gun, it's different. With one of those, you can stand a distance away from your victim, and providing you can point the thing straight and hold it as though you mean business, you have the complete upper hand. And if you've got the balls to pull the trigger...well. How much percentage of the kill would be down to 'you' and how much down to the gun?

British firearms laws are very strict and most handguns are banned outright and cannot be licensed. However, relics from the past may well reside amongst the possessions of older people, dating from times when less vigilance existed. Such is the case of my Great Uncle Jerry, aged ninety-eight and a veteran of World War II. When I was a kid, he often boasted about his Webley service revolver, which he'd retained after being demobbed, and once he even let me play with it – unloaded of course. My mother and other relatives urged him to give it up at various gun amnesties, but he wouldn't, saying that he needed it in case a burglar ever broke into his rural cottage. He kept it in an old tin chest under his bed, along with several boxes of ammunition.

Now Uncle Jerry has got Alzheimer's. He often doesn't know what time of year it is and still thinks Margaret Thatcher is prime minister. Carers visit him regularly at home, entering by means of a coded key safe outside. I know the combination and sometimes drop in to have a cup of tea and say hello. This was the case last week, when in preparation for my endeavour I let myself in, found Uncle Jerry dozing in his armchair and silently sneaked into his bedroom. The tin box was still under the bed and was covered in a thick layer of dust, having not been touched in perhaps a decade. I inched open the lid and found the Webley and about thirty rounds in their original cardboard boxes, all foxed at the edges and corners. The revolver, a Mk IV .38 calibre, was almost as big and weighty as I remembered it from childhood, and my heart thrummed as I hefted it and aimed at a flower-patterned vase on the dressing table.

I put the piece and the ammo into a holdall, and as I was passing the lounge an awakened Uncle Jerry met my eyes.

'Hello Jago. Where've all the monkeys gone?'

'They've taken them back to the zoo, Uncle Jerry. I'll put the kettle on.'

'Oh good...'

Early on the Wednesday morning, I drive past Darren's house in Chertsey and then make my way to a secluded parking spot near the River Thames. The contingencies are in place and all I have to do now is wait. I know from Darren's Nike Running App posts on Facebook that he always goes for a run on Wednesday mornings; moreover the app also conveniently delineates his routes, which take in the Thames towpath. I leave the car and position myself at a vantage point where I can see him coming. Thankfully not many other people are about, only the odd dog walker.

Though the day is overcast, I still wear large black-framed sunglasses, and I have a porkpie hat on my head and the collar of my jacket is turned up. This is in part a disguise and in part an attempt to get 'in character'.

Presently Darren's jogging figure takes shape – the stubbly bullet head and well-muscled shoulders, biceps and thighs in a white T-shirt and blue lycra shorts. As he gets closer, I step out and say his name, which makes him pull up abruptly with a scrunch and stare at me.

'Jago? Is that you? What're you doing here? What's with the shades?'

'Too many questions, Darren.' I pull the Webley from my pocket and wave its four-inch barrel at him. 'Walk this way.'

Darren gives me a sickly grimace. 'What's this? What's going on?'

'We're going fishing.'

'What the fuck…?'

'Darren…you're nothing to me now. You're not a brother, you're not a friend. I don't want to know you or what you do.'

'Have you got a screw loose?'

'Huh! You thought they'd be no repercussions, eh, for that page unlike, Twitter unfollow and Facebook unfriend? And how did you describe me at the time? "A left-wing putz" – that was the expression you used, was it not?'

'Look…' Darren, now drained of colour and considerably diminished, starts to giggle feverishly. 'Is this some kind of joke…?'

'Yes it is, Darren! And the next part involves a little boat trip.' I jab him in the side with the revolver. 'Come on!'

Moored a short way along the towpath is the twelve-foot dingy with a small outboard motor that I hired earlier, complete with a rod, reel and some bread to use as bait. Under protest, Darren gets aboard and sits at the prow, whilst I start up the motor and take us out into a broader, quieter stretch of river, careful to keep the gun barrel on him at all times. We go around a bend and pass a boat-yard and a small group of youngsters hanging around by a car park. When I reach a suitable spot, away from buildings and masked from the bank by a line of tall poplars and oaks, I stop and kill the motor.

'Okay Darren, bait the hook and cast off.'

'Why?' He gives me a defiant stare.

'Humour me, okay.'

'Why fishing?'

'It'll all become clear very soon.'

Darren shrugs and proceeds to pick up the rod, put a bread fragment on the hook and cast, seemingly wanting to get it over with. When the line is in the water, he turns and scowls.

'What now, Jago? What drugs exactly are you on? Or did you forget to take the medication – is that it?'

'Say your prayers.'

'Pardon?'

'Go on. Say: *Hail Mary, full of grace. Our Lord is with thee. Blessed art thou among women, and blessed is the fruit of thy womb, Jesus.*'

'You're bonkers!'

I raise the Webley, pointing it at his head. 'Just say it or I'll let you have it now!'

'Hail Mary...' a nonplussed Darren begins. Then suddenly his expression changes from bemusement to spontaneous alarm. He's got it. 'No! I'm not Fredo Corleone and you're not Al Neri!'

'I've got two things to say to you, Darren. Ding dong the witch is dead. And *Sunset Street* is a load of pigs' testicles!'

I pull the trigger and the gun goes off startlingly loud and with a fair bit of recoil, the report echoing across the river's rippling surface. A flock of birds screeches furiously overhead and some distance away a dog barks four times. Darren's body is slumped forward, over the bow, as a balloon of dark red slowly expands into the water. My first Facebook murder is complete.

Not bad...I think, reading it back from the computer screen. Quite funny in parts. It's only a first draft and I can improve on it later. The thing is: will readers readily cotton on that the scene is based on the climax of *The Godfather Part II*, or should I flag that up earlier? Maybe I'll say something about the catastrophic rift between the two Mafia brothers, Michael and Fredo, and how it rolled on to produce one of the most harrowing revenge scenes in cinema...Or maybe I won't bother...

Oh here we go...I hear the grate of Robin's key in the lock. The insulation of my creative bubble is rent asunder, and I'm going to have to endure more tedium from him, without doubt. His footfalls take him into the kitchen, he sees I'm not there or in the lounge and he calls out my name in a shrill tone, as if alerting his manservant. I come out of my room and say, 'Hello Robin,' quite magnanimously.

'You haven't cleared up the kitchen,' he says as though that omission were on par with genocide. I sensed he was in a bad mood even before he came home.

'Not yet, I've been busy.'

'Let me guess. Writing your novels? Facebooking and Twittering to your friends…?'

I don't reply.

'You said you were going to do some little jobs around the flat. Dusting. Cleaning the mirrors. Things that would take hardly any time at all. Look up there!' – he points hysterically towards a ceiling corner – 'A cobweb!'

'A cobweb? Fuck me! Lets call out the SAS to deal with it…'

'Why don't you just clear it up instead of making witty remarks? Why don't you take some pride in your surroundings instead of living like a slovenly pig…? I'll tell you why – because you're too busy *pretending* to be a writer and tossing off with your mates on Facebook!'

Robin is determined to keep banging away, and I can feel the swell of real anger building in me now, threatening to wash away my façade of nonchalance and sarcasm. There is only one course of action: counterattack.

'Oh yes, here we go. You've had a bad day at work so naturally it's all my fault. I'm a slovenly pig because I'm not monitoring the activity of every spider in the place on a 24/7 basis. And as for tossing off, who were you tossing off with last week on that night out? What were you doing for seven solid hours? That's a lot of shop talk and goss! You were very vague about it when I asked before. Where exactly did you go and what did you do?'

'Just went to a few bars…'

'Till half past two?'

'We went back to Kevin's for a coffee afterwards, if you want to know.'

'Coffee and what? Coffee and a blowjob most likely!'

'Your jealousy and suspiciousness are really unattractive, Nick.'

'You know, I might take more of an interest in cleaning the flat if you took more of an interest in pleasing me. How about giving me a blowjob now and again – like we used to, remember?'

'Huh! Who wants to suck your ugly old cock?'

Robin says it with such acute venom that all my reserve suddenly gives way, and in a spontaneously spasm of anger I let loose my right arm and punch him on the side of his jaw, medium hard. It's nowhere near a full-bloodied strike, but it's stronger than the poke I meant it to be. Oh dear...Robin lurches to one side, loses his balance and staggers backwards, finding a stool to sit down on. He then gives me his standard very serious frown.

'This is domestic violence. I'm going to call the police.'

'Go ahead. I'm past caring.'

He puts his left hand behind his head and uses his right to wiggle his chin fractionally against the support. 'God...You've broken my fucking jaw.'

'No I haven't.'

'There's shooting pains in it, and it feels all numb and weird and out of alignment.'

'It was nothing. Just a light friendly poke.'

'If I called the police, they'd put you away – what with your past record for violence.'

'I wish I hadn't told you about that – I knew you'd use it against me. Well, whatever, if I get put away, I'd be away from you. Look on the bright side!'

'You're pathetic.'

'Yeah yeah, I know. I'm useless, worthless and a slovenly pig. Anything else you want to add to the record, or are all the grooves full by now?'

Robin continues to manipulate his head for several seconds, then he stands up and casts a hateful glare at me. 'I'm going to have some paracetamol and codeine tablets, and then I'm going out. See you.'

I retire to the lounge, turn on the TV and watch the remainder of the news, as Robin paces back and forth outside in the hallway, making lots of theatrical noise. I try not to think or feel too much, there is no point. He pressed my buttons and I went too far, but somehow it was inevitable. Still, I'm aware that I must be careful of those kinds of outbursts in future. I do have a criminal record, dating from many years ago when I was just nineteen and very volatile. A drunk twat in a pub had a go and called me a 'poof', and I showed him just how much of a poof I was by glassing him in the face with a pint sleeve. It was all over in about two seconds. Luckily he was only superficially scarred, and the fact he'd provoked me with an anti-gay taunt counted in my favour. However, I ended up serving nine months and it ruined my university career. Where might I be now if I'd completed my English Lit degree?

Yes, I must be more careful…How many times have I said that before?

7. Love You Forever

It hardly needs to be said, but I'll say it anyway. My 'Literary Stalker' letter to Hugh, posted a week after my obsessive fixation with him commenced, was not answered, and neither were any of the other numerous missives I sent him over the coming months and years. In the initial stages of the obsession, the bubble of love sustained my illusion that he would reply and even reciprocate my feelings, but after around two months had elapsed and I'd heard nothing, I had to admit that something had gone awry. Perhaps the letter had been lost or mislaid amongst the piles of other fan letters he must receive? Or perhaps there was some other not entirely negative reason he hadn't replied? Whatever, I needed to test the situation by more proactive means than merely sending another letter. I had to try and engineer another face-to-face encounter.

When it came to better knowing the man...my love, my quarry... I'd amassed a fat favourites folder with suitable online links, together with physical newspaper and magazine clippings, and luckily I also had a copy of the *Hello!* that contained the big spread of photographs of Melody and Hugh at their swish Kensington and Chelsea home. I assembled the clippings sheaf into a scrapbook of varied textures, from the old book reviews in the Sunday papers, turning various shades of mustard, to glossy articles and interviews from men's mags and supplements, with their glamorous photos of Hugh looking like a film star. And since the Blackwells meeting, my online research had gone into overdrive as I strove to become an expert in the field.

Progressively I fleshed out the sketchy timeline of his life with which I was already familiar into a more substantial biography. He was born in the mid-1960s, the youngest child of Richard Eversleigh and Olivia Canford, who'd decided to double-barrel their names upon marriage in order to enhance the posh profile they were cultivating. In fact Hugh comes from a long line of overachievers. One of his ancestors was a key ally of the Duke of Buckingham during the Wars of the Roses, and he was amply rewarded when Henry Tudor took the throne. Hugh's grandfather, Air Commodore Bernard Eversleigh, was one of the first Spitfire pilots and a Fighter Command bigwig during World War II, gaining plaudits for his actions during the Battle of Britain and the air offensives afterwards.

Dick Eversleigh, Hugh's father, took a different career direction, attending RADA in the 1950s and becoming a theatre actor, eventually breaking into movies in the '60s, when he became 'Dick Canford-Eversleigh' and got a reputation for playing handsome upper class rakish types – the kind of parts George Sanders excelled at in an earlier era. The 'posh English cad' persona served him well, and he went to Hollywood and had a good run there, before he aged and then popped up in British TV doing character roles. As you may know, he was an alcoholic and died in the 1990s of cirrhosis of the liver.

So Hugh was born and raised within his parents' moneyed, jet-setting lifestyle, and his childhood as reported in the press was one of fantastic adventures in English country estates and exotic foreign trips to the French Riviera, California and the Caribbean, interspersed by spells in a string of boarding schools. Somewhat at odds to this background, as it was spun by feature writers, was Hugh's early interest in the macabre and occult, sparked by reading about the Golden Dawn, Aleister Crowley, W. B. Yeats and others, which led to his absorption of Gothic literature. And in more recent interviews, after his father's death, Hugh hinted at other aspects of his childhood that put these tendencies into perspective – his father's dark moods and rages, and occasional eruptions of domestic violence. Yes, the impulse to be a horror writer doesn't come out of nowhere.

The rest is all so well known it hardly needs reiterating here – the academically brilliant Oxford years, the early success of his short stories and novels in reinvigorating British horror, and the quick rise to a celebrity status yet more illustrious than his father's. What part, if any, of the mass of information I'd acquired about Hugh was useful to me in my next move? That was the question with which I was now confronted. I knew him intimately from afar, but how was I to get to know him close up? Funnily out of all the data and paper artefacts at my disposal, much of it intellectually weighty, it was actually the fluffiest item of all that provided the key – the colourful pages of *Hello!* magazine.

From the feel of the photos in the spread, I got the strong sense that Hugh wasn't exactly happy with this kind of exposure, but he was going ahead with it for Melody's sake and to help with her publicity as a model. In contrast to the moody enigmatic radiance of the solo shots of Hugh that appeared on book jackets and in features, accompanying interviews, he appeared stiff and ill at ease in *Hello!*, wearing the forced unnatural smile of a waxworks dummy. Melody, by contrast, beamed constantly with the ease of a professional poser, her wavy blonde tresses dominating most every shot.

In one especially artificial-feeling set, the blissful couple were depicted cuddling up together on a plump damask chaise longue, their bare feet hanging awkwardly in space, with Hugh looking mildly stunned. In another they were sat sipping champagne in their walled garden, surrounded by mildewed Greco-Roman cherubs, staring lovingly into each others eyes, as if in a contest. But the best set, from my point of view, depicted the pair in front of their Chelsea house, on the steps and coming down to pose with Hugh's classic silver Virage Volante, top down of course.

I couldn't find the address online, but from my reading I'd learnt that Hugh and Melody lived either in or very near Edgerton Crescent, within easy walking distance of Harrods. In the *Hello!* pictures, the actual house number was obscured, but by utilising other identifying features – the design of the front door, including the knocker and letterbox, and the arrangements of bay trees on the balcony and flowers in the window box – I felt sure I'd have no trouble tracking it down and hopefully getting better acquainted with the object of my desire inside. I could almost see myself in that *Hello!* spread, taking Melody's place, and the flagging fantasies from the bookshop encounter were sparked back into life.

There is a unique sensation to being a stalker on the job. One is perpetually in the grip of an effervescent nerviness, coupled with tremendous excitement and expectation, wired up on topsy-turvy waves of adrenalin. The term 'knotted stomach' is an undoubted cliché, but accurate in these circumstances. It's the kind of feeling you get watching a really edgy movie thriller where you can't work out what's going to happen next, but you know it's going to be tasty, whatever it is. With stalking, though, you're actually in the movie, making it up as you go along, and at any time it might run away from you and assume a life of its own.

Hugh's area was an oasis of comparative calm and seclusion within such a busy part of London, with bustling Knightsbridge and its big museums and shopping streets to one side, and the trendy King's Road district on the other. The crescent itself was pristine in its whiteness, as though made out of cake icing, without a blemishing feature in sight. Indeed, this was a nice millionaire-friendly neighbourhood, with a segment of wooded private gardens fitting into the curve of the house frontage, birdsong in the treetops and a pleasing localised quietness framed by the city's roar in the middle distance. As there was only a circumscribed number of houses to choose from, I soon found Hugh's place, using the *Hello!* photos for comparison and confident there could be no ambiguity. In fact the silver Aston Martin was parked a couple of bays up, and I took down its registration number in my little notebook, feeling like a twelve-year-old trainspotter.

I paced up and down in legs of fifty yards, first on one side of the crescent, then on the other. My casual glances towards the windows detected no activity. Deflation set in as it dawned on me that I could spend all day here and not see anything worthwhile. Earlier I'd told myself that I would need to be patient, though now I was fast becoming irritated. In a pulse of wild abandon, I almost went up the steps and rang the doorbell, but I stopped myself and tried to calm down. Constant imaginary dialogues with Hugh were coursing through my mind, looping around and doubling back on themselves, rehearsals for the real thing...

Look Hugh, we can't go on like this...we've got to get things sorted out...

After more than an hour of circling the crescent and gardens, whilst sinking deeper into reverie, something actually did happen and I wasn't prepared, so it jolted me profoundly as though I'd been woken suddenly by a kick in the ribs. Forty yards away around the curve from my viewpoint, a black front door slammed and a chestnut-haired figure wearing a brown leather bomber jacket and ginger corduroy trousers scurried down the steps and marched stridently away along the pavement. It was Hugh – and I barely recognised him! Here he was, the centrepiece of my dreams, right in my vicinity, practically breathing the same air! It was utterly unbelievable, and my heart went through the gears into overdrive in next to no time.

Hugh didn't look around and see me, so it was a simple matter to run across the crescent and fall in behind him, maintaining a distance of around twenty feet. He turned a corner, crossed the Brompton Road, and soon we were mingling with others and heading up Thurloe Square at some pace. The tall edifice of the Victoria and Albert Museum loomed before us, and it proved to be Hugh's intended destination, a walk of less than half a mile. As it was a Saturday afternoon, the entrance area was overrun with noisy visitors and tourists of all nationalities, many sitting on the steps. I followed Hugh inside and through the labyrinthine structure of corridors, galleries and stairways, eventually arriving on the third floor, where he took a particular interest in the theatre costume displays, circling slowly and pensively whilst writing down details in a flip notepad.

Up till now he hadn't registered my presence, but in the ambulatory flux of the gallery setting I did pass through his field of view more than once, though he didn't appear to notice. I felt I ought to do something proactive, and my heart thrummed as a plan took shape. Earlier I'd concluded that if I'd approached him right outside or very near his home, I'd have given myself away as a stalker; but here in this public space I could just happen to bump into him and it could conceivably pass for a coincidence. Feeling light-headed and silly but determined, I positioned myself in his path and prepared to dive off the high board.

'Hello,' I said as he caught up, 'it's Hugh, isn't it? We met at a reading of your new book in Bristol a few months back…'

Hugh looked at me poker-faced for a good two or three seconds, and then he said, 'Oh really…? And what are you doing here?'

'Just up for a day in town, looking around the galleries, doing a bit of shopping, that kind of thing…'

'Any specific exhibitions on your radar?'

'No, not really…I just like browsing.'

'Oh well, have fun.' Quickly he sidestepped and strode away, passing the oriental costume displays.

'Hugh?' I said, springing to his side. 'You do remember our meeting, our tête-à-tête, don't you…?'

He carried on walking, heading for the exit and the next gallery. 'I talk to lots of people at many, many readings and signings…It all becomes a bit of a blur, you know…'

'I wrote you a letter afterwards, did you receive it?' I was conscious of raising my voice to an urgent pitch in the struggle to keep his attention.

By now we were turning corners at some considerable speed, with Hugh pausing for longer before replying. It wasn't going how I'd hoped at all, and I was feeling most crestfallen.

'I get hundreds of fan letters, if not thousands. I can't read them all.'

'It contained a plot, a story…I tell you what, I'll send you another copy…'

As we marched through the red-walled space of Sacred Silver and Stained Glass, he didn't say a word, but when we reached the stairwell, and it was clear I wasn't going away, he stopped and faced me. 'I wouldn't bother if I were you,' he said with finality. 'I get loads of writers sending me their stuff, and I haven't got time to read it all. I'm not a publisher or a writing coach; I can't help in that department. Sorry! Now if you'll excuse me, I need to be somewhere else.'

'Why are you fighting it…?' I said morosely, and that aroused his curiosity for a second.

'Fighting what…?'

'Why don't we go for a drink and pick up from where we left off in Blackwells?'

'Where was that?'

'You remember, you were telling me about inking in the bad possibilities in life, using your writing as a kind of inoculation. That was really interesting.'

'Phwoar!' he exclaimed involuntarily, turning crimson at this piece of real information undeniably linking us together. 'I'd love to really, but I gotta go.'

'No you haven't. You're just saying that. Why are you fighting it, Hugh, surely you must be feeling it too?'

'Feeling what?'

'This…this tremendous affinity between us.'

'Look…What's your name?'

'You know what my name is. Nick.'

'Nick…listen. I feel nothing. Nothing at all. I don't even remember meeting you. It's all a projection on your part. Do you understand what I'm saying? You should cool it, okay?'

'It's because of Melody, isn't it?'

'What!'

'You've had a change of heart. You don't want to hurt Melody, and that's understandable. But you can't deny this thing, Hugh. You mustn't do that!'

'*A change of heart…?*'

'Yes. From the way you were in Blackwells – giving me those "come-on" looks and chat-up lines. You've got cold feet now…'

Hugh feigned a look of total astonishment, slowly backing away from me. 'This is ridiculous!' he exclaimed weakly.

'Lets talk it out, Hugh, it's the only way.'

His face kind of crumpled hopelessly like a deflating party balloon, and then he gritted his teeth, wordlessly about turned and bounded down the wide mosaic staircase, overtaking other visitors in his hurry to get away. At the bottom he speed-walked though Sculpture, watched by recumbent and gesturing statues as he scrambled towards the revolving doors. Outside, I continued following him along the busy pavement, and he turned at intervals of twenty seconds or so, checking I was still there. At one point he tried to hail a black cab, but it was engaged. Getting the hang of stalking now, I crouched low, using the crowds for cover, and I let him think he'd shaken me off. But I kept an eye on him from a greater distance, and presently I saw him cross the street and dive into Harrods at the Hans Road entrance.

He wasn't going to get rid of me that easily. This was the flowering of something huge, and having tested the situation I knew that plenty of hard work lay ahead in overcoming his resistance. Or was I just kidding myself? I did consider that possibility, but it wasn't important. The only thing that mattered was the enormity of the love between us – a love that I had to get Hugh to acknowledge, no matter what. His immediate compliance or non-compliance was a secondary issue, a mere detail.

Entering the dreamy opalescent spaces of Harrods, I felt like a warrior on a quest for some fugitive and almost unattainable prize, where the difficulty of the undertaking would be quickly out-matched by my limitless resolve. Surreptitiously I floated in the background, spying on Hugh as he perused the Tiffany jewellery, the glittering watch collections, and then went to shop for a few tinned and bagged items from the delicatessen. Presently he exited onto the Brompton Road, crossed over and made his way to Richoux restaurant. When I caught up and slowly passed by the window, I could see him inside having tea with Melody, his equilibrium seemingly restored.

Hugh was part of my life now, and I wasn't going to give up on him or be shaken off. Perhaps he knew I was still stalking him but thought the better of showing it, taking refuge in pretending it didn't matter all that much. Whatever, when he and Melody left Richoux, they got straight into a pre-ordered taxi and drove away, escaping pursuit. But of course I knew where they lived, and as darkness was falling I returned there and hung around, savouring the crisp evening atmosphere and conjecturing what was happening behind the illuminated window blinds.

Just after seven o'clock, another taxi pulled up and Hugh and Melody came out of the front door and she scurried down the steps. He was wearing a slim-fit dark suit and salmon-coloured shirt, and Melody a flowing cream evening dress with a scarf over her shoulders. Before he descended, Hugh pressed the front door three times and then anxiously scanned the other side of the crescent, making minimal eye contact with me and then carrying on as though everything was normal. He was near a Victorian street lamp and I was in the shadows under the trees, a good thirty yards away, but I felt sure he was expecting me to be there, so he would have no doubt it was I, his nemesis. There was no need to do anything more at this stage; after our earlier encounter in the V&A my mere presence spoke for itself.

After I'd watched the taxi's red tail lamps recede away, I crossed over, climbed the steps and posted a little something through the decorative brass letterbox. It was a small but outrageously priced card I'd bought in Harrods, which bore a simple design of a red embossed heart, surrounded by glitter, and the words 'Love You Forever' inside. I'd signed it with my initial, N, and added three kisses – a silly and sentimental gesture, I knew, but I didn't care, everything was out in the open now and I was wildly exuberant as a result.

Contented for the moment, I made my way back to Paddington to get a train home. To amuse myself as I looked out at the nightscapes flashing past the carriage windows, I mentally composed a new letter to Hugh, a continuation of the stalker story of the first one. And this time the finished article would go to his home address, so there was absolutely no danger of it being ignored.

8. The Literary Stalker's Book & DVD Shelf

The Collector by John Fowles should provide the cornerstone of any worthwhile collection of fictional stalking material. It tells the story of butterfly collector Frederick and his growing obsession with pretty, pale-blonde haired Miranda, whom he compares to an exotic specimen of the insect, a Pale Clouded Yellow, and covets her in the same way. His narration is matter-of-fact and wistful, so it all seems quite normal when he subdues her with chloroform, bundles her into a van and then imprisons her in the cellar of a remote country house he bought with his football pools winnings. The rest of the novel concerns what happens between them, from both points of view, but the notable thing is that Frederick remains an ineffectual character, never really nasty or sadistic towards his love object, and tellingly he's unable to consummate the 'relationship' – even when Miranda strips naked and tries to seduce him. So *The Collector* is a comparatively mild literary take on stalking and where it leads, and avoids being a torture-porn shocker or delineating the extreme horrors of real-life examples of the same tendencies.

Published in 1963, it came to exert a great fascination over the modern horror scene, and unfortunately over the actions of real serial killers who didn't possess Frederick's restraining characteristics. Leonard Lake and accomplice Charles Ng, and also Christopher Wilder and Robert Berdella, all claimed to have been inspired by the story in their murderous actions. *The Collector's* ideas appear in horror classics such as *The Silence of the Lambs*, where 'Buffalo Bill' stalks and kidnaps women, imprisoning them in his cellar before killing them and harvesting their skins – and like Frederick, he also has a lepidopteral obsession. Hannibal Lecter too is something of a collector figure, capturing Clarice Starling within his web of control and getting her to reveal her innermost secrets. Moreover, though a prisoner, he succeeds in manipulating all those around him in order to achieve his desired aims. In particular Lecter 'collects' his captor-in-chief at the loony bin, Dr. Chilton, and the novel ends with the anticipated consummation of that process – tasty!

Horror and crime writers love weaving knowing references to *The Collector* into their works. In *The Doll's House*, Neil Gaiman stages a convention of serial killers who are fans of the film version and see themselves reflected within. In Michael Connelly's *A Darkness More Than Night*, FBI profiler Terry McCaleb identifies a murderer on the basis that he has a well-worn copy of the book on his shelf. And in *Thomas's Playroom* by a certain Hugh Canford-Eversleigh, the eponymous teenage narrator dispatches a Swallowtail butterfly in a killing jar before strangling another young girl victim in his secret cellar and mummifying her body so she can become a doll version of herself in the playroom.

Hugh's love of *The Collector* is well known – and one time, a few years after I first met him, his interest in the book backfired on him spectacularly. This was due to Gretchen Mulhoney, a striking angular-faced, copper-haired fantasy author who turned bitter when she was ditched by Hugh following a protracted affair. Gretchen became a bit of a stalker actually, doing a number of kiss-and-tell interviews and characterising Hugh as a manipulative 'collector' figure, like Frederick in the novel.

She was taken in by him when he said that he and Melody had an open relationship, when in fact it was only open for him and he had many affairs whilst keeping Melody on a tight leash and making her play the 'little woman'. According to Gretchen, Hugh 'collected' people and used them like pawns on his chessboard, or butterflies pinned to a board, making them do his bidding by telling whatever lies that suited, backing it up with his considerable charm, until the time came for them to be shafted in some way. She was duped into thinking they had something deep going, but in truth she was just another conquest. As for Melody, she remained in denial, refusing to believe anything bad about the loving father of her children.

When Hugh was tipped off Gretchen was going public on the affair, he served an injunction on her, saying she was unreliable and was motivated by spite – his very action somewhat validating her claims about his controlling nature. But Gretchen must have impressed the judge, for he ruled against Hugh, much to his fury, and by resorting to the law he inflated the story to greater proportions. One can only imagine how Melody's denial held up under the strain, but the couple stayed together.

When it comes to horror stories influenced by *The Collector's* ideas, then the best of these has got to be that horror writers' worst nightmare – that a crazy obsessive fan will gain the upper hand and do to you what you write about in your books – which Stephen King brought to life in *Misery*. He actually includes a quote from *The Collector*, and his writer Paul Sheldon speculates about whether that book sits on the shelf of literary stalker Annie, but concludes it's better not to ask. In a way King was precisely following Hugh's formula of inking in the bad things, the terrible possibilities – and in fact King has said that in childhood he used to put down his anxieties on paper in order to prevent them from coming true, so this idea of writing as apotropaic magic is not exclusive to Hugh.

No real obsessed fan could be as lucky as Annie in having her hero arrive, incapacitated, on her doorstep; nor could one be as resourceful and determined as Annie in wringing out every last drop of satisfaction from the exercise of cruel control. But that's not the point, for *Misery* is a piece of modern Gothic and Annie is a monster, expertly crafted to fit the contours of a writer's specific fears – that the craft he loves could be turned against him so as to induce an ordeal, in which the act of writing itself is perverted to become a torture. But hey, it's a story and he breaks free in the end.

Misery is one of those works where the film version with Cathy Bates and James Caan is at least as memorable as the novel, and indeed it's films about stalking that capture the popular imagination much more so than books. Of these, the one which has pride of place on the stalker's DVD shelf is *Fatal Attraction*, an '80s shocker that still stands up well by today's standards. Everybody has seen it, everybody knows the plot, and everybody is familiar with the term 'bunny boiler', a perfect four-syllable alliterative catchphrase that has come to define the dangerous erotic obsessive.

What's good about *Fatal Attraction* is that it's solidly written and directed, and the characters are believably drawn, including the secondary ones. Glenn Close's Alex – all big hair and shoulder pads – makes for a marvellous obsessive, pathetic and needy one minute and a vicious steely warrior the next. The way she establishes a viable claim on Michael Douglas's hapless Dan, based on one weekend of shagging, is most effective, so her demands don't at first seem that unreasonable, whilst his attempts to wriggle off the hook turn more and more desperately tenuous. (Oh, to have had a weekend of shagging with Hugh, just one!) And Douglas himself is a terrific 'everyman' figure, registering the increments of distress on his face as the walls close in, a warning to married men far and wide to keep their snakes in their pants.

As it's a 'stalker story' the ante has to be upped quickly, from hassling to harassment to bunny violence in a smooth trajectory, and a similar real-life account would undoubtedly be more elongated, complex and convoluted. It all gets over melodramatic towards the end, as Alex becomes completely unhinged, but such a tale requires a grand cathartic climax – the evil stalker shot through the heart, or near enough, by the aggrieved wife, an act that combines vengeance, forgiveness and closure in an ideal instant formula. Bravo! And this ending was indeed changed from the original, which was much more low key and involved Alex committing suicide.

So both *Misery* and *Fatal Attraction* inform us about the shape stalker stories tend to assume – the stalker wrecks havoc of every imaginable kind but must never win in the end. That formula holds true for a host of other movies about obsessive headcases, including *Play Misty for Me*, *The Crush*, *The Fan*, *The Hand That Rocks the Cradle* and *Single White Female*.

A far superior exploration of obsession in film is Hitchcock's *Vertigo*, where the subject, James Stewart's Scottie, is an everyman figure rather than a nutcase, but the progression of his hopeless love for the unreal creation that is Kim Novak's 'Madeleine' persona is every bit as intense. *Vertigo* show us that stalkers get hooked on an idea or an image of a person rather than the flesh-and-blood reality, and the way this is conveyed through acting, photography, costume design and Bernard Hermann's rhapsodic score makes this movie into a masterpiece that can be savoured endlessly. But it still had to have a sad ending.

Stalker novels and films lie thick on the ground, and I won't attempt an exhaustive compilation. But one other film that is definitely worthy of mention is Michael Powell's uncharacteristic shocker *Peeping Tom*. So far ahead of its time, this is metafilm horror, where filmmaking paraphernalia itself becomes the weaponry of a diseased psyche. The opening big close up of protagonist Mark's eye, followed by the viewfinder POV of his stalking camera, set a style which would be imitated again and again in the slasher genre.

Mark is a film focus puller and compulsive home moviemaker; but his activities also extend to impaling women with a sharpened tripod leg, whilst filming them watching their own distressed faces in a distorting mirror as they die. Horrible! But it is the film's mission to explain *why* he does this, and not to exploit the material for any form of sicko gratification. By deconstructing Mark's motivations, the film invites sympathy for him, and this was too much for the cinemagoers and critics of 1960, who rose up in a combined out-pouring of disgust, and Powell's brilliant career was sunk. It certainly serves as a lesson to those writers and filmmakers who would take the stalker's side. Beware! But hey, times have changed, haven't they...?

So, having initiated my own 'stalker novel' with the first letter I sent to Hugh, I carried on into a second one, detailing the events of the London episode, and as I wrote I became increasing aware I was contributing to this great tradition of book and film stories. That process proved to be a long and unexpectedly fraught one, and now a decade or so further along, it's finding its apotheosis in the com-position of *The Facebook Murders*. When I've finished, I will make my mark on the genre with that novel – it'll be the thing I'll be remembered for.

In that second letter to Hugh, I found it easier to articulate my feelings about him by referring to 'the stalker' in the third person, as I'd done in the first letter, putting everything at a convenient remove. Similarly I sketched out the thoughts of 'the author', who was reluctant to take the plunge into a new relationship, denying there was anything between the two of them, but secretly battling with his urges to go with the flow and damn the consequences. Even at that point I could see this was the germination of something big – on paper at least if not in actuality!

I ended the letter with an invitation for Hugh to get in touch, so we could discuss everything on an equitable basis. Posting it, I got a flash of futility and knew he wouldn't reply, but I fought it back, taking satisfaction in having made my position absolutely clear. Undaunted by the continuing lack of feedback, I sent further letters to Edgerton Crescent and an expensive Christmas card to boot – at least I knew they were reaching him without any doubt.

And in riding the stimulus that the literary stalker letters had given me, I threw myself more wholeheartedly into other fictional writing, composing new and better sinister short stories and sending them out to magazines. By this time I'd already had three or four stories published – or awaiting publication – in lesser small press zines, but with the boost provided by this new creative wave I would get many more acceptances on a more regular basis. I was partly fulfilling my ambitions for their own sake, but I was also taking steps to get closer to Hugh by rising within the writing business.

Winter became early spring, and I made a couple more weekend trips to London and paced around Hugh's house and neighbourhood, but he failed to make an appearance. One thing I did notice were several discreet CCTV cameras on his balcony which I'm sure weren't there the first time. It occurred to me that if I were in a novel or a film about stalking, the story would be flagging at this point and folk would be complaining that they weren't getting their money's worth. This thought was reflected in the notion that I didn't have enough material for a worthwhile new letter to Hugh, and gloomily I considered that he might be winning the struggle, the tug of war, between us.

What I needed to do was bide my time and wait for an opportunity to get to him again in an enclosed situation, where he couldn't easily fob me off. Having long finished off the round of promotional appearances for *The Major Arcana*, he was now in a quiet phase regarding public events – unless I fancied jetting of to the USA, where he was scheduled to do a couple of talks and interviews, but I let that pass. However, as a member of the horror community, I received a regular newsletter, and within the pages of the next issue there was a notice that reinvigorated my quest, and I saw a beacon of light and hope begin to shine in the not too distant future.

9. The Outer Limits

Since the unfortunate punching incident last week, Robin and I haven't had a proper conversation, and the rapprochement that usually follows our quarrels is more in abeyance than ever. When we do talk we're perfunctory and matter of fact, only communicating out of necessity, and in moving around the shared spaces of the flat, we carefully sidestep one another, as though contagion might ensue from physical contact. On the Saturday night, he went out alone, didn't come home at all and stayed away for most of the Sunday, his main day off and our customarily closest time together. He behaved huffily and prickly on his eventually return, daring me to pick up the gauntlet and challenge him, but I let it pass. If he is making it with Kevin, then that's that.

I don't care, so I tell myself, though I have to fight the fits of rage that crop up for all sorts of disconnected reasons, such as triggering references in newspapers and TV programmes, but underneath I know it's mostly about Robin. To find equilibrium, I'm focussing on what really matters, which is the writing of *The Facebook Murders*, taking the anger out on my characters in the persona of my alter ego, Jago Farrar. It really is gelling this time, and I haven't felt so enthusiastic about an extended work in recent memory. Constantly I'm getting fresh ideas and scribbling down notes for future scenes, and I'm reworking the structure, making it more believable, solid and load bearing. This novel will go the distance, of that I feel sure.

I'm still working when Robin comes home around seven o'clock, and he doesn't call out to me, but instead makes a few noises in the kitchen, no doubt getting himself a cup of tea and something to eat. I hear the TV come on and the cadences of *The One Show* rumble away for around ten minutes, then he turns it off and goes to his room. No accusations about wasting my time on Facebook and Twitter, and no summary of my housekeeping shortcomings…? Well, that's hardly unwelcome. After a further fifteen or twenty minutes, during which time I find it hard to concentrate on anything, Robin enters my room, showing me he's changed his clothes and is now dressed to kill in new skinny jeans and a rose-coloured shirt.

'I'm off out,' he says flatly. 'Don't wait up for me, I might not be back.'

'Oh okay. Have fun,' I reply, attempting to overtrump his dead-pan approach.

'Arrivederci,' he concludes, tossing his hair with his hand before departing.

I exhale long and deeply before looking disconsolately at the work I've got open on the computer and the row of browser tabs. For something to do, I update the Facebook news feed but don't really take any interest in its contents. Well, I'm not going to get any more done today, so I shut everything down and think about where I'm going to go out drinking myself. Robin still retains the knack of bringing me down when I'm otherwise in an okay mood, and if he is going to have another night on the tiles then so am I.

Naturally I decide to avoid the Tavern and the other pubs in the Old Market scene, where I'll bump into people who know Robin and I as a couple. I don't want to face questions about what we're doing, or worse see Robin himself out and about with Kevin and his other exclusive cronies. Instead I take a head-clearing walk on the Downs, eventually arriving in Clifton Village, where I stop off for fish and chips in the shop on Princess Victoria Street. I eat them with a plastic fork as I head over to gaze at the Clifton Suspension Bridge, its towers, chains and rods all delineated in lights and spectacular as ever in the progressing summer evening dusk. Then I make my way down the gorge to Hotwells, where I know I'll find several straight mates who are drinking regulars in either the Mardyke or the Nova Scotia.

Down on the Cumberland Basin, I pause and take in the nearly full moon shining over Leigh Woods, making a pretty composition with a partial view of the bridge lights high in the distance; and unbidden I have thoughts of former good times with Robin that create a twang of nostalgic sorrow. But quickly I shake them off and hurry into the Nova, where Patrick, Barry and Gordon greet me with a cheerful, 'Hello Stranger!' and I set about the serious business of getting hammered on cider and trying to obliterate Robin from my psyche.

Towards twelve o'clock we stagger out into a pleasantly balmy night, and I feel a counterbalancing inner glow from having had a good non-judgemental conversation about my writing and a dose of simple bonhomie. I say cheerio and find myself wandering along past the waterside, feeling that the night is yet young and not wanting to go back to an empty flat or else bump into a returning Robin for another bring-down moment. Vacantly I look over at the marina and the many-masted SS Great Britain, knowing I'm heading for the centre but not thinking too hard about why.

Inevitably I reach St George's Road and then approach the axis of late-night gay fleshpots. Firstly I pass Pineapple, think twice and walk on, sensing I might be getting an attack of cold feet. No way am I going in Queenshilling – it's too flamboyantly camp for my tastes, and besides there's a fair chance Robin might have found his way in there; it's his kind of place. We had his birthday celebrations within its hallowed walls last spring, which seems like eons ago from this present perspective. Instead I decide I'll try the new club on Frogmore Street, The Outer Limits, aware that the stalker feeling is creeping up on me quite noticeably now, a cocktail of excitement and mild trepidation, throttling smoothly with the alcohol.

It's only two quid to get in, which isn't bad, and the guy on the door gives me a friendly smile. The interior is dark and cavern-like, apart from the dance floor, pulsing in pinks and purples, with Pharrell Williams's 'Happy' booming out at a fair volume. Am I feeling happy? I ask myself, not completely sure. I do have a dread of going into unfamiliar places on my own, knowing the regulars are sizing you up from the moment you appear, and soon someone will pounce – usually the person you least fancy in the entire joint.

I approach the horseshoe-shaped bar, where two guys with matching tall undercut quiffs and lush beards are holding court.

They pan their heads as I pass by, but I avoid eye contact. On one side table there's a raucous mixed group, including a lesbian with large tattooed biceps, facial piercings and an electric blue wig. At another table, two skinny old geezers with stubbly heads, wearing tank tops and leather wrist bands, positively leer at me, increasing my sense of discomfiture. Finding a free piece of bar space, I order a bottle of Bulmers Bold Black Cherry and try to relax. Over on the other side, there's a large and exuberant gathering of young lads, obviously students, and one or two of them are pretty okay.

After drinking the bottle, I order another and then saunter towards the dance floor. A tall lantern-jawed drag queen of around fifty-five is cavorting merrily with a spaced-out-looking bald bloke. Her name is Foxy something, and I've seen her around before. Wearing a bright ginger wig and a flouncy black goth dress, she comes across as an aged, alternate-reality version of Gretchen Mulhoney in some weird Pasolini-like sci-fi movie. Further back, two young guys in skin-tight vests are smooching and kissing, whilst a few other males are dancing singly, filling the gaps. Near the DJ, a striking girl in a red satin dress with a blonde bob is doing a kind of tango with her partner, a rangy brunette, and the pair remind me of Naomi Watts and Laura Elena Harring in *Mulholland Drive*.

Furtively moving around, I circle the pack of students and catch the attention of one for the second time. His hair is styled in a neat blonde wave, not too severely undercut, and he has a round cherubic face and very pale blue eyes. I casually stop and smile, and take a swig of cider, the old confidence returning now.

'Hello. Haven't seen you around before,' he says with a velvety touch.

'I don't get out much. I usually spend my evenings in my garret.'

'What – painting?'

'Writing actually.'

I get him a drink and we sit down, further away from the noise, and then I come out with a lot of spiel that makes me sound like five times as prosperous a writer as I really am. His name is Marcus and he's an anthropology postgraduate who likes older men. After fifteen minutes, he asks if I want to dance, and I'm not too keen, but I go along with the suggestion and respond to his probing kisses as we smooch.

At around three o'clock, he goes down on me in the bushes half way up nearby Brandon Hill Park, overlooked by the appropriately phallic edifice of Cabot Tower, pointing upwards into a moon-enhanced violet sky. Because I'm well pissed, it takes me a long time to climax, but I enjoy the build-up and the sense of rediscovery – after all it's been over two months since my ugly old cock has been near Robin's gob or any other orifice. And man cannot live by bread alone. As my excitement multiplies, I grip Marcus's head tighter, holding his ears between fingers and thumbs. Finally I make it to the top of the heavenly stairway, and I groan a couple of times and my body shakes with the explosion of pleasure.

'Looks like you needed that!' Marcus exclaims, standing up.

'You can say that again!'

He already has his jeans undone and has been playing with himself, so I go down and finish him off, and it doesn't take long. Afterwards we kiss briefly and exchange numbers, but I don't have strong feelings this will turn into something significant. Still, I need to keep my options open, what with the deteriorating Robin situation.

The following day, I'm at my workstation at the crack of twelve-thirty, with just the mild residue of a hangover that is quickly dispelled with strong coffee. Robin didn't come home last night, nor have I had a single call or text from him, all of which rather validates my activities on Brandon Hill in the small hours. If he wants to raise the stakes then so can I.

Anyway, I must now return to the business of *pretending* to be a writer, as the little prick would describe it. The 'pretence' is going well actually, with my magnum opus, *The Facebook Murders*, good and ready for the next bit. As I sip my coffee, I take stock for a moment, reviewing progress to date. The *Theatre of Blood* premise has been established and Jago's background and motivation given some shape. His murder victims have been lined up for dispatch, and the individual rationales worked out in note form. The 'Hugh' character's details and the lengthy history of Jago's obsession with him is being spliced into the narrative at intervals, with more to follow. And the first film-themed murder is done, and Darren Winterbottom sleeps with the fishes. I've even started to sketch out some scenes involving Jago's annoying partner, but that's a bit too close to home. No matter, the fictionalisation can be deepened later, and the important thing now is to get a skeletal first draft completed.

And what precisely comes next? I've been relishing this moment, anticipating it all through my night out yesterday, for now is the time to execute my second Facebook murder. Today is the day I shall off Eustace Crimp.

From the moment I first met him, back at a convention in the early 2000s, at the same time as Darren and the others, I never really liked Crimpy, but I did think his stories were clever and thought-provoking, and I made a big effort to be affable. For a start he is one of those guys with absolutely no sense of humour, who takes every-thing literally and at face value – or at least that's how he behaved with me. So when I made a joke where the logic was a bit askew, but it didn't matter because it was meant to be funny, he would give a twitchy frown and then correct my faulty logic, engendering a cold silence in place of laughter. And if I attempted to discuss the science behind the rationale of one of his stories, he would lecture me in a dry schoolmasterish manner as if talking to an idiot.

Funnily enough Eustace is gay, which should have given us something in common, though we're not remotely one another's type. But when it came to addressing issues from the gay perspective with a mutual sense of playing on the same side, that too hit the impenetrable wall of uptightness that operated in other areas. The ice just wouldn't crack with him, or else it quickly reformed if ever a slight fissure occurred. He wasn't like that with other gay writers on the convention circuit though, often air kissing on both sides and going into effusive greetings rituals – he never did that with me.

Like a number of people in the genre-writing world, Crimpy has a singularly odd appearance, and doubtless he's perpetually on his guard against any signs of disrespect or mockery in the behaviour of those he meets. Perhaps in our early interactions something about my body language or attitude put him off. Who knows? – that's pure speculation. He is very tall, well over six feet, and exceedingly thin – he probably barely weighs eleven stone – which lends him a somewhat alien 'stickman' image. On top of this, he has a narrow elongated face, a prominent nose and large sticky-out ears, which because of their misshapen edges give the impression of being pointed, like Mr Spock's in *Star Trek*. He not only resembles Spock, but also his Spockness comes through with his attitude towards everything – emotionally cool, logical and analytical in a most superior fashion. And his high reedy voice adds to the irritation of his outpourings no end.

In an interview, Crimpy admitted that his school nickname had been 'Spock', and in an effort to make himself look less like the famous Vulcan, he'd taken to having his hair cropped very short. But this only served to create the aspect of some weird steampunk villain or convict type in a graphic novel – an even more cartoonish character. The fact is that Eustace is a weird-looking guy, and whatever he does he cannot disguise that truth.

People have picked up on this, sometimes placing it in a humorous context. For example at one convention, when Eustace won an award and Stanley Grainger was master of ceremonies, Stan delivered a long eulogy before the presentation, praising Eustace's talents but slyly remarking that it can't be easy going through life as a cross between Mr Spock and Dobby the House Elf. This generated a huge laugh from the audience – and indeed Eustace himself – everybody taking it in good part. But that's because it was Stan, charismatic Stan, who made the joke, and I can only imagine the different reaction were I to have made similar comments.

When we writers all got on Facebook, things didn't improve with Crimpy, in fact the platform only served to accentuate his bad tendencies still further. Building on the themes of his short stories, his novels incorporated erudite hard science into far-flung fantasy and surreal scenarios, some of them quite camp to be honest, so he had a foot in both the sci-fi and fantasy genres. I did read several of his novels and thought them interesting if a little difficult, so I could call myself a worthy follower. One work that came under discussion on Facebook was *Palaestra*, an ingenious post-structuralist exploration of the quantum many-worlds interpretation that involved activities in gymnasia throughout history, from the Greco-Roman to the present, with understated male love, contact sports and saunas hovering over the experimentalism and the theoretical physics.

Based on past experience, I should have known better, but nonetheless, almost aware I was riding for a fall, I posted a comment on Eustace's wall about the book – a bit of random jive talk incorporating eigenstates, the uncertainty principle, waveform collapse, Schrödinger's cat and Gore Vidal for good measure. His reply was one of the mostly lengthy I've seen on Facebook, clinically taking each of my assertions apart and explaining my misinterpretations of quantum theory in a tone of amused lampooning, and then pontificating on the true meaning of Vidal's *Duluth*, which unlike me he'd actually read. His clever mates joined in the discussion, praising his incisiveness and heaping more opprobrium onto the pitiful twat who tries to talk about matters in which he's out of his intellectual depth – me.

Crimpy is also a staunch atheist and paranormal sceptic, and never loses an opportunity to ram home the commonsense materialist angle in any discussion. What's more, after not interacting with me for months on Facebook, he'll suddenly parachute in from nowhere to give out a hefty dose of his wisdom, if the situation suits. Once I posted a link to an article that claimed quantum theory proves consciousness moves to another universe at death. It was no big deal and I didn't expect the Spanish Inquisition, but I got it in the form of another *War and Peace* comment from Crimpy, which took the position of holding me personally responsible for every aspect of the piece's content. He droned on about how biocentrism is pseudoscience, unfalsifiable claptrap, and its proponents misunderstand the observer effect, and all that. I became weary reading it, but then to make matters worse the post inevitably entered the news feeds of Crimpy's clique, and they too parachuted in with supporting comments of the 'woo-woo mysticism' type, which pissed me off no end.

So, Crimpy on Facebook proved to be an even bigger pain in the ass than Crimpy in the flesh. But it was when my short story collection, *Dark Undertows*, was published by Decahedron Press that things really deteriorated between us. Naturally, after supporting various writer friends for many years now – buying their books, commenting constructively, and liking their pages and joining their groups on Facebook – I now expected them to do the same for me. Of my real friends and those writers with whom I rubbed along well, they all liked my new author page and joined my *Dark Undertows* group without hesitation; but it was the ones who didn't that marked themselves out for special contempt.

In those days Facebook groups were different and you invited people rather than adding them, and they could either accept, decline or do nothing. Of those that did nothing, their faces remained in the 'invited' folder, but when they declined they would disappear. Eustace's ugly mug was one of the first to go, which hardly surprised me, and I reacted by unliking his author page. He then counteracted by sending me a new 'like' request. *Where is he coming from?* I asked myself. Did he really expect me to remain liking his author page after he'd rejected mine, together with the group invite? Did he somehow want me to capitulate in the acceptance of his superiority by supporting his authorial position even in the face of his non-support of mine? Who did he think he was – Neil Gaiman?

Then, through one of the quirks of Facebook, a conversation featured in my news feed between Eustace and someone else, who wasn't a friend of mine, but whose wall was still accessible to me because of his privacy settings. And they were talking about me! It seemed as though Eustace, notwithstanding his planet-sized brain, had slipped up here, thinking that what he was saying was confidential – or maybe he just didn't care.

It's one of those standard fears of the paranoid – that people are saying disparaging things about you behind your back, though usually you can't establish proof. But thanks to Facebook it was all there, in blue, black and white! Firstly Crimpy asked if his friend had heard of the Decahedron Press, adding they looked to be a down-market pulp outfit who published paranormal exploitation crap and borderline porn. The friend asked why was Crimpy interested, and Crimpy replied that some 'peripheral acquaintance' of his had a short story collection out with them. The friend then said, 'So he's no Poe or O. Henry, I take it?' To which Crimpy responded with the killer comment:

'Not exactly. He's some pillock who labours under the delusion that the nonsense he scribbles down is actual writing as written by real writers.'

A pillock who writes nonsense? Clearly, as with the case of Darren Winterbottom, a line had been crossed here and retributions must follow. *Putz…? Pillock…?* It's time to unleash Jago from his coffin to set the world to rights.

10. Stuck in the Middle With You

As shafts of morning sunlight create bright rhomboid shapes on the walls of my attic garret room, I get onto Facebook and post a link to an article in which Vincent Price's daughter confirms he was bisexual. No surprise there! Next thing I go to Eustace Crimp's wall to check if there are any further updates about his book launch at Blue Nebula bookshop in Birmingham later today. Everything looks on track, and several of our mutual writer friends say they will be attending and are looking forward to it – smiley, smiley! I've made my own 'special preparations' concerning the event, and after shutting down the computer, I get changed into my bespoke outfit for the day and set out for Temple Meads Station to catch a Birmingham train.

Blue Nebula is a large specialist sci-fi, fantasy and horror independent bookshop, which is popular for launches because it has a private backroom that serves as an after-party venue. The interior is a wonderland of shelf after mammoth shelf of flashy riotously coloured comics and graphic novels, many rare and collectable, together with a very broad selection of genre titles and merchandise, such as superhero T-shirts, figurines and magic wands. I saunter upstairs and catch sight of Crimpy with a group of helpers, standing at a table bearing scores of hardback copies of his latest epic tome: *Jack Daedalus's Nirvana*, with eye-catching posters behind. Crimpy sees me as I walk across to the backroom, and he does a quick surprised double take before adopting an inscrutable Spockish frown.

At the entrance to the backroom, a red-T-shirted employee asks me if I have an invite, and I say I've forgotten to bring it along. Luckily Stanley Grainger is standing nearby, and he comes forward and vouches for me. Good old Stan – a highly successful fantasy author and a really nice guy. He's always warm and affable, and there's never any side to him.

'Hello Jago, didn't know you were going to be here.'

'Hi Stan. Oh, I never miss Crimpy's launches if I can help it.'

Stan smiles somewhat incredulously and waves me in, holding up a pina colada in a large poco grande glass. 'Come and have one of these poncey drinks – I could do with a pint of Guinness, myself, but got to go with the theme!'

It turns out there is an array of cocktails to choose from, including margaritas, various rainbow shades of daiquiri and the speciality of the day: the Blue Nebula Hawaiian, seductively coloured with curaçao liqueur. There is even a selection of leis hanging up, and several guests are wearing them, but not Stan. This Hawaiian theme comes from the rationale of Eustace's new novel, where protagonist Jack Daedalus builds a super-dooper island paradise on a newly colonised planet, evoking the magic times of his childhood spent on the actual Hawaii. The book is a post-global warming, post-Armageddon cautionary tale, with lots of heavy science in its six hundred-odd pages, and it's being marketed as Crimpy's most ambitious to date – a breakthrough work – hence the generous booze and food spread laid on by his publishers. Sipping a potent Blue Nebula Hawaiian and eyeing up the canapés and other nibbles, to be consumed after the reading, I feel really glad I came along. What's more, the strongly flavoured cocktails are a gift, ideal for what I've got in mind.

Stan and I chat whilst I wave and say hello to other writer friends working the room, such as Darius and Otto. I ask Stan about his latest project and in return tell him how enthusiastic I am about the developing Facebook murder novel, feeling pleased as he nods approvingly.

'Talking about murder,' Stan continues, 'strange that – what happened to Darren Winterbottom. Almost like something from out of a mystery novel…'

'Yeah, absolutely…'

The story of Darren's slaying has been all over the TV and the newspapers, following the discovery of his body, washed up near Chertsey Marina a couple of weeks back. Several people distantly heard the gunshot, but without a scene to attach it to, they assumed it was an extreme case of a car backfiring. Beyond that, there are no leads, no witnesses, and the police can't establish any kind of a motive.

'Why would anyone want to do that to poor old Darren?' says Stan, shaking his head. 'He didn't have any enemies.'

'No, no one had anything against Darren.'

Stan narrows his gaze quizzically. 'Mind you, he was a UKIP supporter…'

'Very true Stan. I think you've nailed it.'

We hear an amplified shout out from the main room, asking everyone to gather for Eustace's reading, which is about to begin. So us special guests file through, carrying our cocktails, and we join the general public in the well-filled floor space. It's an impressive gathering, and Crimpy manages a thin smile as he comes to the mike and thanks everyone for attending.

Shuffling against a backdrop of large poster versions of his book cover, Crimpy begins by describing the work. The cover itself features a retro Heinleinesque painting of an otherworldly palm tree-studded landscape in soft pinks, turquoises, lime greens and violets, and Eustace says he's trying to recapture the enquiring spirit of the Golden Age of Science Fiction, but invest it with today's concerns and technological know-how. Though there's plenty of hard science in his novel, he wanted to write a more metaphysical story, with Jack Daedalus asking himself the big questions as he attempts to recreate 'paradise' with mounting difficulties.

So far so good, but typically Crimpy starts to drag philosophy into the equation, going on about Aristotle, Hegel, epistemology and the implications of Korzybski's principles of general semantics as they apply to Daedalus. Some in the audience laugh politely, indicating perhaps that they don't have a clue what he's on about – lucky for them they're not friends with him on Facebook! Presently, to everyone's relief, Eustace commences the reading, and in his thin whiny voice, he tells of an engineering nightmare brought on by fluctuating gravitational forces, and compares it interestingly to Isambard Kingdom Brunel's problems in constructing the Clifton

Suspension Bridge. Then there's a round of applause, the punters line up to get their copies signed, and I make a beeline for the canapés next door.

By the time Crimpy joins the after-party, I'm on my third or fourth cocktail and practically levitating. Cheering, Darius puts a multi-coloured lei around Crimpy's neck, and though he's a touch embarrassed he keeps it on, going with the flow. Systematically he works the room, sipping gingerly on a Blue Nebula Hawaiian as he banters with the people who matter in order of priority. I can tell Crimpy is very aware of my presence, but keeping me at arms length, putting off an encounter for as long as he can. Eventually he looms up unexpectedly, just as I'm stuffing another absolutely delicious luau glazed pineapple and ham bite into my mouth.

'Jago Farrar?' he says, as though there's doubt about who I am. And typical of Crimpy to use my full name as a form of address.

'Hello Eustace,' I say as I masticate. 'The lei suits you.'

Crimpy gives me a denigrating frown. 'And what brings you here today? Is it a love of cutting-edge science fiction or the free drinks?'

'Oh the free drinks – and very good they are too!'

His gaze wanders down to my feet and then back up to my face. 'Why the black suit and tie? Are you going to a funeral?'

'Er…not just yet.'

'Do you think cowboy boots are a suitable accompaniment to such an outfit…?' Crimpy then manages a restrained Spock-like smile. 'Or are you trying to be a Blues Brother perhaps? Ha, ha, ha.'

'You're close.'

'Well I hope you enjoy the book – you can get signed copies at the desk.'

'Looking forward to it,' I say as Eustace turns his back on me to talk to someone else.

The circulating and bantering starts to flag after about an hour and a half, and a few people have now drifted off. Crimpy takes an age to finish his first cocktail, and I fear he won't go for a second one, but luckily Stan fetches him another Blue Nebula Hawaiian.

He looks at it disconcertedly for a couple of seconds, takes a sip and then puts it down on a side table and heads for the gents. This is my moment to pounce, so quickly I sidle over to Crimpy's drink, making sure no one is watching, and with my back to the room, I reach into my jacket pocket for a small phial of liquid. It contains a prepared solution of Rohypnol, and I deftly pour this into the Blue Nebula Hawaiian and give it a quick stir with the little red umbrella. Then I casually sidestep towards the buffet spread, where the last of the luau meatballs and a couple of honeyed shrimps are waiting.

Another half hour takes us to late afternoon, and the party is beginning to break up properly. Stan and Darius have already gone, after saying their goodbyes to an unsteady-looking Eustace. He's almost finished the cocktail now, and as he blinks his eyes and glances around in befuddlement, its contents appears to be taking effect. I walk up to Eustace and he seems surprised to see me, almost as though he's forgotten the other time.

'I didn't tell you, Eustace – I really enjoyed your reading and the talk you gave about the book. I can see that you're counterbalancing the metaphysical centre of the characters' plight with a Socratic dialectic, aiming to get at the true meaning of the logos in other-planetary terms.'

Crimpy gawps at me, sways from side to side and almost falls, before quickly steadying himself.

'What...? What...on earth...are...you...talking about...Farrar...? I don't feel quite right...Everything's swaying...'

'You look as though you need some fresh air, Eustace. Cocktail too strong, was it?'

'I don't know...must've been.' He is now slurring his speech and sounding like a Wodehousian buffoon.

'Come on, this way.' I clasp Eustace around the back and he lays a bony piston rod arm over my shoulders and staggers a little as he walks. A couple of people smile at us, and I say, 'He's had a few too many!' and they laugh and nod.

I steer him into the kitchen area and then slowly down the back stairs into the loading bay. The area is practically empty, so our exit has attracted far less attention than if we'd gone out the front way. 'Take a few deep breaths, Eustace,' I say as I lead him onwards, out of the back gate and down a side street. By now he's barely able to walk, his long spindly legs threatening to fold under him, and I reflect that perhaps I overdid the dosage of the sedative. But better too much than too little. Luckily, though he's tall he isn't heavy, and I manage to hold him up by the armpits and half drag him along the pavement.

'Where...are...we...going...?' he says, as if in a dream.

'Somewhere to have a nice sit down, old boy.'

Passersby give us quizzical smiles, and I repeat the 'few too many' comment, which satisfies for the moment. Crimpy becomes so groggy that I fear he'll pass out altogether before we reach our destination, but we just manage to arrive at the door as he crumples. Quickly I undo the padlock, open up and then drag him inside. No one walking in the vicinity or driving past seems to have registered anything untoward.

The premises are a small railway arch lockup that I rented under a false name. It's centrally situated on the Birmingham-Oxford line and fortunately within walking distance of Blue Nebula. Inside I turn on the neon strip lighting and take in the miasma of dampness and residual engine fumes as I track the rows of ancient painted bricks curving across the ceiling. A train rattles past overhead, making the whole space momentarily vibrate. Crimpy is virtually senseless now, so he hardly registers my actions as I sit him down in a heavy oak chair and secure his arms, body and ankles to its frame with copious lengths of grey gaffer tape. His head bobs forward and sways to one side whilst he moans and mumbles incoherently. Trussed up good and proper, he really looks the part and the setting is pretty spot on too – not quite a warehouse but close enough.

Now all I have to do is wait for him to return to some level of consciousness, and I boil some water in a grubby plastic kettle in order to make myself a cup of coffee. Through the little back window I watch dusk turn to night, then Crimpy's monosyllabic grunts start to turn into half sentences as he gradually becomes more aware of his surroundings. Suddenly he attempts to stand, realises he's bound to the chair and then looks up at my face as I loom before him.

'You – Farrar! How did I get here? What's going on…?'

'Doesn't quite conform to Vulcan logic, does it, Crimpy?'

He looks down at his bonds and struggles against them futilely with rising panic. 'I demand that you stop this and release me before it goes any further.'

'It's already gone too far, Eustace, old bean. All those attempts to belittle me and bulldozer me flat with your intellectual might – now's the time for the reckoning. And how did you react to my years of support for you as a writer? When my story collection came out, you wouldn't join my group or like my author page, and on top of that you described me – and I quote – as "some pillock who labours under the delusion that the nonsense he scribbles down is actual writing as written by real writers". Didn't think I saw that on Facebook, did you? But I did see it, Eustace…'

Crimpy's eyes go bright with alarm and his whole posture kind of withers as he finally regards me with some respect and awe. 'Now…now…I think you're maybe exaggerating or taking things out of context…'

'Well it hardly matters at this point, does it, Eustace? I've got the upper hand. I'm calling the shots. And for your information, I'm not dressed up as a Blues Brother, I'm dressed up as Mr Blonde – and it's time to face the music!'

'Jago! Get a grip on yourself, man. See sense.'

'Ever listen to *K-Billy's Super Sounds of the Seventies*?'

'What…? This is preposterous!'

I saunter to the workbench where I've positioned my iPod in its dock, cued up and ready for play. As the intro to the Stealers Wheel number fills the small space, I reach into the top of a cowboy boot and extract the tortoiseshell-handled cutthroat razor I bought in Bristol Market the other day. I do the little dance steps, forwards and backwards, opening the razor and smiling at Crimpy as I mime the act of shaving. Next I perform a pirouette, watching as he becomes convulsed in terror, bawling like a two year old. Then I lip synch the lyrics and hum the tune as I menacingly converge on Crimpy's person.

'You're insane!' he whines with a slight interrogative edge, as if finally coming to that dreadful conclusion.

Cackling like a madman, I point to my left. 'Look over there, Crimpy – clowns!' Then I whip my hand across the other way. 'And over there – jokers! Ha, ha, ha…'

'Now…now…now look, Jago, old chap. I think we may have got our wires crossed here. You are a good writer. Your work is…is… interesting and shows plenty of promi – Arraaagghhh!'

I slice down on one of those big Spock ears, and it offers a surprising amount of sinewy resistance…And the blood – far more blood than in *Reservoir Dogs*! Crimpy cries and screams and wails and bellows…Yeah, yeah…

Where do I go from here? I wonder. How do I find out exactly how much resistance an ear would offer to a cutthroat razor and does it really matter? It's the sort of thing Hugh would research thoroughly and then render elegantly in viscerally-gripping prose. As for Tarantino, he dealt with the issue by simply panning away.

So, Crimpy is minus an ear, but ear removal isn't of itself fatal. In the film, the suavely psychopathic Mr Blonde intends to finish off his cop captive by dousing him in petrol and setting him alight, but Mr Orange blows him away before he can light the trail. The cop is eventually shot dead by Nice Guy Eddie, so perhaps Jago could let Crimpy have it with the Webley and be true to the storyline…? It does seem a bit anticlimactic though. Hmmm…this needs more thought…

And just as I'm thinking the story needs more thought, I hear the grate of Robin's key in the lock, and I look at my watch and see it's nearly six o'clock. A whole working day gone in creative reverie, and I realise I haven't given Robin a single thought, I've blanked him out completely – until this moment. Now I wonder what's next in the story of my life. More stony silence, or something else?

Robin comes to my door and peers in at me, clearly intending to stage the confrontation he's had bottled up inside him for days and days. His face looks all askew and lopsided like a Picasso portrait. I return his look and say nothing, waiting for him to start.

'I nearly didn't come home at all, almost resolved to stay away for good,' he says, tossing back his hair, 'but then I thought: this is my flat too and I'll come and go as I please. If you're curious about where I've been, well I don't owe you any explanations – and if you're going to react by punching me again, well this time I shall call the police, no danger.'

'I've been too busy getting on with my own life to bother about your whereabouts. As for that punch, it was nothing. Let it go, chill out.'

'Huh! The universal call of abusing husbands. "Let it go." "Didn't mean anything." "Why are you making such a fuss?" Well it's not that simple, Nick…Anyway, I'm going to stay in tonight, make a stir fry and watch what I want on my telly.'

'That'd be *The Real Housewives of Atlanta* and *Vicious*, I take it?'

Robin tosses back his hair again and leaves, and we proceed to have the most terrible evening where he keeps picking at me, baiting me, and trying to get me to react. He admits he went to Queenshilling with Kevin last night, but I ask no questions and don't volunteer the fact I was only a short distance away in another club and up to no good myself. I won't give him the satisfaction of showing my anger, though I still feel it percolating away and know that he's aware of it doing just that. At midnight he goes off to bed, declaring that he may well stay away tomorrow night and the next, if he wants. I feel crestfallen and exasperated, anticipating the war of attrition going on and on, ruining my otherwise contented creative headspace.

Desultorily I switch channels, watch part of *Scarface* on ITV 4, then turn off the TV at around half one and prepare for bed myself. Passing Robin's partly open door, I hear him snoring away, dead to sentience, and suddenly I'm seized by a perverse whim. I go to the cupboard under the kitchen sink and get out the rubber-handled claw hammer, brandishing it and swinging it about like a Viking warrior. Then I sneak into Robin's room, and I stand over him in the darkness, listening to the rhythm of his snoring as I raise the hammer over his head. Here is a chance to dispatch an actual human being – not some phantom I've made up on paper. The sense of power at the ease with which I could end his life is quite heady, intoxicating, and I drink it in as I hold myself back from accomplishing the deed.

I could do it if I wanted to, just like that. Maybe not now. But soon…eh? We'll see.

11. In the Teeth of Hell

Medusacon 2006 was held at a big swish hotel in London's Docklands, with commanding views of the Thames, Canary Wharf and the pristine Docklands Light Railway providing a cool backdrop to the proceedings. All the 'usual suspect' horror, fantasy and sci-fi writers were present, including Stan, Darren, Crimpy, Otto and Darius, together with more illustrious scribes and the Guests of Honour. Film critic and writer Kim Newman attended, in Victorian Gothic mode as usual, with his long flowing hair and full moustache, silk waistcoat and cravat. Horror veteran Brian Lumley enlivened the atmosphere, looking awesome in a white suit and shirt with silver collar tips, and a leather bolo tie and ornate aiguillette around his neck. And horror newcomer Joe Hill floated around enigmatically, with his jet black hair and equally jet black full beard, having recently come out as the son of Stephen King. I liked the look of him, but of course he was married and straight. And besides I was after bigger fish, as the Guests of Honour were Neil Gaiman and the man himself: Hugh Canford-Eversleigh.

At the Friday night initial gathering I watched Hugh circulating and pumping hands in the red-carpeted main bar space. His chestnut hair had grown out and was a little curly at the edges, in need of a cut, which made him appear more boyish. He wore an open waistcoat over a loose shirt and close-fitting jeans, showing off his ass and legs majestically and giving him the air of a tights-clad duellist. If only I could have injected him with some memory-wiping drug and then re-programmed him to be as I wished – but that was impossible. Instead I could just ogle and savour, which contented me for the while, and when he happened to pass my way and we made eye contact, I said 'Hi Hugh' in the most natural casual non-invasive way ever. 'Hello…' he replied under his breath, moving on without a break of stride, his face falling like a building under the wrecking ball.

I was expecting this and I didn't let it faze me, quite the opposite in fact. The rules here were different to those of the general outside world, where Hugh could walk away and keep walking, jump in a cab or shut the door on me in some other way. We were within the bubble of the convention, circumscribed by the walls of the hotel and the commitments that bound Hugh to the event, and to his larger career. He was limited in the distance he could put between himself and me, and he would have to manage the situation accordingly. Because I knew this, and knew he knew I knew it, I was prepared to cut him a bit of slack and go easy and not be an annoying stalker. In a sense I had 'collected' him temporarily, and I wanted to rub along well in these circumstances – and perhaps even overcome earlier bad impressions I might have created.

That was the theory at any rate, but of course in practice it always works out differently. Like a bad gambler I had to keep doubling up the stake in an attempt to cover earlier losses, and after Hugh kept cutting me dead when I tried to contribute towards shared chats, I got that old urge to 'have it out' and put everything to rights. Fuelled by alcohol late on the Friday, I circled and waited to pounce. When I spied Hugh walking on his own, I sprang out from behind a pillar and blocked his path in a no-nonsense manner.

'Hugh…why are you avoiding talking to me? Lets just be normal – two writers at a convention.'

He gave me a deadpan stare, like a gunslinger in a western. 'Normal? That is a word you know the meaning of, is it?'

'Ha, ha. Very funny! Is that one of Wilde's or one of Shaw's? How about you let me get you a drink and we'll sit down and have a proper chat?'

'How about a solution of cyanide – and have one for yourself?'

'Oh very good! I like it!'

At that moment Neil Gaiman strode past and Hugh quickly latched on to him, turning his back on me, putting an arm around Neil's shoulder and walking away. Nonetheless I felt pleased that I'd got a reaction out of Hugh. I'd burrowed my way under his skin sufficiently for him to be critically aware of me, no doubt thinking about me a lot of the time. I was a feature in his life and he couldn't easily make me go away. In several letters and greetings cards I'd made my amorous position clear, and I'd tried to engage on a literary level with the ongoing stalker story – which was at this moment having its next chapter written. I knew he'd continue fighting our love, and I knew his denial was very strong, but I remained undaunted.

He must be feeling the love too on some level, I reasoned, it seemed a logical impossibility that he wasn't. Every rebuff registered as a disguised expression of desire – he was doing the opposite of what he actually wanted. In fact it didn't really matter what Hugh did or didn't do, I applied a heads-I-win-tails-you-lose rationale to it all. The fortress of my obsession was impregnable…or so I thought. One particular element that had buttressed it up to this moment was the idea that Hugh couldn't countenance being unfaithful to Melody or facing up to his bisexual side, which together constituted an enormous barrier to be overcome. But as Medusacon wore on into the Saturday, I discovered I was being naïve – certainly in regard to the former aspect of this trait.

There are certain people, often beautiful people, who naturally stand out in a crowd, making you register their presence, sometimes peripherally or subliminally when you are occupied with other things. Hugh was such a person, naturally, and another who caught my attention for the first time at Medusacon was Gretchen Mulhoney – who would become a watershed figure in the trajectory of my obsession. Tall, gauntly thin, with heavy make-up on her angular features and big curly copper hair, she was given to extravagant gesticulations and made for a kinetic focus of hand-waving and elbow-pointing, accompanied by animated facial expressiveness. I found myself studying her frequently, and I asked who she was, finding out about the tetralogy of fantasy novels she'd then published.

I must have been slow on the uptake because it took me until the Saturday to deduce that the reason I was often in Gretchen's vicinity was because I was shadowing Hugh and she was working the same circles – more regularly than by pure chance. By Saturday, when Hugh was mercilessly cutting me dead, he and Gretchen were talking more effusively and at greater length, sometimes in one-to-one situations. At a mid-morning panel on the future of the horror novel, I saw them sitting side by side in the audience. And later in the afternoon when Hugh was interviewed on stage in his main appearance as a Guest of Honour, I couldn't help but notice the eye contact and smiles he exchanged with Gretchen, sitting in the audience front row, and it took me right back to our first meeting in Blackwells and the attention he'd given me then and had now transferred elsewhere.

Watching them flirt so sweetly, I became engulfed with jealousy and instantly felt the fabric of my starry-eyed delusions about Hugh begin to tear. The bitch was trying to pick him up and he was clearly game! So infidelity was not a barrier, it was just *me* he didn't want. The simple fact that I was of the wrong gender didn't press at this point – in order to keep the flame of hope burning, I had convinced myself that Hugh was bisexual. I had no other choice! The pieces had to be made to fit together, by force if necessary – but witnessing Gretchen and Hugh paired up had caused the whole jigsaw to fall apart in disarray.

As the false picture I'd created broke down still further, I saw that my mind had two distinct modes. The first was the rational one, which having computed the information told me that my quest to have Hugh was hopeless. And the second was the obsessive one, which suppressed the former and thundered on regardless like a train with no brakes, making up its own rules and pushing aside anything contrary to its wishes. Now I had achieved clarity and it was unbearable. The obsessive runaway train had switched points and could only go in one direction.

I'd been angry with Hugh and his recalcitrant attitude many times before, but I'd always managed to beat it down and return to looking on the bright side. Now rage erupted as never before and I felt myself twitching as I visualised beating him, kicking him and eventually pummelling him to death with a variety of weapons as I explained in detail what a total bastard he was. My equilibrium had been rent asunder and I was no longer in the groove of the convention happenings and just wanted to go home. Even my mates, such as Stan and Darius, remarked that I seemed downcast and out of the flow.

Later on the Saturday night, when Neil Gaiman gave a talk and a reading from his story collection, *Fragile Things*, Hugh and Gretchen were sitting together again in the audience front row, cosily close to one another, and once I spied them surreptitiously holding hands. He would fuck her tonight, no doubt in his suite in the penthouse upstairs, whilst a clueless Melody minded the kids back at the Chelsea home. Following Neil's reading, everyone converged on the launch party for some fat fantasy novel whose title I've forgotten, and I got stuck into the punch that was on offer, and it tasted good and strong. Hugh, still with Gretchen, flashed me a victory smile from across the other side of the tightly-packed throng. I sensed he was challenging me in a *What are you going to do about it?* manner.

I'd been drinking beer steadily all day and after the punch and another couple of pints I was well loaded and had reached that couldn't-give-a-damn stage. Sauntering around the bar space, I saw Hugh and Gretchen talking with Neil Gaiman and Kim Newman in a lovely animated grouping, these talented successful people interacting so wondrously, as they do. Hugh was now wearing a silk waistcoat and black leather trousers, and was seemingly having a waistcoat-comparing session with Kim. I passed right next to them and waved my index finger in a *naughty naughty* rebuke towards the couple.

'Hugh!' I exclaimed. 'If only Melody could see you now!' And I smacked my lips in mock disapproval, shaking my head.

Hugh, Gretchen, Neil Gaiman and Kim Newman stopped talking, and with a synchronised shared expression they looked at me as though I had a live lobster crawling out of my mouth. Then they turned away, huddled together and recommenced their conversation, making a point of acting as if I didn't exist.

*   *   *   *   *

If nothing else, the events of Medusacon boosted the literary stalker novel. After the hiatus in which there was no worthwhile new material, I suddenly had a shedload, and I got down to it with a renewed vengeance. Also my count of published stories appearing in small press magazines was steadily mounting, which was satisfying. So if my dreams of being joined with Hugh were shattered, my literary ambitions were actually shaping up well. Love and cards, and all that.

The literary stalker novel now had a definite ending, whereas before it had been only hazy and theoretical. The Obsessed Fan must kill, or at least attempt to kill, the Famous Writer – that had always been the rough plan, but now I saw the scenario vividly. It would take place at a bookshop reading for the writer's next novel, making a nice elliptical symmetry with regard to the beginning, which also concerned a book reading. Thwarted in love, the demented fan tools up with a handgun and mows the writer down as everyone shrieks and runs for cover. He will shout out something like: 'Describe that in one of your books!' I would need to beef up the fan's motivation, invent something more to get him to the state where he's prepared to do such a thing, and make it convincing.

What I couldn't resist doing, though, was a quick draft where I took what happened at Medusacon and elided it into this blood-splattered ending – and then sent it to Hugh as my next literary stalker letter, written in the third person, of course. I'd thought of other horrible things I could do, such as send a dead rat through the post, trash his Aston Martin or put the family poodle in the micro-wave, but instead I opted for the psychological warfare approach. Yes, part of me wanted to act like Alex in *Fatal Attraction*, but I was aware that if I became an overtly violent stalker, I'd give Hugh the excuse to get the law onto me – and I already had a criminal record. Perhaps even this new letter could be construed as a threat, but if challenged I'd simply say: *It's only a story.*

However, stories have a habit of coming true, and Hugh would be precisely aware of this, and it would taunt him throughout his waking hours, and give him bad dreams that would wake him with a start at four in the morning, and he wouldn't be able to get back to sleep. For he was a famous writer, undoubtedly working on a new novel that he would eventually publish, and then he'd inescapably go out on reading events, potentially putting himself in the firing line. How could he avoid it without giving up his career and becoming J. D. Salinger or somebody similar? This would be my strategy from now on, and as the months accrued I sent out other versions of the denouement to him, with different twists and curlicues, but always concluding the same way. So this was how I kept the furnace of my anger stoked without doing anything overtly indictable. It's no good getting older if you don't get more sophisticated.

Now in mid-career, Hugh published novels on a schedule of one every two or three years, with occasional graphic novels, other collaborations and smaller books in between. His next novel came out around three years after *The Major Arcana* and was a serial killer shocker entitled *Necropolitic*. It was far more extreme horror than anything he'd recently written, with extended descriptions of no-holds-barred violence. It was constructed as partly a police procedural and partly a diary of a madman – the killer himself. It starts with the discovery of a horde of creatively mutilated corpses in the cellar of a disused house – the mutilations appearing to represent cryptic messages in some bizarre puzzle which the investigators become tasked to solve. The critics praised the brilliance of the writing, but remarked on the gut-churning nature of the carnage, some venturing to say that this time Hugh Canford-Eversleigh had gone too far. My own opinion was that Hugh was clearly in a dark place when he dreamed it all up – and I knew precisely where that dark place was.

Things didn't get any better for him, for coinciding with *Necropolitic's* release Gretchen went public with her kiss-and-tell story, classifying Hugh as a 'collector' figure and boosting the wave of publicity higher still. That was doubly satisfying for me, firstly to see Gretchen shafted, as I had been, and secondly to see Hugh exposed as the philandering bastard he was. And then I had my ace-in-the-hole to play – my attendance at one of his readings for

Necropolitic. Just my mere presence should be enough to send shock-waves running through Hugh as he attempted to perform, with the memory of my stalker letters echoing through the vaults of his being.

His Bristol appearance was elevated from a mere bookshop reading to an arts event at the Arnolfini, involving an interview, a reading and a question-and-answer session before the signing. I was half expecting security men, metal detectors and pat-down searches for weapons at the door, but I bought my ticket and entered without hindrance. However I did detect the presence of a couple of guys who didn't fit. They were casually dressed like literary luvvies, but the style clashed with their weightlifter bodies, gorilla faces and boxing glove hands. When Hugh was on stage they guarded each end, and they flanked him constantly when he was at large and at the signing afterwards. What was their plan if I actually had a gun, I wondered – dive at me like Clint Eastwood dives at John Malkovich in *In the Line of Fire?*

As he came on stage to the applause of several hundred people, Hugh seemed tensed up and ill at ease. He'd just had his hair cut, so in contrast to its state at Medusacon, it was now tidy and formal-looking. That, together with the Armani suit and bright silk tie gave him a much more urbane overall appearance than usual, like some aristocratic playboy. His discomfiture turned to clear embarrassment when the female interviewer heaped effusive praise on him and then read some favourite quotes from his previous works. And during the interview he glanced into the audience, made brief eye contact with me and missed a beat in his answer, though he recovered quickly, ever the professional. The passage he chose to read was from the killer's diary, detailing the capture and sadistic torture of a victim, and it was so gruesome and palpably realistic that it had one poor girl leaping out of her seat and rushing away hurriedly, as though she might be about to throw up.

At the point of interface afforded by the signing, I'd intended to do something menacing, such as point my index finger in gun mode and say, *Bang bang, you're dead!* or make a catty remark about Gretchen. But seeing Hugh close up as I approached with my hardback, I just felt all gooey about him again, as if I were thirteen, back at school and trying to act naturally with someone I fancied like mad. All the animosity that had built up stalking him in London and at Medusacon melted away, and it was like we were back in Blackwells that first time, starting over again. But now there was no way forward; a complete stalemate had been reached.

Bashfulness affected us both as I handed over the book for signing, and Hugh did the deed in a buttoned-up English reserved manner.

To break the frosty silence I found myself saying, 'How have you been? How's Melody and the family?'

'All very well. Thank you for asking.'

Hugh handed me back my copy of *Necropolitic* and I was left with no choice but to walk away under the smirking gazes of the two bodyguard goons. Despite everything I still loved him – I couldn't help it.

Unsurprisingly the literary stalker novel flagged at that point. I no longer had the heart to compose and send out any more nasty letters, and to try and remonstrate further and 'put everything to rights' was clearly a dead duck too. The material I had so far wasn't enough to make a substantial novel; to have the fan murder the writer over the failure of their love seemed too simplistic as it stood. I did however ponder deeply over that last encounter with Hugh. All the freight of the stuff built up between us, the unaddressed emotions, the unprocessed interpersonal business, lay walled behind a façade of genteel English politeness, expressed at a level of Jane Austen formality – though Hugh turned out to have none of the redeeming features of a Mr Darcy, as it happened.

But life has a funny way of making bad things better again – if only temporarily. A few months after the Arnolfini event with Hugh, and just a short distance away across Pero's Bridge, in the Watershed complex, I met someone new. His name was Helmut and he was blond but nonetheless very intellectual, and he talked with a sweetly high-pitched German accent. There was a David Lynch season on in the cinema, and we were both, as singletons, watching *Lost Highway* and exchanging furtive glances from a distance of around five seats width. It was the first time I'd seen this particular work of Lynch's, and I was totally knocked out. When it was time to exit, Helmut and I converged and openly grinned at one another.

'What did you think of it?' he said when we were outside.

I laughed. 'I thought it was absolutely fucking marvellous – almost as good as *Mulholland Drive*, with which it shares many similarities.'

'I totally agree. A work of genius. A completely deconstructed film noir rebuilt as a piece of pure Gothic surrealism.'

I nodded, showing I was impressed by this analysis. 'Yeah…it's Billy Wilder morphing into Luis Bunuel.'

'Ain't it the truth?' Helmut punched me softly on the shoulder.

'I need a drink,' I said, smiling broadly.

'Right. I'm buying.'

It turned out that Helmut was a psychologist, and as our relationship progressed he proved most willing to help me deal with the issues surrounding my obsession with Hugh. He made me understand that much of it was projection on my part, leading to the creation of a self-sustaining bubble that became more and more divorced from reality. Helmut said that I should try to wean myself off Hugh, much as an alcoholic or drug addict should renounce the troublesome substance. That meant avoiding triggers, such as reading articles or news reports about him, and visiting his website or Facebook page. If I found myself thinking about him and wishing to be with him, I should not indulge the process but should instead try to divert the tendency towards other ends – those ends being Helmut and I together. Progressively he cured me from the fixation on Hugh and offered himself as the prize in Hugh's place.

After all, I hadn't had a proper relationship in the years since I'd met Hugh, only casual encounters. Hugh was supposed to be 'the one' for that period in my life, so I could have hardly sought out another love interest. Now it was different, I told myself. Helmut asked me to move into his house in Bishopston, and we had a good life there, with little of the domestic animosity I later experienced with Robin. I achieved a quiet, relatively contented existence, if sometimes rather boring. Helmut was a nice guy and that made for easy living – but somehow I just couldn't see it lasting forever.

When Hugh's next novel, *Valkyrie*, came out I avoided articles and reviews, didn't read the book itself and would hardly countenance attending a reading and signing! Helmut was most impressed and really thought a corner had been turned, but in truth I still felt the old itch to jump on the Hugh bandwagon, though I kept it to myself. We remained a stable and averagely happy couple for a further two years, and would have managed longer, but for a totally unforeseen event that completely upset everything at a stroke. And who was the instigator of this event? Ironically it was Hugh, the completely passive party in the obsession, the man who wouldn't react or hardly bat an eyelid no matter what I did. Finally, almost eight years after that first Blackwells meeting, he did show a reaction. He published his next novel, and he entitled it *In the Teeth of Hell*.

12. An Inspector Calls

The doorbell rings downstairs, causing a seismic shift in the dream I'm having, which concerns a gathering or shindig in some large non-specific interior. I open one eye, see the hands on the alarm clock forming five minutes to eight, and close the eye again, wishing to pick up the dream's threads before it's too late. No one I want to see would be calling at this hour; it's even too early for the postman. Just as I parachute back, and I'm talking to Darius and Otto, drinks in hand, the damn bell goes again – a more persistent ring this time. I'm going to be very annoyed if it's some opportunist cold caller.

Gluey-eyed, I open the street door to reveal two figures. The first is a portly middle-aged man in a raincoat, suit, tie and trilby hat, who gives me an implacable stare through gold-rimmed bifocals. The other is younger, slimmer, taller but also wearing a cheap-looking dark suit. My first thought is Jehovah's Witnesses, but they don't seem religious and they aren't carrying Bibles.

'Jago Farrar…?' the portly one says.

'Yes…'

'I'm Inspector Leopard of the Birmingham CID, and this is Constable Hawkins. Could we come in and ask you a few questions, please?'

They each hold up their ID cards side by side, and I crouch to read the details, but they snatch them away before I can finish.

'We're investigating the disappearance of a Eustace Crimp and we'd like to take a statement from you.' His accent is unmistakably Birmingham.

Upstairs in my flat, Leopard sits down next to me on my thread-bare ratty sofa, removing his hat to reveal a bald pate with just a few wispy hairs on his crown. His neat greying moustache curls as he smiles disingenuously, establishing the high ground before the interrogation gets underway. Meanwhile Hawkins hovers, looking around inquisitively and smiling similarly in an unnerving fashion.

Empty cider bottles and dirty plates, glasses and cutlery are piled high on the dining table, undoubtedly creating a bad impression. As the preliminaries begin, Hawkins flips open his notepad and parks himself on a stool. I tell myself to keep calm…keep calm and think carefully before I speak.

'Now…' Leopard continues, 'I understand you attended a book-signing event at the Blue Nebula bookshop last Saturday. Is that correct?'

'Yes.'

'You travelled from Bristol to Birmingham especially to attend?'

'I did.'

'And what mode of transport did you use?'

'Train.'

'Hmm…' Leopard consults a page in his notebook. 'You weren't actually on the invited guest list, were you?'

'Er…no.'

'But you still undertook a not inconsiderable journey to attend. Why was that?'

'Oh well, I had a free day, and I heard about it on Facebook, and I knew friends would be there, so why not?'

'Are you a particular friend of Mr Crimp?'

'Er…I wouldn't say a close friend, more a professional acquaintance.'

'Are you a writer yourself?'

'Oh yes, I've published many short stories.'

At this both Leopard and Hawkins give simultaneous involuntary nasal laughs, and I feel I'm being bullied. Perhaps I should have refused to let them in, asserted my rights more stridently.

'So…when was the last time you saw Mr Crimp at the event?' Leopard teases out the sentence slowly.

'Umm…I saw him outside at the back, after he'd gone out for some fresh air. He'd had a few too many of the strong cocktails, I think.'

There is a pause and I become aware of Hawkins scribbling down these details in his notepad. I sense I'm about to fall into a trap.

'And why were you outside at the back yourself?' Leopard continues.

'Er…I helped Crr…Mr Crimp down the back stairs. He was a little groggy and unsteady.'

'So you took it upon yourself to help him outside for some fresh air. How long were you out there?'

'Er…perhaps five or ten minutes.'

'And what did you do then?'

'I went off.'

'You went off and left him in a groggy state outside in the loading bay? Was that a responsible course of action?'

'Uh…he was taking in some lungfuls of fresh air and seemed a little better.'

'Really?' Leopard says sardonically, most unconvinced. 'Where did you go after you left Mr Crimp?'

'I wondered about a bit.'

'You weren't in a hurry to get home?'

'Not particularly.'

'Did you catch the train back to Bristol?'

'Yes, eventually.'

'And what time was that?'

'Er…I don't remember.'

'Was it an hour after you left the bookshop? Two hours? Three hours?'

'Around two, I'm guessing…'

'And what did you do in that time?'

'Wondered around, went for a drink in some bar, I forget the name…'

'So you left Mr Crimp in a groggy state outside in the loading bay, wondered around, went for a drink in a bar, and got the train back to Bristol around two hours later?'

'Yeah, that's about it.'

'Then, according to other witnesses, you must have been the last known person to have seen Mr Crimp before he, uh, disappeared without a trace. When his friends tried to phone him to find out where he was, his mobile was turned off. And he didn't respond to any text or voice messages. That's odd, don't you think, Jago...?'

Leopard's use of my name in an insinuatingly familiar manner unnerves me further. But quickly I see I have the perfect response at hand.

'I'm pretty sure Mr Crimp turned off his mobile so he wouldn't be disturbed during his reading and signing. He most likely forgot to turn it on again – especially as he got drunk soon afterwards!'

Actually I know this for a fact, for I checked Crimpy's mobile in the lockup and found it to be conveniently switched off.

'Mmmn...' Leopard is set back by my excellent answer, but tries not to show it. 'So...what then do you think happened to him?'

'Umm...I don't know...Maybe he wondered off, still a bit drunk and got lost? Who knows?'

'Well, someone knows, Jago...' Leopard smiles and holds my gaze for an unnaturally long time, the 'o' of my name seemingly echoing in space. 'Another thing...Do you – or should I say *did* you – know Darren Winterbottom?'

'Er...yes...'

'Was he a friend or perhaps a professional acquaintance?'

'Yes, both of those.'

'You know what happened to Mr Winterbottom last month, I take it?'

'Of course, it's all over the news. A terrible thing!'

'Indeed...Funny isn't it that two writers from a specific, ah, area – science fiction – who, on top of that, knew one another should suffer, hmm, unusual misfortunes close together in time? Might be more than a coincidence, don't you think?'

'I don't know...'

'And did you ever have, err, any fallings out or disagreements with Mr Winterbottom – or indeed Mr Crimp...?'

'You're joking! We always got on famously well.'

'And I don't suppose you might have any theories about who could possibly be responsible for these, uh, occurrences?'

'I don't, I'm afraid, Inspector...'

'Well, our colleagues in the Surrey force might want to have a further word with you about that…'

After that comment, Leopard goes through it all again in greater detail whilst Hawkins compiles the account as a statement. Clearly they don't have anything definite to pin on me, but they're suspicious. When they finish, I have to sign to say it's a true and accurate account of what took place. I get a strong impression that Leopard is disappointed that he couldn't trip me up, but we both know this is only Round One.

'We just have to check a few things and we'll be in touch again, if anything crops up. You aren't planning to go away, leave the country or anything like that, are you?' Leopard stands and replaces his trilby hat at a jaunty angle on his head.

'No…no…' I say, relief overtaking me now. 'I'll show you out.'

Crimpy's body is still in the railway arch lockup, swaddled in several layers of plastic sheeting and gaffer tape in order to contain the smell. So long as I continue paying the rent, no one should have any reason to look in there, but I'll have to dispose of him sometime. The poor bugger begged for his life in the end, crying and mewling and slobbering. Seeing him broken like that I almost felt sorry for him! But what could I do – give him back his ear and send him on his way? Apart from anything else, it wouldn't have fitted the script. Instead I found an old cushion and some canvas dust sheets and used them to muffle the report of the Webley, which I had stashed in the lockup for this eventuality. So my second Facebook murder was enacted – and the manner remained true to *Reservoir Dogs*.

But now the cops are putting two and two together. If the motivation remains cloudy, then the connection between the victims is readily apparent, once people start talking and comparing notes. I hadn't considered that before, and it means I've got to act fast. I made sure there's no CCTV coverage on the streets between the bookshop and the lockup, but several people saw Crimpy and I together, staggering along, and if Leopard can trace such a witness then I'm in trouble. And on the Darren front, if ANPR cameras can place my car in the vicinity of Chertsey on the day…well, how do I explain that away?

While I still can, I have to get moving on to my third victim, and that is none other than the acclaimed critic Simon Ongar. I wonder if he has any inkling that he is next on the hit list, but I doubt even his enormous facilities can stretch that far. However, when I next check Facebook, I find that the news of Crimpy's disappearance has broken big time, and everyone is linking it to the Darren shooting and speculating about connections. Oh, these daft internet conspiracy theorists! But several of the comments do skirt close to the truth, conjecturing some putative psycho nutter who's out to murder writers…not to mention critics. Perhaps Ongarface will work it out and be ready for me with his pitchfork!

My grievance against Simon is a simple one. Critics possess a certain amount of power which they can either use responsibly or otherwise. And in a small almost hermetic world like that of genre magazine stories – and collections of such stories – there are few critics, and of those few Simon reigns supreme. Decades ago, the legendary critic Pauline Kael could chose to make or break a film with her *New Yorker* reviews, and the same applies to Simon and his pronouncements in *The British SF & Fantasy Review*, the magazine of which he is also editor and publisher.

Ongarface was never a fan of my work, I knew, but when I published my story collection, *Seriously Unhinged*, I had little choice but to send a copy to the *BSFFR* and hope for the best. I was taking a risk, but I had to publicise it amongst its target audience. The review was unusually lengthy for a fairly minor work, and Simon relished outlining several of the stories and gently lampooning them from a position of huge superiority, clearly building up to saying something much more heavyweight. Several years later I can almost quote his final paragraph verbatim, and it still pains me to recall it now:

When writers start out composing fiction, they often take real-life incidents and embroider them at the edges in order to buff them up into stories. One might call this the tadpole stage of development. Later, writers dream up all-of-a-piece ideas for plots and invent wholesale to furnish the scenarios, which constitutes the frog stage. On the evidence of *Seriously Unhinged*, Farrar is stuck with embroidering real life, and not very skilfully at that. One assumes that his plots are autobiographical, if for no other reason than they are not interesting enough to have been made up. He is a tadpole that might well grow fatter over the years, but will doubtless never accomplish the metamorphosis into a frog.

Wrong! Wrong! Wrong! On so many counts! I do make stuff up and my work isn't fucking autobiographical! This is a classic example of a critic warping the truth in order to say something 'clever'. In other words, an abuse of power that must be avenged – Edward Lionheart style, naturally!

Simon lives alone in a cottage in a remote Somerset village. He has posted many photographs of the place on Facebook, displaying both the inside, outside and the garden, and in one street shot I discovered you can see the post office and grocery store almost opposite. Therefore it will be easy to locate, and losing no time I disinter the Webley from its hiding place and throw it in the boot of the car, along with an Ordnance Survey map and some other relevant items. If the police stop and search me, I'm fucked, but that's not likely at this precise moment. Bearing in mind the issue of my car registration being captured by traffic cameras, I avoid the M5 and other major routes, and wend my way down country by the back roads.

Before I reach the village, I pull over and reconsult the map. I'm looking for an entry to the footpath that I know runs behind Simon's back garden, to which there is a gate – again all discovered from good old Facebook, the stalker's friend. I end up parking off the road in a deserted woodland clearing where my car shouldn't attract any attention, and I gather my stuff into a small backpack so I look like an innocent rambler. A three-quarter-mile walk later and

I'm at his back gate, having not encountered another human being up to this point. I have a feeling it's all going to go very well, and after two Facebook murders my confidence has blossomed.

Sneakily I edge past the vegetable patch and across the lawn, keeping my head down, and I try to peer into the cottage without being seen myself. I must make sure Ongarface is home alone before going any further. Staying close to a trellis of pink roses, I advance on the back reception room sash window, and I make out his bulky form sitting at his workstation in the gloom, banging away on a keyboard, probably disparaging some other poor writer's efforts. I wait perhaps a couple of minutes, just to be sure. Satisfied he is without company, I go in through the unlocked kitchen door, pulling out the Webley and feeling gloriously crazy.

'Ongarface!' I shout as I come up behind him.

Simon jolts in his chair and swivels around to meet my gaze. He is quite a bit older than me, around fifty, and has wild bushy brown hair and a bristling moustache dividing a long gaunt unshaven face. We had an uneasy encounter at a convention two years back, so he's able to recognise me without difficulty. His black beady eyes register first astonishment and then pure incredulity.

'Jago…? Is that a real gun?'

'Not much point if it isn't!'

'W-why are you here…? God…I think I can guess. It's you, isn't it? You're the one everybody's speculating about…'

'You're quick on the uptake – I'll give you that.'

Keeping the Webley on Simon, I position the backpack on the sideboard and dig inside for a clear plastic breathing mask that I put to my face and inhale through, adopting a gurning expression. Then I go to iTunes on my phone and start up Roy Orbison's 'In Dreams' at not too high a volume. I lip synch the opening lines, mockingly serenading Simon with tales of candy-coloured clowns, sandmen and drifting off into sleep…

Simon stares with rising horror and fascination, his mouth contorting in a sickly fashion. 'Who are you meant to be – Frank Booth?'

'Got it in one!'

'So what's this? Some half-arsed recreation of *Blue Velvet*?'

'I can assure you, Simon, that it's completely fully arsed…as you'll find out…'

The alarm increments on Simon's face as his brain performs the calculations. 'So you're murdering writers – you shot Darren and no doubt Eustace too – and you're doing it *according to the plots of movies*! Oh my God, what a terrible idea!'

'But just the sort of idea you'd expect a "tadpole" writer to have, eh Simon? That was the word you used to describe me, was it not – "*tadpole*"…?' I use a sardonic Vincent Pricey tone of voice, which frightens Simon still further.

'My God…you're doing *Theatre of Blood* – you're copycatting Edward Lionheart!'

'Well deduced.'

'And what film plot did you use for Darren?'

'*Godfather II*. I took him out in a boat with a fishing rod!'

Simon grimaces and recoils. 'You twisted fuck!'

'Wait till you hear about Crimpy – I did him according to *Reservoir Dogs*.'

'You didn't cut his ear off?'

'What do you think?'

Simon winces and momentarily closes his eyes, then hastily looks right and left, vainly hoping for an avenue of escape. Suddenly he straightens in his chair and regards me with anger and defiance – the Simon I know from his review work.

'It doesn't matter how many writers or critics you slay, Farrar, it won't make *you* into a decent writer.'

'Well, *you* won't be around to besmirch my new ongoing work, Simon, which is some consolation.'

Simon opens his gimlet eyes wider. 'New ongoing work…? That's what this is, isn't it? You're murdering writers and critics *for a novel*!'

'This isn't a novel. It's real.'

'Can you tell the difference?'

'Maybe not, Simon.'

'You're a malignant tumour, Farrar – a foul growth on the body of British genre fiction!'

'Good piece of crit. Pity no one will hear it. Actually I prefer that to "tadpole"…Oh, how that word has rattled around in my brain for all this time…Do you think it was right or responsible to say what you did – to strike so decisively at the existential heart of a writer's nature?'

That makes Ongarface swallow the lump in his throat and pause for thought. 'I only gave an opinion. Maybe it was a kind of wake-up call to do something else other than write.'

'Be a serial killer, perhaps?'

He is stumped for a reply and his gaze goes misty and loses focus.

I'm becoming aware we're talking too much and not getting on with the re-enactment. 'In Dreams' has finished now, and I take a hit on the breathing mask to get back in character.

'Hang on…' Simon says. 'How does this work? If you're Frank Booth who am I?'

'Take your pick – the Yellow Man, the husband, Jeffrey…'

'But Frank gets shot at the end. You haven't thought this through, have you?'

'I just like films with a combination of severed ears and lip-synched songs containing references to clowns, not to mention gas masks. And Frank is such a good psycho role model – "Baby wants to fuck!"'

Ongarface is desperately improvising to buy time, but we both know the denouement is fast approaching.

'Look, Jago…' he intones softly. 'Why don't you put down the gun, turn yourself in and plead diminished responsibility? Your actions are not those of a sane man.'

'What, and spend the rest of my life in a nuthouse instead of prison? That doesn't greatly appeal, Simon. And anyhow, if I'm a nutter why would I do something sensible like that? It doesn't hang together. As a true psycho, I'm going to carry on till some external force stops me. I've killed twice now. You know it really does get easier.'

I move to the backpack and exchange the mask for a makeshift silencer that I put together out of PVC piping and cotton wool, following on from the noise issue with the Crimpy shooting. As I position it in front of the Webley barrel, Simon rushes out of his chair and tries to cross the six feet of space between us as quickly as he can. I simply whack him on the bridge of the nose with the pistol butt and affix the silencer as he crumples onto the floor.

'I tell you what, Simon, you can be Frank now and I'll be Jeffrey. That'll work...'

I aim and shoot him right in the centre of the forehead, remaining true to the plotline of *Blue Velvet*. The silenced bullet makes a pleasing *phokk* sound as it travels to its destination. A hat-trick of Facebook murders is now in the bag.

13. The Red Pill

Robin has changed tack since the night he came home all obstreperous and laying down the law, yet again making a big deal out of that little poke he calls a punch. He still stays away much of the time, but when he's home he acts matter-of-factly, neither aggressive nor conciliatory. I doubt this is indicative of a thaw in relations and eventual forgiveness; it feels more like a tactical stance, as if he's planning something but being careful not to show his hand yet, which might arouse my ire and retribution before he's ready. I'm convinced he's getting it on with Kevin and it's just a matter of time till the announcement. Perhaps when he does tell me he'll employ a couple of bodyguards as Hugh did, just to be on the safe side.

As for myself, I didn't follow up on the encounter with Marcus at The Outer Limits, though I vacillated a few times. However, after nearly a week he texted me, and being at a loose end I met up with him again at the club, and I represented my reserve as being due to my relationship with Robin and its fragile state of balance. Leaving earlier than last time, we went back to Marcus's room in his shared student house and had a great night of fun, which was welcome and another *up yours* to Robin and his attitude. Still, I feel doubtful about embarking on another relationship at the moment. I just can't be doing with the emotional entangling and scapegoating and counter-scapegoating that inevitably happens once the novelty stage has worn off.

I will have to see how it pans out, but my paramount concern is to keep my mind clear for the most important thing. *The Facebook Murders* is streaking ahead, regardless of my personal issues, and I want to remain focused to thunder on to the finish of the first draft. It's actually turning out to be a lot grittier than I originally envisaged, not a tongue-in-cheek black comedy like *Theatre of Blood*; and my inspector on the case is quite formidable, far from a genial fool like Milo O'Shea. I have niggling concerns that the reader might not identify with Jago on any level, finding him utterly without redeeming features – and in addition find the work as a whole as devoid of a moral centre, gratuitous. But, hey, it's customary to have such doubts half way through a draft. One must just forget them and press on.

A thought that occurred to me whilst writing the Simon Ongar chapter is that if Jago is composing a novel based on the actual murders he's committing then I should say more about his novel. He would require a protagonist within the narrative doing his bidding, say, Miles Hunniford...? And then Miles could also be writing a novel based on his murders within Jago's novel, so he himself would need his own man. That would be Damien Smithson, and the way this is heading, there would be another Russian doll narrator/protagonist inside Damien's novel, and he'd go by the name of Archibald Wetherell...and yes, yes, he'd have a narrator too, a certain Donald Ponsonby, whose novel would be propelled forward by none other than Aaron Slingsby...and so on down the line, to a more improbably exotic creation, say, Ezekiel Fazackerley!

I'm running out of silly names and I can't keep this up. Theoretically it could go on forever, and it's just like the amazing model village in Bourton on the Water in the Cotswolds, which contains a model of itself, and a model of the model, and a model of the model of the model. And indeed it's also like that marvellous movie *Synedoche New York*, starring Philip Seymour Hoffman, about an autobiographical playwright who gets to workshop his own life story, eventually arriving at the point in his life where he started work on the play itself, needing to dramatise that, and then inevitably moving on to where he started the play-within-a-play and so on infinitely, with actors playing actors playing actors and Chinese box sets filling New York...

Seriously though, with three murders down and two to go, one thing that's playing on my mind is the need for greater realism in the story. Perhaps I should actually visit the putative locations of Darren's, Eustace's and Simon's slayings and record ambient details to give more verisimilitude, rather than just relying on Google Earth,

Street View and my imagination. And I've used the Webley three times now, and it would be getting a bit tired to trot it out again. Regarding the fourth murder victim – Neil Hornblower – I have a special non-firearms-related fate in store for him, but when it comes to Hugh, the last and best, it has to be a gun again to fit the whole historical sweep. I can't use the Webley on Hugh, I'll have to find something different – and make it more real.

The village of Coombe Monkdown lies in rolling, picturesque Cotswold countryside, about fifteen miles east of Gloucester. There's an imposing medieval church at one end, a village green with a butter cross and an olde-worlde free house pub a short distance away, and a main thoroughfare with traditional cream-coloured stone buildings, housing shops and other amenities, with quieter residential streets fanning off. It's such a pretty and unspoilt village that it's been used several times as a location for country-orientated TV dramas, representing the nostalgic middle England of people's finer memories.

I drive there by a circuitous rural route, taking in the sights along the way, and indeed it's a pleasant day for such an excursion, with high scudding cumulus clouds in hazy blue sky. After parking my car discreetly in one of the side streets, I have a wonder around, using an Ordnance Survey map to get a better feel for the layout of the place. Presently I make my way to the lower boundary of the village, where I'm faced with a half-mile walk past open farmland to get to my intended destination. From a distance I can't make anything out, but as I get closer, nestling in the trees, I spy a green sign with white lettering: Coombe Monkdown Shooting School.

I hear multiple shotgun blasts as I walk down the gravel drive, reaching a car park delineated by half-round log rails, with similarly styled fencing for the paths and shooting stands around the grounds. The main building is a large log cabin with a covered veranda running around, where members can sit with a beer, tea or coffee. Several backwoods-type guys in Barbour clothing and cloth caps watch me as I approach, their guns lying at their feet in slipcases, and

I have that sense of entering a closed subculture sealed off from the mainstream of regular life.

A small office window opens onto the veranda, and I tell the girl about the half-price introductory lesson that I booked over the phone. She takes payment and then fetches my instructor, a handsome young man called Gilbert, who has a Roman nose, ash-blond floppy hair and talks in a posh accent. We shake hands warmly, and instantly he reminds me of a straighter wax-jacketed version of Marcus, and I wonder if he's gay, but I strongly suspect not. Gilbert asks if I've ever fired a gun before and I say no. He fixes me up with a 12 gauge over-and-under Beretta entry-level model, and tells me how to stand in order to fire, adding that I must always carry the gun broken when away from the shooting stands. I like the feel of the firearm and also the sense of superiority I get pointing it and looking along the barrel to the front sight.

Now wearing ear protectors and safety glasses, we walk to the first stand, passing a group of five laughing lads having a jolly day out. Gilbert explains that this trap will eject the clay vertically into the air, and I should aim at the lower end when it reaches the top of the trajectory. He loads two green 21 gram cartridges into my barrels and I get ready, holding the stock tight to my right cheek as I take aim. After I say 'pull', the clay floats up before me, and as it slows I blast away, smashing it to smithereens. The recoil isn't as strong as expected, but the surge of pleasure – coupled with an element of beginner's luck – is tremendous. Gilbert gives me a smile and says, 'Well done!'

I try again and miss this time, and my overall hit rate comes to average around sixty percent, which isn't bad for a first timer. The different stands and traps afford left-to-right and right-to-left trajectories, plus greater heights, double clays and ground-level rabbit-shooting simulation. The whole experience really takes me out of myself, what with the gun smoke wafting out of the barrels and the smell of cordite, conjuring up a thousand film scenes, and the keen sense of concentration in the effort to do better. A recurring fault, a common one, is a tendency to lift my head before firing, causing my aim to falter, and also to pause the gun rather than fire on the swing. When I either successfully hit or miss a clay, it's hard to know exactly what I've done right or wrong and to capitalise on that knowledge, but I suppose it will all come with practice.

On my way around the stands I twice passed a pair of giggling women shooters, making brief eye contact; and returning to the main lodge with Gilbert, I see them again, sat at a veranda table with coffees and biscuits. One is a bird-like bleached blonde of about forty-five, and the other is younger, around late thirties, with a cheeky smile and big curly auburn hair. After shaking hands with Gilbert, telling him how much I enjoyed it all and that I'll definitely come again, I get my complimentary coffee and ginger nuts, and I smile at the girls as I hover nearby.

'Enjoy yourself?' says the auburn haired one.

'Yeah, had a great time!'

'Your first time, was it?'

'Yes…I'm a virgin.'

'Ooh I doubt that…' She arches her eyebrows. 'Join us, have a seat.'

It turns out the pair are local members and very experienced shooters, their guns under the table in slips. They introduce themselves – the blonde is called Marjorie and the other Pippa, and Pippa asks me my name.

'Rodney,' I say.

'Rodney, eh – not "Ronnie"? You look a bit like Ronnie Wood – in his younger days, of course. I bet you get that all the time.'

'Yeah, well, there are worse people to look like.'

'Where're you from then, Ronnie? Sorry! I mean Rodney!' Pippa gives a high trilling laugh.

'I'm from Gloucester,' I reply, affecting a mild Gloucester accent. 'Thought I'd have a change and come out and try some country pursuits.'

'Go wild in the country, eh?'

'Yeah, that too!'

Pippa gives that laugh again, even higher and more trilling.

Marjorie looks at her watch and stands, shouldering her gun slip. 'Go to go. The brood need to be fed. I'll text you tomorrow, Pip.' She turns to me. 'Nice to have met you, Rodney, see you again maybe.'

'Yeah, I hope so.'

After she's gone, Pippa says, 'Another coffee? Or maybe a beer?'

'A beer would be great, thanks. Lager if they've got it.'

As she rises and goes inside to the small wood-panelled bar area, I study Pippa more closely. She's buxom and full hipped but trim in the waist, an apple-cheeked fecund country girl. There's an air of sartorial affluence about her, represented in her burgundy fleece gilet with leather trim, Dubarry-tagged equestrian knee boots over tight beige cord jeans, and jewelled Tag Heuer watch. Clearly a woman of some substance. While she's waiting for the order, a middle-aged bloke in a hacking jacket says something funny to her, attempting to flirt, and she laughs and responds with gaiety. But I don't fancy his chances somehow.

Pippa returns with two bottles of Budweiser, and now she has me in a one-to-one, she launches into a full exposition of her world, with me nodding and asking the odd encouraging question like a canny interviewer. She starts by talking about the shooting school and how it's the hub for the country set, along with the golf club, of which she's also a member, and together with the three village pubs they combine to give a lively, even racy, local scene. It turns out her parents own a nearby farm and she's been shooting ever since she could hold a gun, and she often hunts pheasant and sometimes rabbit, fox and various wildfowl. I ask her what kind of cartridge type is needed to kill a fox or a goose, and as hoped I get an in-depth expert answer.

She explains that for clay shooting one usually employs 7.5 shot – fairly small – with a 21 or 24 gram load – fairly light. For pheasant one uses slightly bigger 5, 6 or 7 shot and a heavier load – 30 or 32 grams – as obviously one's trying for a kill. When it comes to larger birds, 3 and 4 shot are good for duck and 1 shot for geese, with loads of around 42 and sometimes over 50 grams. With fox, one would use the very large BB shot or perhaps AAA buckshot to make sure of wiping the buggers out. Larger sizes of buckshot are available, but single slug cartridges are only legal with a firearms certificate. I'm confused at first, but soon realise the smaller the number the larger the shot size, and I ask what's the biggest she's used and she says BB.

'You could kill practically anything with that at close enough range, even your husband!'

Simultaneously we break into uproarious laugher that has people nearby turning their heads to glance at us. I finish my beer, wave the empty bottle and say, 'Another one?'

Pippa gives me a thoughtful look, saying, 'Are you in a hurry to get away?'

'Not really.'

'No wife or girlfriend waiting at home?'

'Nah, I'm single.'

'Me too…' She beams a protracted smile. 'Look, they do very good food at The Stag and Hounds in the village – moules marinière, a sirloin steak, or fish and chips if you like. I was going to head over there, have a glass of wine and eat later. You're welcome to join me.'

The day is turning from singular to positively surreal, but avoiding hesitation I say in a casual tone, 'Sounds like a good idea, why not?'

On the way out to the car park, gravel crunching underfoot, we pass Gilbert who says cheerio with a smiling face, and makes brief amused eye contact with me. Pippa gets out her keys and beeps open a newish black Land Rover Discovery, unshouldering her gun slip and placing it in the boot.

'What kind of gun have you got?' I ask.

She takes it out of the slip, breaks it and shows me. 'It's a Beretta side-by-side – more traditional style, you know.'

'Nice engraving,' I say, stroking the side panel.

'Yes, rose and scroll. It was a birthday present from my dad.' She snaps it shut, returns it to the slip and stows it away amongst the clutter of various footwear, shopping bags, golf clubs and boxes of balls and gun cartridges. 'Which is your car?' she asks.

'Oh I left it in the village.'

'Right. I'll give you a lift then.'

Zooming back down the road, gripped by the plush comfortable leather passenger seat, I reflect that Pippa showed no curiosity as to why I left my car in the village and walked, which registers as another strong positive in the way things are going.

We pull up on the drive of Pippa's detached house at the north end of the village at just before eleven o'clock. By now she's had two glasses of Sauvignon blanc, most of a bottle of red Bordeaux and two, perhaps three, gin and tonics. She's way over the limit for driving, but the journey from The Stag and Hounds was less than a mile, and no one here's going to breathalyse her anyway, she said on departure with another trilling laugh. Now she drops her car keys getting out of her door, sways slightly as she goes to the boot to collect the gun, and fumbles a bit opening up her Victorian-style front door, casting dreamy-eyed glances in my direction. Once inside, she puts the gun in the umbrella stand and holds me by the forearms.

'From when I was a young girl I had a fantasy about bedding a Rolling Stone...' She leans inwards and we commence an energetic and protracted kiss.

In the five or so hours I spent with Pippa in the pub, I got the full history of the acrimonious split from her rich former husband, leading to a generous settlement and the wonderful life she has now – as well as shooting and playing golf, she has two horses and rides with the Heythrop Hunt. I also ate an excellent ten-ounce sirloin with chunky chips and portobello mushroom, and was left to my own devices for periods whilst she went to chat to people who'd just come in. Even from a distance, her laugh registered constantly above the general pub hubbub, like the call of some exotic bird. Presently I was introduced to several of her cronies, and with the drink flowing, I was inducted as an honorary member of the Coombe Monkdown jet set. Throughout Pippa drank profusely and assumed I'd done the same, hence the friendly offer of a bed for the night; but I'd actually been careful with my own intake and wasn't smashed at all, just a little merry.

Wasting no time on preliminaries, Pippa leads me up the stairs to a spacious bedroom with fitted wardrobes, chests of drawers and an ornate dressing table with a large round mirror and padded stool, every surface covered by product containers of varying sizes, standing like chessmen. Giving me a sexy leer, she turns on a couple of lamps and kills the ceiling light to create a subdued effect. The huge floral-carved bed has plump pillows and a silver silk duvet cover, and the sight of it gives me a mild attack of anguish. Pippa pulls off her boots and invites me to do the same and get comfortable, whilst she enters an adjoining dressing room to change.

I have had a few 'relationships' with women in the past – the very distant, much more experimental past. Now I try to recall how I managed it back then and wonder if it's still viable. Pippa re-enters, wearing a towelling dressing gown and mules, just as I'm struggling to get out of my jeans. She gives me a hand and then pulls me further onto the bed, kissing me and groping inside my shorts at the same time. Amazingly the frisson is having the desired effect, and I take off her robe and reciprocate, causing her to writhe and roll on top of me. I get a twang of nostalgia at that long lost smell, the scent of a woman – so far removed from that of a man – but somehow on a purely chemical level it is working, bypassing the higher brain centres.

Pippa halts proceedings at the critical moment and reaches over to her bedside drawer, fishing out a Durex Thin Feel from a box of twenty-four therein. I let her put it on and encourage her to go down on me, which she does; and then quickly, for fear of losing the moment, I take charge, roll on top and give her what she desires, watching her large breasts jiggle while thinking abstractly about how odd women's bodies are in general. If Pippa's fantasy is being ravished by an exalted Rolling Stone, then mine is my emergency backup *Matrix* one. I take the Neo role and stop all the bullets in bullet time in mid air…next I effortlessly parry Agent Smith's attacks, showing him who's boss…and then I karate kick him to the floor, rip off his trousers and shag him senseless in showers of sparks and electrostatic effects. So Ronnie Wood makes it with Hugo Weaving – that must be a first!

Soon afterwards an exhausted Pippa turns over, gets herself under the duvet and enters an alcoholic post-coital slumber, her snoring almost reaching male volume levels. I try to clear my mind and remember what I touched within the house – nothing with my fingertips, I reckon, as by that time I was being careful and using my knuckles to push open doors and so forth. In the bathroom I get rid of the condom and use toilet paper to handle the flush and the sink taps. Then with Pippa still dead to sentience, I dress quickly and go downstairs, taking some more toilet paper with me to touch objects and grip handles.

Her gun safe is under the stairs, fixed to the wall, and nearby there's a large walnut cabinet, with its folding doors and drawers left fortuitously unlocked. Inside, to my delight, there are many boxes of cartridges, stacked in columns, with printed specifications facing outwards on the lids. Using the knowledge gained today, I identify the heavy-load variety of preference – extreme hunting, BB shot size – and I stuff two boxes into my jacket pockets. I freeze and hear nothing from upstairs, so now is the moment. With adrenalin flooding my system, touching every nerve ending, I walk to the front door, open it with tissue, and taking the slipcased shotgun carefully from the umbrella stand, I shoulder it and glide out into the night. Then I quickly wipe the Land Rover passenger door handle, hope-fully eradicating all traces of my fingerprints.

When I finally get back to the flat at past three in the morning, Pippa's shotgun still in my boot and the car parked in a side alley, I collapse onto the leather sofa and stare at the walls in stunned disbelief. I went along to the shooting school with the vaguest, most fanciful and half-baked notion that I may be somehow able to lift a gun…and I succeeded totally – lock, stock and barrel, I'm tempted to say! *What is happening?* I ask myself. I really have taken the red pill tonight, and I'm tumbling down the rabbit hole and passing through to the other side of the mirror.

14. Piranhas in the Jacuzzi

The four years I spent living with Helmut constituted the longest continuously stable period of my adult life. There were the usual vicissitudes one gets in any relationship and occasional fallings out, but it was all mild and short-lived by comparison to other lovers. As I've thought many times since we broke up, often with regret, Helmut was a kind, logical person with a placid temperament, and being with him served to flatten out the inherent volatility within myself. When I think of what I got in his place – the irritating, over-controlling Robin – I shake my head in disbelief and wish I could press 'undo'.

For a start Helmut and I had a similar taste in film, as evinced by our first meeting, mutually eulogising David Lynch. As well as more contemporary edgy movies, we watched the classics together on DVD – *La Grande Illusion, Bicycle Thieves* and *The Passion of Joan of Arc*, for example – and discussed them afterwards. In fact *Bicycle Thieves* was Helmut's all-time favourite film, as it crystallised his anti-capitalist tendencies in a near perfect poetic form. Helmut was also supportive of my writing and unjudgemental when it came to its commercial prospects, or the lack of them. During that time with him, after the literary stalker novel had been mothballed, I concentrated on short stories and eventually worked up to compiling my collection, *Dark Undertows*, taking on board his helpful suggestions.

Money-wise things were fine, and we never had any of those who-should-pay-for-what arguments. Helmut had a prestigious job as a psychology senior lecturer at the university, and I worked intermittently in bookshops. He paid the mortgage and all the bills for his roomy Bishopstone terrace and didn't ask me to contribute. In one way it meant I had no stake in the accommodation where I was living, but that didn't bother me much. My own earnings were therefore all personal spending money, and so my cash flow was good.

However Helmut was stricter when it came to anything political. As an ideological left-winger he was stridently opposed to abuses of government power or the bullying tactics employed by big institutions and corporations. His angry side got expressed in this way – for example he called, only semi-humorously, for the lynching of bankers in the long fallout from the 2008 financial meltdown; and whenever there were news reports concerning far-right groups such as UKIP and the BNP, he shook his fist at the TV. Conversely when Julian Assange came on, he cheered. It was in the area of politics that his customary broad-mindedness was circumscribed; he just couldn't countenance right-wingers as simply people with a different point of view. If you harboured right-wing sentiments, you were a bad person, or at best deluded, in Helmut's reckoning.

It was a similar case when it came to food, for Helmut was a staunch vegan. Again he didn't see meat-eating as simply an alternative choice, but as intrinsically bad, bordering on evil. He regarded my omnivorousness as something he could cure me from – like obsession. However no amount of indoctrination on the cruel conditions animals endured on their way to the table, or lectures on the morality of taking away another creature's life, had any effect on me. I told him I just didn't think about that stuff, and simply regarded meat and fish as food – a dimension of eating of which I wouldn't want to be deprived. But in order to please him, I played his game, at least for the while. I didn't like soya milk in tea and on cereal, and whilst he was most creative with vegetable dishes, they just got so monotonous over time. Eventually I went out for cod and chips or a kebab, or visited restaurants for steak or a rack of lamb. A crestfallen Helmut would eat alone on these occasions, sulking, just as if I'd been unfaithful.

When it came to sex, we had a fulfilling, fairly adventurous time – in fact Helmut had several books on gay erotica that informed our sessions. But as we know, going with the same partner eventually becomes repetitious, no matter how many twists you weave in. After almost a couple of years, I went out clubbing with other mates, got drunk, met someone and was actually unfaithful for the first time.

More encounters followed sporadically, and when Helmut became suspicious I didn't try to hide it, I confessed. He was deeply hurt but surprisingly understanding and soon forgiving. Promiscuity was another of my faults that he could work on, and he knew that it didn't actually threaten the love that we shared. In truth, I think he regarded an opportunist blow job as a lesser evil than a full English breakfast.

I go into detail on these points of Helmut's character in order to make it clear how damning it was when my obsession with Hugh became rekindled so dramatically by the publication of his next novel. For me to get back into the saddle over Hugh like this was a fundamental transgression that Helmut couldn't bear – as bad as if I'd announced I was standing for election as a UKIP MEP. All the work he'd undertook to move me away from Hugh unravelled catastrophically, and it led inexorably to the destruction of our relationship.

When a prominent writer has a new novel coming out, we get to hear about it several months in advance of its release to the world. Firstly it's just the title and date of publication that are given out, and the title alone of Hugh's latest – *In the Teeth of Hell* – was enough to make the small hairs stand on end and give me a most unpleasant creepy sickness in the stomach. Looking back, I felt I'd had a clairvoyant premonition of what was to come. A few weeks on and a short synopsis appeared on various publishing-related sites, which was reproduced on Hugh's site, his Facebook author page and in news articles. That one paragraph absolutely sealed all my worst fears. It was as if Hugh had thrown down a massive armoured gauntlet, clattering at my feet, daring me to do something and prove I wasn't completely impotent:

When rock guitarist Rory Gibson and his band play a private gig for a billionaire's birthday party, he has a chance encounter with gay part-time waiter Alfonso, Rory's biggest fan and a dangerously unstable psychotic. Relentless primal forces are unleashed that lead Rory and those close to him to the edge of madness and death itself. In this tale of erotomania and violence, set in the colourful milieu of indie rock, Hugh Canford-Eversleigh shows he's lost none of his power to shock and transport us into the darkest realms of the human condition.

I, for one, was certainly shocked and transported into the darkest realms of the human condition. My first reaction, naturally, was to talk it over with my lover, Helmut. After I'd outlined the situation in a breathless frantic voice, he patted a space on the sofa and told me to sit and calm down.

'This is a test,' he said, his German accent sounding thicker than usual. 'Ignore it, don't react and you've got it beat.'

'But...but...it's different this time, don't you see that Helmut? Before it was me doing all the running, chasing Hugh, trying to get a response and getting absolutely nothing back except avoidance. Now *he's* done something – and not only that, something big. Very big! He's written a book based on what happened between us – the very thing I was trying to do myself!'

'You don't know that for sure absolutely.'

'I will once I've read it!'

'You shouldn't read it...' Helmut sighed and his expression hardened, seemingly accepting he'd lost the argument already. 'If you read it, whatever the outcome, it will suck you back into the architecture of the obsession, reinforce all the old patterns – hate, love, it makes no difference, it's still obsession.'

I exhaled and thought over what Helmut had said. 'I understand where you're coming from, my dear, but your proposed alternative – *not* to read it, not to bite the bullet, never to know for sure how things stand, is equally unappealing. I need to find out exactly what he's done – how much he's extracted from our liaison together and how he's used it.'

'And what then? If you find out he's extracted and used much of it, what do you do about it?'

'I'm not sure at this point.'

'If you go on the rampage, it could destroy you...destroy us...'

'I won't go on the rampage, but I need to have a full picture of everything. I can't live in limbo.'

Helmut put an arm around the back of my head and wiggled an ear under my hair, a customary affectionate gesture. 'If I told you to leave it alone for the sake of us, would you do that for me?'

'Helmut, this isn't about you and me. Don't put you and me in the firing line, you daft apeth. I love you, and I don't want to compromise that.'

'You love Hugh too – or hate, which is the flipside of the same thing. I'm not happy, Nick. I don't think this is going to end well.'

Embarking on *In the Teeth of Hell*, I was initially lost in the rapture of Hugh's prose, made to experience the sights, sounds and smells of the fictional island within Saint Vincent and the Grenadines where the billionaire hedge fund manager's fiftieth birthday party is set. I felt the bake of the Caribbean sun, the intensity of electric blue skies and shimmering turquoise waters, and the gentle sway of palm fronds in the warm breeze. It had been over four years since I'd read *Necropolitic*, having passed on the historical saga reboot *Valkyrie*, and in truth I was missing the unique Hugh buzz. I almost forgot I had a vested interest in the text as I turned the pages and got into the story.

Presently I became bedazzled by the precision with which Hugh drew Rory and his band, a set of blingy, leather-clad, shades-wearing, messy-haired rockers, a bit like a Brit version of The Killers, The Strokes or Imagine Dragons. Rory, a virtuoso on guitar, a nouveau Jeff Beck or Eric Clapton, is trying to make the best of the occasion whilst having problems with his clingy girlfriend Alicia, who insisted on coming along and is now demanding attention when he's busy setting up for the concert. However, the evening's entertainment goes well, and it's only afterwards, when Rory is relaxing that the shadowy Alfonso makes his presence felt. He serves Rory a glass of Cristal and commiserates with him on his woman trouble, some of which Alfonso overheard. Rory is happy to open up to this friendly stranger and becomes impressed by Alfonso's knowledge of his oeuvre, right down to the notations of individual guitar breaks.

That first chapter was written in the third person, with Rory as the viewpoint character, and it was only when I reached the second chapter that alarm was triggered and my system started to go into emergency mode. For the second chapter employed Alfonso's point of view, and it became clear that Hugh's intention was to play off dramatic ironies between the two leads and the reader.

We are plunged into Alfonso's obsessive delusional world, and of course he sees his meeting with Rory as divinely ordained, the beginning of something beautiful, which fulfils the promises in the messages Rory has been sending to Alfonso through his song lyrics. Alfonso's obsessive fandom is detailed in bursts of unpunctuated Joycean stream-of-consciousness that are taken *right out of my fucking literary stalker letters to Hugh!* Whole passages are reproduced virtually verbatim, apart from changes to factual details. In one of my letters, outside of the third person stalker narrative, I suggested that perhaps Hugh had been sending me messages in his prose – but I meant it as a joke! Now my entreaties of love had been warped into the fantasies of a fictional nutcase!

I became numb reading it, paragraph after paragraph of my own stuff, too stunned to be able to be angry. It was mid-evening and Helmut was downstairs reading a book himself and listening to Mozart. By now we'd been through many variations of the argument about whether to read *In the Teeth of Hell* or leave it alone, and I knew it was unwise to reignite it all, but I just couldn't help myself. I dashed into the lounge, turned down the volume on the music and began reading passages aloud, annotating them with contextual comments. Though I knew there was nothing to be gained from informing Helmut, I wanted to prove I'd been right all along in my suppositions about Hugh.

'So what now…?' Helmut said wearily. 'He's nicked your ideas. What are you going to do? Get a gun and shoot him?'

'Sounds like a plan.'

Helmut shrugged hopelessly. 'This is what I was afraid of…'

'I'll tell you what I'm going to do – I'll go along to a public reading and confront him from the audience in the question-and-answer session.'

'And say what exactly?'

'Well…I'll put it to him that he used my letters for the character… And there may be more to it – I've only read two chapters so far.'

'If you say that, people will think you're a crackpot. And I'm sure Hugh will have a good answer ready to rebut such a claim.'

My spirits sank further as I saw Helmut had a point. 'Yes, I'd better think it out again then. And I'll read the rest of the book and know the worst.'

Helmut just sighed and diverted his eyes back to his book. I'd never seen him so disconsolate.

And there was worse to come, much more, much worse. As the story progresses, Alfonso's obsession pretty much follows the trajectory of mine with Hugh, at first friendly and amorous and then reaching the key tipping point where love sours and curdles. That is prompted when Rory ditches girlfriend Alicia, and Alfonso approves, believing Rory is freeing himself up for Alfonso himself. But instead Rory commences a new relationship with flamboyant Lady Gaga-like pop star Moonchild Clytemnestra (real name: Stacey Burnside), and naturally Alfonso goes ape. It was the Nick-Hugh-Gretchen triangle all over again, and when Alfonso's intentions turn nasty, Hugh used my later post-Medusacon letters to furnish the mindset.

Nearing the end, it all gets much more Gothic and Grand Guignol in Hugh's customary style, with Alfonso becoming a supercharged gay male version of Alex from *Fatal Attraction*. In one attempt on Rory's life, he wires up his guitar strings in order to deliver a fatal electric shock when touched, but an unlucky roadie gets there first and is blown off the Glastonbury Pyramid Stage in flurries of sparks and smoke. Another involves placing a shoal of piranhas in the dimly-lit outdoor jacuzzi of Rory's Italian villa one night, but it's Moonchild who dips her foot in the water and loses two toes in a fit of blood-chilling screams – brutal. Finally Alfonso, who is very adept and resourceful in many practical areas, constructs an elaborate spring-loaded mantrap – similar to the one featured in the movie *Apocalypto* – with the intention of impaling Rory through the heart, head and genitals should he step onto the plate. But in the confusion of the chase that follows the discovery of Alfonso in Rory's garden, it is – you've guessed it – Alfonso himself who gets the sharp end of the deal.

In a really bizarre way I found *In the Teeth of Hell* a fairly enjoyable read. It was beautifully written, with Hugh's trademark touches of making the improbable seem utterly convincing, and if I put the part of my mind that contained my personal issues on hold, I could admire it just like any other normal fan. But I was in shock from the whole experience, not my usual self at all, suffering from a weird bout of Stockholm Syndrome. The novel was indeed a piece of pure fiction, carrying over hardly a single factual detail from the real story of Hugh and myself, and Hugh could argue that point if challenged. Nonetheless that real story lay at its core and formed its DNA, and it couldn't exist in its present form were it not for what had happened.

On top of that, sizable sections of *my own actual writing* had been incorporated into the text and were crucial in the development of Alfonso's character. If nothing else, there was copyright infringement here. However one looked at it, as a literary crime it was heinous indeed, a staggeringly momentous act of revenge. Hugh had paid me back for the hassle of all that stalking big time, and Alfonso's fate at the novel's conclusion was a neat metaphor for what he'd done to me in real life. He'd inked me in and then inked me out of existence in a flash!

I analysed my feelings as they gradually started to come back to me. It was as if an expert pickpocket had brushed past and lifted my wallet so deftly that I'd hardly noticed, yet I was left patting down my trouser pockets, noting the wallet's absence, and sighting the pickpocket in the distance, now too far away to catch. But it wasn't a wallet, it was a novel that Hugh had pickpocketed – my pet stalker novel. I might have abandoned it, but Hugh, with his superior literary prowess, had taken it over and made it his own – much as a big conglomerate gobbles up a small struggling firm and takes possession of its valuable patents, cashing in and giving little or nothing in return. That was a phrase that echoed in my brain over the coming days: 'nothing in return'. In a way *In the Teeth of Hell* was a kind of joint venture, a collaboration between two writers, such as might take place in the development of a screenplay. But did I get a co-screenwriting credit? Did I get percentage points of the profits? No fucking way! It was winner takes all.

Next I was thinking about poor Moonchild Clytemnestra with her two missing toes, and reflecting that she was so clearly a portrait of Gretchen Mulhoney. Then it hit me in a flash – Gretchen's kiss-and-tell article all about Hugh's real character, the man the public never saw. Of course! It all came back to *The Collector*, a favoured novel of Hugh's. I'd been so preoccupied regarding Hugh as my muse that it never occurred to me I might be his muse. He had *collected* me as surely as he'd collected Gretchen and no doubt many others. I was now locked in Hugh's basement, made to do his bidding, or else snuffed out in the killing jar like one of his Pale Clouded Yellows.

On the night I started reading *In the Teeth of Hell*, I carried on till I'd finished it – all three hundred and twenty-odd pages – at around five o'clock in the morning. Needless to say, I wasn't thanked in the Acknowledgements on the final page. Helmut didn't look in on me in the study, and went to bed alone without a word. In the coming days he was sulky and circumspect in his dealings with me, and both of us avoided mentioning what had now become a taboo subject. Eventually it was Helmut who made the first move, asking me to sit down again and explain my current feelings, now that a bit of time had passed. As constructively as I could manage, I outlined how my attitude to Hugh had hardened to stone, now I had conclusive evidence of the way he'd ripped me off. I did intend to do something about it, but I assured Helmut I wasn't going 'on the rampage'. Nonetheless he looked at me with a woeful expression of utter defeat.

'So that's it then,' he said. 'You're just going to go on and on and on with this.'

Trying to be conciliatory, I said I agreed it wasn't a good idea to confront Hugh at a reading, where I'd be at a natural disadvantage. Instead I was setting up a blog in order to tell the world about Hugh and his dirty dealings. My hope was that it would start something and gather momentum, and others would rally to my cause. Helmut just shook his head despairingly and made no reply.

A couple of weeks later, several blog pages were ready and I launched the thing, publicising it on Facebook, Twitter, Reddit and Stumbleupon. Predictably my proper friends on Facebook were supportive and took an interest, whereas my enemies posted sardonic comments, Darren and Crimpy amongst them, which made for further nails in their coffins as far as I was concerned. Over the coming days I added more posts, further beefing up my arguments, such as actual comparisons between the texts of my letters and passages within *In the Teeth of Hell*. I was careful to present my letters as containing fictional narrative ideas, not real stalking sentiments. I got a fair number of hits and some interesting comments from other bloggers, plus the usual input from the loony fringe.

My next step was to try and interest the press in what I hoped was developing into a viable story. I contacted news desks, agencies and some promising-looking individual journalists, giving a brief outline and links to the blog pieces. A few did reply, requesting more information, which I found heartening. I told Helmut the campaign was ticking along in an orderly fashion, devoid of any hysteria, and I hoped he would start to come around. But he wasn't interested; his moroseness was deeply ingrained and he now seemed to regard me as some form of reprobate – a brand of far-right-winger or animal abuser, perhaps. Then after another few days of prolonged sulking, he confronted me.

'Nick, I can't live like this. Everything is out of kilter, in chaos. It's like you're having a relationship with him, not me. Perhaps it would be an idea for you to move out for a time, so we can take stock over a longer period – a trial separation.'

'Helmut, if I move out that'll be it. Is that really what you want? Why do you insist on controlling me in this matter – like you want to control what I eat? Just let me do what I want regarding Hugh.'

'Look, you're suffering from an obsessional disorder. Until you get back to recognising it as such and treating it as an illness, there is no hope.'

'Why don't you tell Hugh that?'

'I don't know Hugh, I know you. And besides Hugh is a professional writer – he's just doing what professional writers…do…' Helmut trailed off, realising he'd gone out on the wrong tack.

'Oh he's a professional writer, is he? And what am I – a fucking circus clown…? He's doing what professional writers do, is he? And what should I do according to you? Back down with my tail between my legs because he's a professional writer and I'm just some sad unprofessional obsessive headcase? I'll pack some things and stay at Patrick's tonight.'

My anger was surging now and buoyed up on a wave of adrenalin, I transferred the bad feelings about Hugh onto Helmut's shoulders. If the twat couldn't be supportive in this important matter, then fuck him! I went upstairs and carried out my threat, and he made no move to stop me. In truth though, regardless of Hugh, I was getting sick of Helmut and his whining, and his balanced approach to everything and his vegan attitude to life. I wanted to get back to being red in tooth and claw.

15. Attack of the Kamikaze Writer

I think I'm starting to crack up. Earlier today I was in Bristol city centre, doing a few errands, and I became convinced I was being followed. Walking through the Broadmead precinct, I passed a man in a raincoat and trilby hat, and he did a slight double take when we made eye contact, but he tried to hide it as best he could. Later, I was coming out of Marks and Spencer, having bought a bacon sandwich for lunch, and there he was again, lurking over by the entrance to the Galleries and Pret A Manger, pretending to be looking at his phone.

It's Leopard! I thought, and then I heard a disembodied giggling voice at the back of my skull and tried to play down the implications to myself.

Minor though this incident was, the damage had been done, and I was on the lookout for Leopard throughout the rest of the afternoon. I felt him peering over my shoulder or lying in wait around the next corner, or else just generally monitoring me by supernatural means. Of course I knew I was paranoid and had good reason to be. Heading up Park Street in the direction of Clifton, I looked over at Queenshilling on the street below the bridge, and I happened to brush too close to a heavy-set guy with a long beard. On receiving his hard stare I thought: *he knows!* It was definitely a *you've-got-a-stolen-shotgun-stashed-away* kind of look without a doubt.

Because I've become so wary about my image being generally captured on CCTV, I bought a wide-brimmed leather hat and took to wearing it with my long hair stuffed behind my ears and inside my turned-up collar, with the further addition of wraparound shades. But even with this obfuscation of my appearance, I still feel trepidation about somehow being caught out. The same anxieties extend to my phone and internet activities – I want to be in a position to call, text and surf anonymously. To this end I bought a cheap SIM-free phone and a pre-paid card in town today, using cash naturally. Providing I don't use the phone at home, there is nothing to link me, Nick Chatterton, to its activities.

So I headed up through Clifton to the discreet, wooded, camera-free downs and sat on a bench to set it up. Indeed, if anything blows up and I'm subject to a police search of my home computer or regular phone usage records, I wouldn't want them finding evidence of the search I was about to perform: *how to saw off a shotgun*.

Even with all these precautions in place, my hat pulled down over my brows and only the odd jogger and dog walker about, the idea of Leopard's watchful gaze just wouldn't go away. Nonetheless, I got a wikiHow link on the first results page and it gave a simple step-by-step guide to the process. I'd need a circular power saw, a vice, a file and emery paper, and a hacksaw to cut down the stock into a pistol shape. As the site is American, there aren't the same legal constraints as exist in the UK, so the information isn't sensitive. Feeling a little better, I switched off the phone, donned the shades and headed back into Clifton to meet Marcus for a coffee. With the information I now possessed, I could turn Pippa's beautiful engraved Berretta into a twenty-four-inch-long concealable weapon.

It's really sinking in now that writing about Jago's murderous adventures has made *me* more devil-may-care on a fundamental structural level. That tryst with Pippa was fugitively opportunistic; it could so easily not have happened, yet it did. My first heterosexual fuck in almost twenty years, followed by a definitive criminal act. I've definitely crossed a line – I know it in my head and feel it in my bones. Reality is not the same anymore, and I now have no choice but to go on living in the terms of the new rarefied world in which I find myself. There is no going back. I wanted more of a sense of realism for the composition of *The Facebook Murders* and now I'm getting it in abundance!

In an effort to ground myself, I have to keep saying *I'm not Jago Farrar, and my actions have real consequences.* Stealing Pippa's shotgun was an incredibly impulsive act, but rendered irresistible by the enabling factors of the moment. Now it seems ludicrously reckless, bordering on madcap. I have a criminal record – from nineteen years ago, but I'm still on the database. What if Pippa is asked to look at some mugshots and happens to identify me? I haven't changed much over the years; the Ronnie Wood resemblance might be the key that clinches my fate. I've kept my nose clean for two decades, but a shotgun theft prosecution, following on from a conviction for grievous bodily harm would not be good for my prospects.

Why did I do it? I've asked myself. I could have legally applied for a shotgun certificate and bought one from a retailer. *Oh yes...?* I would have had to pay eighty quid, provide four passport photos, fill out a form declaring my GBH conviction, get someone to counter-sign, and then install a gun safe in the flat that Robin is about to break up, and have the police come around to inspect it for security. And after all that, in the unlikely event that my application is successful – in about a year from now – I'll illegally saw off my new gun. *A likely course of action?* Not really.

Looking on the bright side though, it's highly possible that Pippa won't report the theft. It's circumstances would reflect very poorly on her and might even jeopardize her own shotgun certificate. There was no break-in; her gun was left unattended and out of the safe while she had sex with a strange man she'd only known for five or six hours. Would she really want to give out that information to the police and face the music? Then again she'd know that if the gun was discovered in criminal hands it might be traceable to her, and she'd be in greater trouble for not reporting the theft. It's a difficult call, but I reckon if I give it three weeks and there's no knock on the door, then I'm in the clear. I might be terribly edgy now, but by then I'll be feeling better.

Even if there is a knock on the door and a police search, they won't find anything. Pippa's Berretta currently resides in my old mate Patrick's garden shed, concealed within a bag of ancient dusty golf clubs that belonged to his father or grandfather and probably haven't been used to hit balls since the 1970s. There is no chance that Patrick will venture into the shed and discover the gun. He gave up gardening and DIY about fifteen years ago, after his wife left him, and all he does now in his spare time is drink cider and bet on the horses. I often see Patrick for a drink in the Nova Scotia and then sometimes crash in the spare room at his house in Southville after a nightcap of Old Rosie. I was therefore able to secrete away the shotgun as he snored and will retrieve it similarly, when the time is right.

When I met Marcus in Caffe Nero on Queens Road, he was intrigued by the hat, the turned-up collar and the shades, saying it added to my mystique. In a nice way, he said he could tell I was a bit of a wrong'un, and that made him all the more attracted to me. What he termed 'badass' older men were his special interest and I fitted the niche perfectly.

Ah, the guilelessness of youth! I thought as I watched his sweet full lips talking away, and I tried not to fall for him too much, recognising he was clearly falling for me in a big way. He's a great kid, but it's not the time for me to be getting all lovey dovey again; there are too many wild cards in play and I want to cool it, at least till I've completed *The Facebook Murders*. That's what I keep telling myself at any rate.

After we finished our coffee, Marcus asked if I wanted to go for a drink tonight, and I told him maybe, but first I had to see what Robin wants. He phoned yesterday to say he was coming around at six for a chat. That sounds ominous, as Robin has never before announced that he's dropping into his own flat to 'chat' to his own partner. Even after our big bust up, he made a point of coming and going as he pleased. I told Marcus I'd contact him afterwards and let him know the score.

Now I'm at home waiting for the man himself, and the edgy feelings of earlier are creeping back up as I anticipate the nauseous scrunch of his key in the lock. Sure enough, I hear it a little after six, and Robin enters smiling and acting uncharacteristically sheepish. I offer him a cup of tea and we sit together on the leather sofa in the lounge, the BBC news ticking away at low volume on the TV. After a little bit of weird small talk, he comes out with his news: he and Kevin are starting a new salon together, taking a lease on premises in the Village, and he wants us to give notice on this flat and go our separate ways. As he imparts this final bit, I see him twitch involuntarily, perhaps expecting to be spontaneously punched again, but I remain calm as I respond.

'Robin, tell me, why does starting a new salon mean that we have to break up this flat?'

'Because there is accommodation above the shop premises, and it makes sense to live there – economic and practical sense.'

'Live there with Kevin…?'

'Uh huh.'

'And not me…?'

Robin straightens in his seat, more businesslike now. 'Look, Nick, I think we both know it's run its course. Why don't we agree to part amicably?'

'So you are getting it on with Kevin?'

'That's got nothing to do with it!'

'Robin, I'll find out sooner or later. Why don't you just be a man and admit it?'

'How is Marcus Hudson at the moment?' he retorts, all flustered now.

'Marcus Hudson?'

'The pretty blond young student you hang out with at OMG and The Outer Limits. The Bristol gay scene is a small world, ducky. People notice what's going on.'

'I'm shagging him, okay? Now how about Kevin?'

'I don't want another punch in the mouth. I know you, Nick.'

I give Robin my standard evil smile. 'I'm not in a punching frame of mind tonight, dearie. You're right. It's run its course. Lets part amicably. So you and Kevin are a couple now, partners in life as well as business? You're staying at his place now, aren't you?'

Robin just looks at me blankly and remains silent.

'I'll take that as a "yes" shall I? And it started some time ago, didn't it? Around the time we stopped having sex?'

Robin shuffles out of his seat and stands up. 'I think it's best if I go now, Nick. We'll talk about giving notice on the flat sometime soon. Ta-ta.'

As he reaches the door, I shout out 'Hey Robin!'

'What?' He looks really petrified.

'I shagged a woman the other day too!'

'Jesus Christ, you must be more desperate than I thought!'

After he goes I feel all light-headed and dissociated, and I reflect on what a surreal day it's been. First Leopard and paranoia in town, then the new anonymous phone and the sneaky searching, and finally Robin makes the declaration I've been expecting for weeks. So none of it was my imagination – I was right in my suspicions all along! I know I should feel angry at being cuckolded first, but I don't have the inclination for that, not right now. I get out my regular phone and text Marcus that I'll meet him in The Hatchet for a couple of beers prior to hitting the clubs. Then I change into funky evening wear and go out for a double lamb shish kebab on Whiteladies Road.

Marcus asks about Robin, but I keep it vague, mentioning only the new salon and not the impending break-up. I want to leave things ticking over in second gear and not press the accelerator too hard. Anyway Marcus doesn't ask any probing questions and seems content to carry on under whatever terms I present. He makes some philosophical comment from Confucius or Lao Tzu, still being young enough to derive inspiration and succour from such enlightened sayings.

After the pub, we move on to The Outer Limits, though I'm careful not to drink too much and ruin my head for work tomorrow. We go back to his room, but following an hour in bed I get up and say I'm returning home for a good night's sleep in order to remain fresh and alert. In no uncertain terms, I tell Marcus that I'm a working writer, a serious novelist, and putting together seventy or eighty thousand words of carefully crafted prose is a job and a half. He is really impressed by my discipline and gives me an extra passionate goodnight kiss as I hover in the doorway. Once I'm outside on the empty small-hours streets, I regret going, but the next chapter of *The Facebook Murders* is beckoning me.

Up, breakfasted and full of coffee, I'm at my desk ready to start at just before eleven. I intend to motor on for eight to ten hours and get a lot done. It's three down and two to go on the kill list, and Number Four is, of course, none other than that little prick Neil Hornblower. He is genuinely little and slight of build, a ratty gingery presence like a half-pint Uriah Heep. It's just as well that he is a small weedy guy – what I've got planned for him wouldn't work if he were six feet four and weighed sixteen stones.

I remember Neil at those first conventions I attended, back in the early 2000s, and the way no one took any notice of him then, ignoring him when he made a contribution to a group chat, or not including him when we mustered to go out for a curry. However, that all changed rapidly as the years progressed. The horror story magazine he founded, *Tamaghis*, started like so many as an amateurish-looking A5, monochrome-covered, saddle-stitched and flimsy-of-feel little booklet; but it came out regularly and on schedule, and writers of reasonable repute soon contributed. I had two of my early stories published in issues 3 and 5 respectively, which gave me reason to become matey with Neil. And that established itself as the general pattern online and at conventions, for soon most everybody wanted to be matey with this reliable editor who was clearly going places.

By the time *Tamaghis* had graduated to being a perfect bound, colour-covered, Royal format and substantial-of-feel anthology, Neil had achieved the status of a little tin god, included in the best writerly circles, and with aspiring contributors fawning and creeping to him, saying *Yes, Neil, yes, Neil, three bags full, Neil.* Typically he became much more high-handed and pompous in his attitude at conventions, and was distinctly less friendly towards me than he'd been in the past. Portentously, this behaviour just preceded or slightly overlapped with a long drawn-out issue I was to have with Neil – an issue that eventually escalated into a dispute.

Another story of mine had been accepted by Neil, and on the basis of *Tamaghis's* regular schedule I would have expected it to appear in issue 10, 11 or 12. But the issues kept coming out, going up to 15 and 16, and still no sign of my story. I compared notes with other contributors – Stan had a story in issue 15, and Darius in issue 16; and both confirmed they'd had their acceptances from Neil long after mine. So I sent Neil a polite email asking when I could expect my story to appear. He didn't reply. I left it two months and sent a reminder email, reiterating the issue. He didn't reply to that either, and my fears were pretty much confirmed.

When the next regular convention came around, I made a point of asking Neil if he'd received my emails and could he now give me an answer regarding the story. He dissembled like a master, first mentioning some server trouble that could have wiped out a cache of emails, and then professing not to know anything about the story, acting surprised that a story could have fallen through the cracks like that. He said he'd check his records when he got home, and I said I'd forward him his own acceptance email, which I did. Neil was extra frosty to me for the reminder of the convention, and naturally he didn't contact me with an answer in the coming weeks and months.

It was clear that Neil was going to perpetually stonewall me on this matter, so when my subscription to *Tamaghis* expired, I didn't renew. As far as I was concerned it was a lost cause and I was walking away. But that's not how Neil saw things. From a situation of receiving no personal, non-generic communication from him for over two years, I was suddenly bombarded with emails and Facebook messages reminding me that I hadn't renewed. I ignored them, of course, but when they continued so unrelentingly I became exasperated and replied to Neil, once again reminding him of my unpublished story that had 'fallen through the cracks' and the fact he'd not answered my many queries.

Neil then emailed back, unleashing the most incredible torrent of bile against me. Firstly he reiterated that he didn't know anything about the story and recommended that I forget it too and move on. Then he contradicted himself by saying that the standard of .

acceptance for *Tamaghis* had risen considerably since its early days – that is, he gave an excuse for reneging on the acceptance of a story he'd supposedly forgotten about. On top of that, he said it was very bad form of me to cancel my subscription as a retaliation, and subscriptions are a magazine's life blood, and all that. Then, as if *my* blood pressure wasn't already high enough, he added the killer final comments. He said I was being childish, petulant and acting with the brainless misguided resolve of a 'kamikaze writer', and I really ought to change my attitude!

I almost put my fist through the computer screen after I'd read that! *I* was guilty of bad form, childishness, petulance, brainlessness and being a kamikaze writer – what about the little fucker himself? His ego and self-image were so bloated, he regarded himself as the completely blameless injured party in the dispute. I replied, telling him where he could stick his pious sentiments; then I unfriended him on Facebook, unliked the *Tamaghis* page and unfollowed it on Twitter. But it wasn't anywhere near enough. Those comments of his, and particularly the term 'kamikaze writer', went around in my mind over and over, joining the ranks of 'left-wing putz' and 'tadpole'.

Right, Neil, you want to see a kamikaze writer in full combat action? I'll show you one!

16. He Comes as a Fool!

The Simon Ongar tragedy is all over Facebook. Some are linking it to Darren's shooting and Crimpy's disappearance, and others think it's unrelated, just a coincidence. The split is roughly fifty-fifty and the debate is fierce – Monty Python's 'Argument' sketch has got nothing on this! What happened was Simon's cottage was totally destroyed in a massive gas explosion that shook the village like an earthquake and sent a ball of flame and smoke over a hundred feet into the air, according to news sources. All that remains is a pile of rubble, timber and smashed household appliances and furniture. The cause appears to have been a faulty gas cooker, and due to the severity of the blast, Simon's body was not recovered intact. There is no evidence of foul play...not yet.

Which is jolly lucky for me! Using a scenario drawn from *The Bourne Supremacy*, I opened all the internal doors upstairs and downstairs, then turned on the gas rings and went out into the garden to wait half an hour for the cottage to fill with gas – a much longer period than the relatively short time in the film. Then I held my breath, went back into the lounge and turned on the toaster with the magazine inside, positioned next to Simon's head, and ran off as fast as possible back down the path towards where my car was parked. It took a good three minutes for the magazine to burn sufficiently to ignite the gas, by which time I was nearly half a mile away. But wow, what an explosion! It was like a thunderclap raised to the power ten. The magazine I used was one of Simon's own *British SF & Fantasy Review* copies – at last it was put to some good use!

On the drive home along narrow country roads, I had to pull over to allow fire engines, ambulances and police vehicles to pass, their sirens wailing frantically. None of them were interested in me, of course. However, a couple of days later the doorbell went at half past seven, and I knew beyond doubt that it was the police again. This time it was a couple of local Avon and Somerset detectives, and they asked if I would voluntarily accompany them for an interview at the

Trinity Road station in town. I agreed, as I felt sure they would arrest me if I didn't. Also I felt a small measure of relief that they didn't automatically arrest me – if they possessed something hard, they certainly would have.

Nonetheless, I was still cautioned and provided with a duty solicitor, and the interview was taped, so this was a major attempt to 'break' me. Over the course of six hours or more, I was interrogated by Avon and Somerset detectives about Simon; Surrey detectives about Darren; and, naturally, Leopard and Hawkins of the West Midlands about Crimpy once again. There was also a National Crime Squad superintendent hovering, reflecting the rising seriousness of the whole affair. But it soon became clear none of them had anything on me; they were simply fishing in the absence of leads.

Fortunately they'd turned up nothing to link me to the scenes of Darren's and Simon's demises, and Leopard had nothing more on the Crimpy affair. That is apart from establishing that I'd caught the 21.10 train back to Bristol that evening, leaving a four-hour gap from when the Blue Nebula function wrapped. Leopard badgered me for answers as to how I'd passed the time, but I was suitably vague, saying I went from bar to bar, sampling Birmingham life, but as I was a little drunk and didn't know the city I couldn't remember their names. His cop's instinct told him I was lying, but he still couldn't get me to trip myself up.

Finally the NCS superintendent, whose name was Steele, told me they were deeply concerned because the three incidents appeared to be linked by the commonality of the genre-writing community. All three victims knew one another, and all three knew me, he added menacingly. 'That applies to a lot of other people,' I replied, shrugging my shoulders. He then probed me on the subject of any animosity I might harbour for the three, and again I laughed at this like it was the silliest joke, denying it nonchalantly and feeling I was in the clear.

Yes, they knew the incidents were connected, all right, but they didn't know how and couldn't see the keyhole that would open the door to evidence. If Steele were Morse or Poirot, he might work out that the key to the Facebook Murders is Facebook itself! How does the genre-writing community exchange information about everything – through Facebook, of course – and the victims, and doubtless the perpetrator, are all in the same circle of friends. They didn't trawl back three years or so to find Darren's 'left-wing putz' comment, or Crimpy's aspersions, or indeed scour the back issues of *The British SF & Fantasy Review* to discover Simon's disparaging review of *Seriously Unhinged*. And obviously none of them had seen or remembered *Theatre of Blood*! They were investigating a community of writers, but they failed to look for clues within the weave of the writing itself. This ensemble of top cops just weren't thinking outside the box. Like the Nazis in *Raiders of the Lost Ark*, they were looking in the wrong place!

With great reluctance I was released for the time being, but storm clouds are gathering in another part of the sky. In a few days a new episode of *Crimewatch* is being aired, and it will contain dramatic reconstructions of both Darren's shooting in Chertsey and Crimpy's disappearance in Birmingham. These visual mock-ups have a habit of jogging people's memories, and witnesses who may not realise they have seen something important could now come forward. So, another thing to worry about for Jago, the Facebook Murderer, and I must now quickly get on and deal with my fourth victim.

The small market town of Tormartley, in the East Midlands, is a fair drive away from Bristol, and I'll use the motorways to take a direct route, as I'm not worried about traffic cameras this time. That's because I'm driving a newly bought cheap car that I paid for in cash whilst providing the seller with a false name and address. I'm convinced the police are watching my movements, so I leave the flat by the building back entrance and do several circuits of the streets to make sure no one is following before I pick up the car. My usual car is parked out in front to create the appearance that I'm home. Later, when it gets dark, lights will come on in the flat, enabled by timer switches, to further that impression. Satisfied that I'm in the clear, I drive off, making Tormartley by mid-afternoon.

Neil has lived there all of his life, and the correspondence address for *Tamaghis* is, naturally, his own, so no big investigation required in that. The town has a certain charm, with a wide main street and parking along the centre, a busy market square overlooked by a railway viaduct, and picturesque back streets, some of them cobbled, housing many eclectic old buildings clustering together, with business signs jutting out over the pavements. Neil's house is nearer the edge of town, in a typical 1950s estate of redbrick semis, most of them bay windowed, and from his Facebook feed I know he's very active within the local community. I might have unfriended him after our altercation, but he has many followers and his posts are set to 'public', so it makes no difference.

So, what am I going to do to apprehend Neil and bend him to my will? Well, thanks to Facebook it's simple. I know that around dusk Neil will be undertaking a short journey from his home to the Tilsley Recreation Ground, and I plan to grab him en route. My backpack is bulging with the necessary accoutrements – a dark longhaired female wig and flowing coat dress, some old tracksuit bottoms and a similar sweatshirt, a ball of strong twine, some heavy-duty cable ties and a big roll of gaffer tape. In addition, I have a mask made from a pillowcase with a face drawn on in magic marker and, most importantly, a three-pronged multicoloured jester hat that I bought from the Christmas Steps Joke Shop in Bristol. I also have a bottle of chloroform and some absorbent cloths, plus the Webley and a box of rounds, just in case things go haywire – but I don't plan to use it this time around.

The short November day is disappearing into gloom by four-thirty, and I make myself ready. When Neil comes down the lonely crepuscular footpath, with high fencing on one side and trees and scrubland on the other, I leap out behind him, grab him around the neck with my left arm and chloroform his face with my right hand. He struggles and squeals, but he's a little fella and I hold on tight, forcing the cloth hard down on the nose and mouth whilst pulling him backwards to unbalance him and make it harder for him to jab me with his elbows. As he becomes more quiescent, I drag him off the path and into the trees, and I begin to talk into his ear.

'Welcome, fool. You have come of your own free will to the appointed place. The game's over!'

At that moment there are a couple of small explosions in the middle distance, and presently there's a *whoosh!* and a trail of red sparks crosses the indigo sky.

'You have angered the gods by insulting Jago Farrar, withholding his story from publication and then calling him a "kamikaze writer" for complaining. There must be a sacrifice to atone – a sacrifice of the right kind of adult…You, Neil…'

He squirms as he comes around a little and opens his eyes to stare, so I dose the cloth with more chloroform to put him under, and, trying not to inhale the pungent fumes myself, I then get to work. Firstly I wind gaffer tape around his mouth to keep the cloth in place. Next I turn him over and secure his wrists behind his back with the cable ties and similarly truss up his ankles. Then I bind his arms more closely to his body by wrapping around the twine, and do the same to his legs, with the intention of minimising his ability to move.

Again, partly as a disguise and partly to be in character, I proceed to transform my appearance. I don the wig and the coat dress, then apply a little foundation makeup to my face, to cover up the beard shadow and make me look more of a woman than a man-woman. Finally I add a touch of pink lipstick, using a hand mirror to see my face. It's a good job – I'm almost emulating Christopher Lee in drag!

Now I have the difficult job of carrying Neil by the waist through the scrubland to the far perimeter of the Rec, and with aching arms I reach my destination. Luckily there's no one around yet and it's almost fully dark, with little ambient lighting. Neil begins to wake up a little as I push a long wooden pole under the twine bindings on his legs and upper body, and I use more twine and gaffer tape to hold it in position. Then I pull the sweatshirt over the pole and his head and body, and stuff the loose arms with old rags and newspapers to give them form, finally tying off the cuffs with twine. Similarly I place the waistband of the traccy bottoms around Neil, but I've cut away the seat, so the legs just dangle in front. These too I stuff and tie off, and then I place the pillowcase mask over his head, smiling as I address him.

'You have come with the power of a king – of the horror small presses. You have come as a virgin – never had a partner, have you Neil? And you have come as a fool!'

I take out the jester hat and wave it in front of a groggy Neil momentarily, before putting it on his head, pouring on a final dose of chloroform through the mask and hoisting him up in the air on the pole. With a bit of jiggling around, I get him to appear to sit on top of the bonfire, his fake arms and legs sticking out appropriately from the wigwam of sticks, branches, garden cuttings, old floorboards, broken furniture and other bits of assorted timber.

'You have accepted the role of King for a Day – and who but a fool would do that, eh Neil…?'

Out of the moonless, foggy evening gloom, several anoraked figures now present themselves. They include a middle-aged man with a grey beard, a younger man of around thirty and a gaggle of chirping children in the seven-to-ten age group. A boy points at the bonfire and titters gleefully.

'Look! He's got a pointy hat on!'

'Yes, it's a fool's hat,' says the younger man. 'Nice touch.'

'Hello…' says the older man to me. 'I see they've managed to put together a decent Guy Fawkes – excellent show…And you are…?'

'Stacey – Stacey Burnside,' I reply in a falsetto voice. 'I've recently moved into Watling Street.'

'Ah ha, well, it's a lively community here.'

'I look forward to integrating.'

'Jolly good. So, lets start the blaze!'

The children spring up and down with delight, clapping their hands, as the man gets out a big box of matches and lights some scrunched-up newspapers at the bottom of the pile. A few initial flames soon peter out into thick smoke, and it's a while before the centre of the fire begins to glow and then give out definite tongues of orange. Other people have gathered now, mainly young families, and some are setting off fireworks and launching rockets. I glance up at Neil and feel an icy stab to the stomach as it appears he's trying to shake himself free. A young girl sees it too and points.

'Look...!' she exclaims. 'The guy is moving!'

The younger man, probably her father, crouches down to speak at her level. 'That's the effect of combustion underneath, makes it look like he's doing a merry dance, doesn't it?'

At that point the stuffed arms and legs frazzle and burn, and then the whole guy goes up in a strong bellow of flame, doubtless accelerated by the chloroform. Everybody cheers and claps their hands, and grinning fire-lit faces bob in the night. It's not quite on the scale of *The Wicker Man*, but pretty damn good nonetheless. Soon the sacrifice is done, the gods are appeased and next year's harvest in Tormartley will most certainly be fecund. Momentarily I feel sorrow for Neil, but the memory of what he called me – a fucking kamikaze writer – quickly wipes it away. Now is the time for me to slip into the shadows, and once I'm back on the path alone, I lose the man-woman disguise. Facebook Murder Number Four is complete, without a single shot being fired.

It's not my intention to drive back to my Bristol flat tonight. If Neil's charred remains should be discovered in the morning, or if tomorrow's *Crimewatch* gets a result, the police will be on to me again, and this time I won't walk away. When rolling the dice, you can only win so many times in a row, and I'm due for a fall if I wait around in the line of fire.

Back at the car, I adopt another disguise, this time a flat cap, false beard and geeky horn-rimmed glasses. I drive away to the anonymity of a commercial centre off the M1 near Leicester, and check in to the cheapest-looking hotel I can find. It's my intention to hang out here for a couple of days or so and see what transpires. There's plenty to do in these soulless labyrinths, the same the world over, their businesses identically cloned. One day they'll be all over Mars and

Venus. Nobody stands out because most everybody is just passing through.

So, I get a burger and chips in McDonalds and go and see the latest *X-Men* movie, losing myself in the whizzy computer-generated action scenes and not paying much attention to the plot. Neil and the bonfire now seem dim and faraway; they might not have happened at all. Back in my hotel room around midnight, I turn on the TV and find the BBC rolling news. Nothing of interest. I sleep about four hours and then wake up and commence a cycle of falling asleep and waking again, my dreams overlaying the impersonal walls of the cubicle space. After a dried-out unappetising English breakfast, I try the news again and still no hue and cry.

I go out and walk around the shopping mall, feeling like one of the zombies in *Dawn of the Dead*. Everybody here looks like a zombie, I realise, and they're all thinking zombie thoughts and leading zombie lives in a zombie world. In the evening, after a pizza and a few beers, I'm back in my room ready to view *Crimewatch*. I suck from a half-bottle of Scotch to calm me down, trying not to drink too much too quickly. Darren's reconstruction is first up, and it's eerie to see a lookalike actor in white T-shirt and lycra shorts, jogging along the Thames towpath on his regular route. Afterwards they show a CCTV still of two women walking dogs, and ask for them to come forward in case they may have seen something. Did I pass these two…? I can't be sure.

But it's the Crimpy reconstruction that really makes me sit up and glug at the Scotch. They have another lookalike actor, tall and thin with pointy ears, leaving the loading bay entrance of Blue Nebula in a groggy condition – and then they cut to another lookalike of *me*, wearing black suit, black tie and shades! The voiceover says that Eustace may have been accompanied by a man dressed this way, possibly exerting some kind of coercion. As the two figures walk arm in arm along the pavement, there is a plea for people to come forward if they witnessed such a sight.

From early on I've known that this is the weakest link in any of my schemes. There was no foolproof way of getting Crimpy from Blue

Nebula to the lockup without us being seen. Using a car or taking a taxi would merely have presented other risks, so I went with walking and hoped for the best. Sure, I checked there are no CCTV cameras on the route, but the eyes of others are a kind of camera, and now that footage might well be reviewed. In the *Update* follow-on, after *News at Ten*, Kirsty Young says that several promising calls have been received about the Crimpy case, and police are following up leads.

I knew this would happen sooner or later – the tipping point in the Facebook Murders – and as I feel it approach, I congratulate myself for taking the precaution of going underground. I'd love to look at Facebook now, but of course if I access the site from a mobile device I'll give away my location. After finishing the Scotch, I go out and find a late-night bar and have a weird party all on my own, avoiding contact with other drinkers just to be on the safe side. I'm so nervous and excited I can barely sleep, but I manage to doze off properly near dawn after swallowing a temazepam, and I miss breakfast, but no great loss there.

On the TV there's a big breaking news story – nothing to do with Crimpy or Darren, but with missing Tormartley resident Neil Hornblower. After a three-day disappearance and a local search, residents and police have discovered burnt human bones in the ashes of a bonfire, and dental records are being sought in order to establish if they belong to Neil. Police wish to interview a tall, eccentric-looking woman, and a photofit image of myself in drag pops up – not a very good likeness!

I go out for coffee and an all-day breakfast at a café, and when I return to the TV, around lunchtime, everything has exploded into the biggest homicide story of the decade. The first image I see is that of Leopard, talking outside the Birmingham railway arch lockup, which now has yellow crime scene tape around the entrance and forensics people in white overalls going in and out. He says the phrase, '…minus an ear,' and goes on to describe intelligence gained from colleagues of the murderer, and from an examination of his computer, which indicate the killing was carried out according to the plot of the Tarantino movie *Reservoir Dogs*.

Then Stanley Grainger pops up in interview, looking pasty-faced and haggard, saying that on the surface Jago appeared to be a regular bloke, one of the lads, and no one had any idea he was clinically insane. An actual photograph of myself, taken from Facebook, now overlays some of Stan's words, and reflexively I check in the mirror to make sure the beard and glasses are doing their job of concealment. A psychiatrist then speculates about a delusional state, similar to '*Truman Show* Syndrome', where the sufferer believes he is a character in a novel, removed from actual real life, and therefore may do terrible things such as murder, because he feels he is 'being written' to do them.

What utter rubbish these so-called experts come out with! I did the Facebook Murders because the fuckers deserved to die – not because I think I'm a character in a bleeding novel! And suddenly there it is on the screen, my soubriquet, obviously taken out of the draft of my novel on the computer: The Social Media Avenger – Jago Farrar, aged thirty-eight. The public are warned not to approach him as he's highly dangerous and probably armed with a .38 calibre pistol. Later, the report reveals the ballistics on Darren's and Crimpy's shootings match, and drawing on the novel, the full extent of the movies which the respective murders are based upon is explained. Then, marvellously, they show a clip from the master movie, *Theatre of Blood* – the scene where Vincent Price makes his big speech to the critics in the Thameside flat.

So most everything is in the public domain, and as the day progresses more speculation swirls about, and later even foreign media become interested in this four-time serial killer who thinks he's living inside a novel. Of course the one thing they don't know is where I am, and as a nationwide manhunt steps up frenziedly through the gears, the next big concern is where I'll strike next.

In truth I was expecting them to find the partial draft of *Social Media Avenger*, and I wasn't too concerned about the plot so far being discovered. But I was careful to destroy any notes and redact other indications of who my next and final victim will be. My narrator, Miles Hunniford , remains tight-lipped on this matter, as does his narrator, Damien Smithson, and so on right down the line to Ezekiel Fazackerley. They won't be able to work it out, and as they mention me in the same breath as Jack the Ripper, Peter Sutcliffe, Fred West and Harold Shipman, they haven't the faintest idea of the identity of the individual whose murder will form the spectacular climax to this novel. Victim Number Five…you know who…

17. Fatal Attraction Goes Gay!

Predictably no news desk editors, agencies or individual journalists were ultimately interested in developing a story about Hugh's use of my material within *In the Teeth of Hell*. The closest I came involved a long and initially promising phone conversation with a senior agency journalist, who probed the details and subjected them to a stress test. He said that I couldn't prove I'd sent the letters to Hugh or that Hugh had read them – I could be making it all up. I said that the original computer files had creation and last-modified dates, well into the past, but he thought that wasn't strong enough. Then he asked if the letters contained threats, and I hesitated a little before saying everything was supposed to be fictional. He gave a long umm and then passed, wishing me good luck.

This happened about a week after I'd moved out of Helmut's and was crashing in mate Patrick's spare room. It served to bring me down still more and intensify the spiral of cider bingeing – as if living with Patrick and pubbing with him most nights wasn't enough to do that on its own! Another really irritating factor was the gush of effusive praise heaped upon Hugh as the loathsome novel was further publicised and became still more widely read. The reviews and interview puff pieces were bad enough, but the Amazon reviews were somehow worse – ordinary punters duped into believing that Alfonso was entirely Hugh's creation, and the authenticity of his mindset exclusively down to Hugh's writing skills. All those adjectives: 'brilliant', 'marvellous', 'wonderful', and phrases such as: 'my favourite writer', 'the best writer ever', really grated and made me clench my fists.

Then, to make things even worse still, news of the movie deal broke. Hugh and his old friend Sam Mendes had been in negotiation for them to respectively write a screenplay and direct a film version of *In the Teeth of Hell*, and it was now a 'go' project. Mendes would fit it around his *James Bond* commitments. Already on board were Robert Pattinson as Rory, Tom Hiddleston as Alfonso and Gemma Arterton as Moonchild Clytemnestra. The budget would be around thirty-five million dollars, and the film would join the ranks of other exalted screen adaptations of Hugh's novels, swelling his sales still further. I told Patrick that Tom Hiddleston was going to play me in a film, and he said that Tom Hiddleston didn't look anything like me. That comment somehow encapsulated the last three months in a nutshell.

In hitting rock bottom, I concluded that maybe Helmut had had something in his analysis. By going full tilt with the righteous indignation element of my obsession, I'd been left high and dry like an impotent beached whale. Hugh held all the good cards and I had no moves left to make. But what should I have done instead? There was no clear answer, and no going back – not to Helmut at any rate; he and I had only spoken perfunctorily to arrange our separation, with neither of us trying to patch it up. And there was no going back on revenging myself on Hugh either – I just had to bide my time and play the long game. After five weeks of terminal alcoholism, I found myself a studio flat in Hotwells and left Patrick to his own devices. It was a big comedown from sharing a salubrious three-bedroomed house with Helmut, but I was moving on. Paying rent and bills out of my bookshop manager's wages wasn't much fun, but I had complete freedom to do as I wanted, with no one looking over my shoulder. What I wanted was more drinking in the nearby Nova and the Mardyke with Patrick and the others, and forays into the gay fleshpots of Bristol centre for no-strings fun; but while I was doing that something important was germinating in my psyche, and I wasn't hurrying it, I was letting it flourish naturally.

All this kafuffle with Hugh over *In the Teeth of Hell* did have an upside – my own literary stalker novel, abandoned over four years previously, was becoming revitalised. Now the Literary Stalker had a much better rationale for revenge on the Famous Writer than mere rejection in love. He could add to that: theft of literary property. It opened up whole new vistas of possibility, the transgression coming to rankle so extensively, so deeply, so bereft of any possibility of redemption, that extreme violence became plausible as a solution. Yes, the literary stalker novel was always meant to end with the Stalker gunning down the Famous Writer, and now I knew that with some thought and planning I could make it work.

I made new notes and recorded ideas, and fleshed them out into passages of prose; but I'd done this with any number of previous putative novels in my then twelve years of being a writer, and I hadn't yet satisfactorily completed a single extended work, only about forty short stories, a dozen of which were collected in *Dark Undertows*. That was the difference between Hugh and I – or Darren and I, or Crimpy and I, for that matter – they delivered on their goals. But it would be different this time – it always was, but of course it wasn't. Working and partying didn't leave a lot of time for writing, and once the new wave of ideas had been inducted onto paper, the project flagged again. And then two big things happened that really pushed it to the rear.

The first was the sad departure of my dear old mum. She had a major stroke and died in hospital three weeks later, which left me shattered and depressed for several months afterwards. Gutted by all this Hugh business, I'd thought I couldn't sink any lower, but I was wrong. Somehow the experience of the death of a loved one left me with even greater and more steely determination to get back at Hugh and turn the tables – what doesn't kill you makes you stronger, and all that jazz. When my mother's affairs were settled, I found myself, along with my brother and sister, with a third share of her estate, and for the first time in my life I had a substantial capital sum. It was not enough to enable a flat purchase – Bristol prices were sky high – but I moved into a better rented studio in Clifton Wood and I got a swankier car – a black BMW 3 series coupe.

Then, when I was on this rising tide of recovery, the second big thing took place. On a drinking session with a few platonic gay mates, we dropped into Queenshilling for a boogie, and who should I end up dancing with? A longhaired, effete, spidery-limbed hairdresser called Robin Frobisher, and we began what can be described as an extended courtship. He said he didn't believe in jumping into bed with someone on the first night, and it was two weeks before we actually did that, by which time we'd decided we were in love. We spent a year having a rumbustious and fairly enjoyable time, and then we took the fateful step of getting a flat together, which seemed a good idea at the time. But it wasn't the same as living with Helmut – Robin was far more controlling on the domestic front, and with the novelty stage now well worn off, we became an average humdrum couple.

But there was enough upside to counterbalance any shortcomings, until the early summer, when he became different, much more prickly and irritating, and went off sex. And I spontaneously had a creative idea – I remembered the old horror movie *Theatre of Blood*, not seen for years, and I got the DVD and re-watched it several times, consequently confirming its usefulness to the future of my writing. Finally after all this time, my literary stalker novel project had reached critical mass and I saw the way forward to its completion.

Now everything has come full circle once again. Robin and I are breaking up, and I will shortly be seeking new accommodation in reduced circumstances, and in the meantime I'll perhaps end up crashing at Patrick's again and getting too drunk for my own good. And Hugh has a new novel coming out, and he's commencing a round of promotional appearances to catapult him high in the public eye once more. Not only that, but the film version of *In the Teeth of Hell* is scheduled to be released at the year's end, and the tagline is already out there, grabbing attention: *Fatal Attraction Goes Gay!* Perhaps I should be all bothered and frustrated like last time, but I'm not. This time I have a plan.

The Elysian Fields, Hugh's latest, is being touted as his best and most ambitious yet, and a pre-publication publicity quote from Neil Gaiman sums it up as: 'The *War and Peace* of supernatural fiction'. I obtain a copy at the earliest opportunity and settle down for an instructive read. Indeed the hardback is a weighty tome, heavy in the hand and clocking in at nearly five hundred pages, with a busy cover that acts as a mild spoiler for anyone who's not read any promotional material. The novel's whole ambience invites careful, unhurried scrutiny – the opposite of speed reading – and on the afternoon I commence it, I have nothing on my agenda to get in the way. In fact this is my agenda – an arm of my research.

Immediately the reader is parachuted into the middle of Operation Granby, the British component of the larger Operation Desert Shield in the First Gulf War in Iraq and Kuwait. Forty-degree heat, sweat and the discomfort of sand and dehydration are high on the agenda, with background apprehension of impending combat also looming significantly. The main protagonist is Captain John Willoughby, a squadron commander in an unnamed regiment within the 1st Armoured Division. Aged twenty-seven, he is popular and charismatic, but is teased for being something of an intellectual, having studied Classics at Oxford. Gulf War army life is presented at a curiously deep level of detail, and secondary characters such as the equitable lieutenant colonel in command, the disciplinary but avuncular RSM and a certain fearful young trooper are fleshed out to a considerable degree. For chapter after chapter, absolutely nothing weird, occult or ghostly takes place, and the work reads as a superbly written piece of naturalistic fiction. But that, of course, is Hugh's trick – to lull the reader into complete acceptance of these terms of reference before executing a rapid volte-face.

With the operation now in combat phase, Willoughby leads a night-time attack on an Iraqi tank position and considerable exchange of fire takes place. At first light, the squadron advances and under bombardment, Willoughby's tank is hit and he suffers a severe head wound. The scene is written from Willoughby's point of view, and after the shock of the impact his perception is undiminished; in fact it is heightened. The battlefield is seen in aerial perspective and shortly Willoughby identifies his own head-injured body being recovered, and concludes he is dead and having an out-of-body experience. He journeys along a tunnel of light and emerges into a landscape of sublime unearthly beauty that he identifies as the

Elysian Fields from his study of Greek mythology and classical literature, such as Homer's *Odyssey*.

Bathed in a glow of peace and serenity, Willoughby floats through this paradise and eventually encounters a giant luminous being who touches him, fills him with love and makes his whole life spool out before him. Next he's taken up into a grand celestial chamber where more luminous beings subject him to a series of visions that unfold like movies in multiple dimensions. The content of these visions is only given sketchily, but their impact on Willoughby is tremendous, and afterwards the council of luminous beings entrust him with a mission and say he must return to the earthly plane to carry it out. He is not in fact dead.

Willoughby re-enters his body and finds himself in the neurology unit of Derriford Hospital in Plymouth, having been in a coma for nearly two weeks. His recovery is protracted and his memory functioning appears to be affected, though he is otherwise in reasonable shape. When he begins to talk about his otherworldly experiences and visions to medical staff, they are divided, with some seeing it as evidence of brain injury and others giving it the benefit of the doubt. That divided approach continues when Willoughby is discharged, and as a wounded veteran he attempts to articulate his heavenly adventures to the world. Soon he falls in with a community of people who've had out-of-body experiences, and receives some affirmation, eventually embarking on public lectures. But even these like-minded folk are somewhat sceptically about his claims that he has been given clairvoyant powers and has seen the future.

Undaunted, Willoughby tells of his visions of future events, which are couched in somewhat Biblical, Nostradamus-like language and are a little vague on names, dates and other hard factual details. But because of his earnestness and absolute self-belief, he does emerge as a figure of interest, and sometimes fun, in the public domain, with steady low level media coverage. Presently he gets a book deal for his life story and prophesies, which he titles *The Elysian Fields*, adding in some Greek scholarship and philosophy to lend weight. The sceptics smile at him and say it's all a result of a laceration of the brain and nothing supernatural is conclusively proved; though his circle of followers gradually expands, some confirming that he can read their minds and has helped with their personal problems.

Then very suddenly Willoughby reaches a tipping point, some six years after he embarked on his new career as a seer. One of his prophesies stated that a much-loved, exalted and charismatic woman will be struck down unexpectedly in a dark underground place, and a whole nation will become united in grief, as a royal house teeters on the brink of collapse. On the last day of August 1997, that prophesy starts to come true, and as the maelstrom of events surrounding the death of Diana, Princess of Wales brew up to a climax, many fingers start pointing at Willoughby and his book, and a clamouring chorus of voices declare: 'He has the gift!'

A few years on, and Willoughby's next big prophesy comes true, elevating him to world superstar status. Two large monoliths in a great city by the sea will be rent asunder by a prince of darkness from a kingdom in the Middle East, and thousands will die, unleashing wars and conflicts for decades to come. It takes a further ten years for the final part to unfold, and by the time the prince has been hunted down and killed at the behest of a leader of African descent, Willoughby has the Second Gulf War, the 7/7 London bombings, the sub-prime financial crisis and Tony Blair being accused of war crimes under his belt.

In the present day John Willoughby, now in his fifties, moves in the same circles as the Dalai Lama, Deepak Chopra and Eckhart Tolle, with several more top bestsellers to his name. He preaches a survivalist philosophy based on the reality of an afterlife, but without the trappings of conventional religion. Hundreds of millions of people around the world look to him for guidance – and they're getting very nervous about his biggest and most apocalyptic prediction, which many feel could come to pass at any moment. A giant celestial body will suddenly manifest in space, set on a collision course for planet Earth, and it will cause earthquakes, tsunamis and dust clouds that block out the sun, and possibly bring about the end of human life...unless we can somehow use the power of love to deflect it away. Willoughby's followers know that only one man can mobilise them to achieve this – he himself: the Messiah.

It looks like Hugh has done it again. His consistent ability to make the far-flung seem palpable has achieved new heights and without doubt *The Elysian Fields* will go down as his masterpiece. The three days I take to get through the novel are a happy uplifting time, and it kind of makes what I have in mind even more momentous and epoch-making. Wanting to join in the celebration, I go to his Facebook author page and see all the links to rapturous reviews – each with tens of thousands of 'likes' – plus visitor posts from fans wetting themselves with joy over the new book. It's all so lovely! Hugh's overall page 'like' count has now gone up to 2.3 million – below Paulo Coelho, J. K. Rowling and Stephen King, but well above his mate Neil Gaiman, who has yet to reach the million mark. He's such a clever man!

But the thing I particularly want to recheck and savour is Hugh's tour of promotional appearances for *The Elysian Fields*. He will be doing Waterstones readings in Tottenham Court Road, Manchester Deansgate, Birmingham and others. Then there's the World Fantasy Convention, Foyles and a few more London venues. But it's his Bristol Festival of Ideas slot that most interests me – Hugh's return to my home turf. There's a banner photo of his smugly smiling face on their website and a pink strap advertising 'a special evening with Britain's premiere horror and fantasy author'. I'll be coming along and it will be special all right – I'll have a little surprise in store for Mr Canford-Eversleigh.

It's Friday night and as arranged I drive over to Patrick's place in Southville, and I park my BMW close to the lane that runs behind the terrace and gives access to the back garden. Friday is the end of the working week for Patrick and a big boozing occasion. I customarily stay over in his spare room on a Friday, as there's no hurry to do anything on the Saturday morning, and he often lies in till eleven. Leaving the house, we stroll across Vauxhall Bridge and take the Chocolate Path alongside the Avon and the Floating Harbour, eventually reaching the Nova Scotia, with the usual row of pleasure craft moored on the landing in front. In the clear autumn sunset, it all looks extra pretty for some reason.

The pub is near full and in raucous mood, with Barry, Gordon, Jemima, Clifford and other regulars determined to start off the weekend on a high liquid tide of amber. I resolve to cap my cider intake at five pints, but I end up going to seven…or perhaps eight. After Patrick and I weave and stagger back home, he gets out the Courvoisier bottle for a nightcap, but I pass, as I don't want an absolutely screaming hangover – I'll make do with the usual fairly bad one. Barely able to stand and slurring his speech, ranting something about the stupidity of the Labour Party, Patrick eventually clumps up the stairs, makes some banging noises in the bathroom and retires to his bedroom, having forgotten to say goodnight. I give him ten minutes, then quietly pad up to his door and check that the rhythm of his throaty snoring is well established, and satisfied I sneak out the back door with a small torch.

I'm so drunk myself that I'm swaying from side to side and my head is starting to do somersaults, and generally everything feels warm, fuzzy and surreal – even handling a stolen shotgun. It's been over three weeks since I purloined it from Pippa, and nothing has happened, so I reckon I'm in the clear to proceed with the next part of the plan. My paranoia has subsided somewhat and I've had no more sightings of Leopard, but still I remain fundamentally changed. It's like the old days when there was a clear split between the mad side of me and the sensible side. Now, as then, the mad stalker part cannot be tamed by the sensible part, only modulated to a degree. There's no point even thinking about the consequences of being caught in possession of the gun – never mind the consequences of actually using it – I just have to go along with the impulse, ride it out and see where it takes me. My cherished fictional life must reign supreme.

As I'm daydreaming, thinking all this, I'm navigating my way to the back of Patrick's cluttered pitch-dark shed, and I accidentally kick something and make something else – a large tin of paint, as my torch beam reveals – fall from a height to the floor with a loud resonant thump. A sword thrust of pure terror slices through the alcohol bubble, as in a single mind-concertinaed flash I anticipate being found out and my whole grand scheme collapsing. But I wait and hear nothing, and then retreat back into the house to check all is silent before recommencing.

Soberer and more careful now, I lift Pippa's slipcased Berreta out of the golf bag and sneak along the lane to my car, making sure no one's around before dropping it into the boot. I treble check the car is locked and go indoors, and I consume a pint of water and three paracetamol, and then have a final piss as quietly as possible. Totally washed out now, I crash in the single bed in the small back room, surrounded by boxes of old clothes, shoes, VHS and cassette tapes, obsolete computer equipment and other assorted detritus from Patrick's derelict life.

18. The Watershed Moment

So, Jago Farrar, four-time literary serial killer, is Britain's most wanted man, and he's currently holed up in a motel on the M1, watching himself on TV and awaiting instructions from above. Now that *The Facebook Murders* is approaching its climax, I want to devote all my time to evolving, nurturing and shaping that climax, but of course I've got the usual shit to deal with instead. Trust Robin to pick this moment to break up the band and force me to look for flats, and deal with the burden of moving, when I most want to get on with my research and writing. What a cunt!

The anger that has been somewhat in abeyance since his announcement is finally bubbling through. Robin has sent me a text message to say he's taken it upon himself to give a month's notice on our flat as from when the rent is next due, which means I have about five weeks to get myself completely sorted out and installed in a new place. A text message! He didn't even have the courage to ring and talk it over with me. I called him and tried to remonstrate, saying I needed more time, but he said his name is on the agreement and he wants out, a clean break, as we agreed; and if I want then maybe I can stay and pay the total outlay myself. But I can't afford that with no job and dwindling savings. And we didn't agree to anything in my recollection!

There might have been the option of moving Marcus in, but because I've been so circumspect about our relationship, he's found himself another 'badass' older man and moved on – or maybe he's just trying to make me jealous, I don't know. Oh, the capriciousness of youth! When I sit down and take stock of my position, I really am in a pickle. Finding suitable new cheap accommodation in a decent area won't be easy – I know from experience. When I split with Helmut, I stayed with Patrick, but left most of my stuff at Helmut's till I'd found a new place; now if I'm not fixed up in time I'll need to put it in storage and face that expense. I'll probably have to take what's going and end up in a crappy studio in Filton with no space for my books and miles to travel to get anywhere. Meanwhile Robin can simply transfer his possessions to his new premises and carry on canoodling with Kevin. The utter bastard!

I'm not that far away from the dreaded age of forty, and when I look at myself in the mirror what do I see? A man of straw. I should have got a civil partnership with Helmut when we discussed it, but I didn't fancy being tied down. If I had, I might have got some money out of him on the split. Or I should have married Robin on the wave of euphoria when it was all new and everybody was doing it, and now I'd be entitled to a share of his legendary nest egg. Instead I'm going to run out of money living in some dour single room in the sticks, and I'll have to go on benefits – and be made to look for work, and end up doing some shitty menial job for the minimum wage. I really have fucked things up…unless I can get that bestseller to market, of course…

No, now is not the time for self-doubt. I will not be a loser, but will go onwards and upwards to glory instead. If it weren't for the fact that I'm in the late stages of gestating a masterpiece, then I might get really down about my situation. As it is, I can heartily recommend the analgesic power of writing a novel!

After a quick bit of online research, I adopt my cautionary CCTV disguise – leather hat pulled low and hair inside my turned-up jacket collar – and drive out to Screwfix in Brislington. Maybe I should get a false beard as well, like Jago, but that's really a step too far – I'm not *that* paranoid! In the well-stocked store I manage to get everything I need for just under two hundred pounds – in cash, naturally. The centrepiece and most expensive item is a power chop saw that sits on a bench or table and comes with its own vice for clamping the object firmly in place – what a brilliant piece of kit! I also get a coping saw, a spokeshave, a selection of files, various grades of sandpaper, some plastic goggles and a pack of dust masks. I think I'm done, but as I approach the checkout, I have an afterthought – some dark oak wood dye, just to finish things off nicely.

I'm back home and ready to get to work. There's virtually no chance that Robin will come in unexpectedly during shop hours, but just to be sure I catch the front door lock. Then I clear the kitchen table, lay newspaper over the surface and underneath, and set up the chop saw, reading the instructions carefully. Satisfied, I get Pippa's shotgun out of its slipcase, break it, examine it and then close it up and practise some shooting manoeuvres, swinging fast to take down imaginary pheasant. It's a 12 gauge Beretta 486 Parabello, classic side-by-side design, as she prefers, and luckily it has a pistol grip which will make sawing and shaping the stock that much easier. Again I admire the lovely engraving on the sides, top lever and trigger guard – rose and scroll patterns – and I recently found out the retail price is around three and a half grand.

The first step is to shorten the twenty-eight-inch barrels to fifteen inches, so as a rehearsal I decide to remove five inches first just to see what happens. I put on a mask and goggles, and with the gun firmly clamped in position I start the saw. It does the job efficiently but makes an incredible din, and I wonder anxiously what the neighbours might think. Probably nothing untoward; I could be a plumber fixing the pipes. The cut is surprisingly clean, so I go ahead and take off the rest, feeling oddly calm now like I'm doing some regular DIY. I also file away the serial number, destroying any obvious connection to Pippa.

After cleaning up the new barrel ends with a file and emery paper, I reclamp the gun, stock pointing outwards and carefully take off the butt with the coping saw, following the contours of the pistol grip but leaving a margin for finishing with the spokeshave and sandpaper. This is turning into really enjoyable work, and I feel like a master craftsman as I shape and sand the standalone pistol grip to perfection. Finally I stain the exposed wood with the dye, achieving an excellent colour match. Then I leave it to dry whilst I have a much-needed cup of tea and a sandwich.

Excited, I unclamp the finished weapon and wipe it carefully with a cloth before hefting it and getting a feel for what I have created and will shortly unleash on an unsuspecting world. It's a good weight for a two-handed grip, and its whole ambience is that of an enlarged flintlock pistol or blunderbuss that an eighteenth century pirate or highwayman might have employed. The ornate engraved panels work even better to that effect in this new truncated version, as they take up more of the reduced surface area. I measure the final length and find it to be half an inch short of two feet, just as I'd calculated. Next, I try it inside the tall forty-litre rucksack I use when I go camping, and it fits fine, the grip reaching almost to the top of the lid, but it won't protrude. I'll wrap a fleece around to pad it out, and no one will have an inkling that they'll be anything other than everyday items and books for signing within the rucksack's innocent space.

Bristol's Watershed holds many piquant memories for me. It's the setting of countless art film viewings, lively get-togethers with mates, and several pickups, including Helmut. So it seems somehow portentous that I should be re-encountering Hugh Canford-Eversleigh here, with an outcome that no one can possibly predict! The entire upper floor conference area has been given over to his *Elysian Fields* Evening, with seating for perhaps five hundred people. I arrive early, having bought my ticket several days before, and already the space is very crowded, with the event certain to sell out or become 'standing room only'.

Naturally I'm very keyed up, with that curious swelling sensation in my head, or external reality, or both. There are butterflies and all manner of other insectoid creatures wafting around in my viscera, and I feel oddly unconnected to the item hanging from my left shoulder – a condition which I'm aware is a psychic defence mechanism. I've made up my mind that at the first sign of any security screening – bag checks or whatever – I shall turn about and quietly walk away; but there's nothing of the kind. No metal detectors, no strip searches, no x-ray machines – not even a pair of dead-eyed goons like the last time I saw Hugh. I take in the fact that it's been more than seven years since the *Necropolitic* reading at the Arnolfini, and Hugh hasn't heard so much as a squeak out of me in all that time. He thinks it's all over and that I've long gone to ground and forgotten. Now all these literary folk assembled here don't have a clue that there's a potential killer on the loose amongst them!

As I head for my chosen seat, near the end of a middle row, I study the expectant fans, ranging from intellectual-looking, horn-rimmed-spectacle types to moody goths in black leather with tattoos creeping up above their collars. Most every age group, social class and grouping is represented, illustrating Hugh's broad appeal, way beyond the traditional boundaries of genre fiction. When we're all seated, my rucksack on the floor by my feet, the loud chatter of voices subsides to a murmur, and a smiling woman comes on stage to tell us that shortly someone will introduce the star of the show. Blimey, he's so important now he needs a person to introduce his introducer!

Sitting there waiting, I try to keep my head straight and remember the crucial thing – I'm a novelist on the job. I have to put myself in Jago's shoes – or maybe Jago has to put himself in my shoes? – and I have to find out exactly what it feels like to have the power, the means and the capacity to end Hugh's life; and then I'll write it all up for *The Facebook Murders*. My hand strays down to the top of the rucksack and I feel the firm bulge there, reflexively looking to my right and making quick eye contact with a woman who has a neat bob and tortoiseshell glasses, and could have belonged to the Bloomsbury Group a hundred years ago. We exchange a smile of unity-in-fandom for our mutual hero, and I wonder what she'd do if she knew I have a loaded sawn-off shotgun within reach. Perhaps she'd stand up and shout it out at the top of her voice, as Paul Newman shouted 'Fire!' in the theatre in *Torn Curtain* to cause a stampede for the exits.

Feeling the pistol grip again, I ask myself how will I know when the time is right, and will I be able to act authoritatively? Having sawn off the shotgun, I had to test it out and get the full measure of its propensity as a weapon. To this end, I drove out to the Forest of Dean and hiked for a couple of hours to reach a really remote spot far away from the regular trails. Once satisfied I was in no danger of peppering innocent bystanders, I set up some homemade cardboard targets on tree trunks, securing them with drawing pins. Each contained three concentric circles, drawn in felt tip pen, which would furnish me with an illustration of the pellet spread at various distances.

Heart thrumming with excitement, I squeezed orange foam plugs into my ears, loaded up two of Pippa's BB cartridges and steadied myself, left foot forward as Gilbert had instructed at the shooting school. This hunting ammunition is twice the load of the clay-shooting variety I'd used before, so the recoil would be that much greater, and the absence of a butt end on the sawn-off stock meant that I'd have to absorb it all with my arms instead of my shoulder.

Holding the gun very firmly in both hands, I raised it and fired at a target from a distance of twelve feet. The blast was tremendous – even through the earplugs – and the kick was strong but handleable. Next I approached the second target and fired from six feet, feeling by now that I was absolute master of my destiny. Yes…I'd made all this happen, I'd put together this scenario with my daring and cunning, and I savoured the feelings and would later write them down in my notebook. This was research after all.

Both shot patterns were a little to the right of centre, and the groupings were fairly tight for fifteen-inch barrels with no choke. Each cartridge contained about a hundred BB pellets, four milli-metres in diameter, the biggest size before the buckshot grades. From twelve feet the entire spread was around ten inches, with a large ragged hole in the centre and a ring of individual pellets around. But from six feet it was practically all hole, with just a few stray pellets to extend the pattern to five or six inches across.

I only had two boxes – twenty cartridges – in total, so I didn't want to waste them, but I tried out another pair on a melon I'd brought, placing it on a tree stump. From twelve feet, I carved off the right corner, peppering the remainder; but from six feet I pulverized the thing totally. In that final shot I conjectured Hugh's face onto the fruit, staring back at me, and I said, '*Bang, bang*, you're dead!'

Now the real face and the rest of the body are about to appear before me, and as the second female compere fill us in with the details of what is about to take place, I analyse my state once again. The sense of swelling trepidation is still strong, and naturally I expect that, but alloyed with it there's something I haven't quite bargained for – a strange schoolgirlish delight at the prospect of seeing Hugh again after all these years. It's just like the other times before, and it doesn't matter how much negative stuff has happened in between, the fundamental emotion remains unaltered, absolutely inviolable. Knowing he's about to step out onto that stage is making me all dreamy and gooey again – not exactly a suitable existential condition for an impending murder. Without really listening to the compere, I wonder how this will play out in the novel?

'Ladies and gentlemen,' she says, practically on the verge of orgasm, 'I give you Hugh Canford-Eversleigh.'

The applause is thundering and from behind a curtain the black-bearded horror critic J. R. Kavener and Hugh himself emerge. Now past fifty Hugh looks older, but not greatly so. The chestnut hair is more brushed back with faint steely streaks at the temples, and there are a few lines around the chin, which is subtly less well defined. As he smiles for the audience, the skin around his eyes crinkles noticeably – another change. He wears an open-necked shirt, a lightweight tan suit and his trademark silk waistcoat, bulging a fraction at the tummy as befits a successful middle-aged man. Yes, he's older but he's still Hugh – my Hugh!

Oh my God...what am I going to do...?

Hugh and Kavener sit down in leather armchairs with mikes positioned on stands at head height. Kavener starts with a description of the key elements of *The Elysian Fields*, adding that he has to be careful as the novel has numerous twists and surprises, and he doesn't want to spoil it for upcoming readers. Framing his first question, he suggests that many writers of supernatural fiction are sceptics who don't actually believe in the reality of what they create, and he wonders where Hugh stands on that score. Smiling, Hugh says that he's in many ways a sceptic, and in the past has noted the lack of decisive evidence when it comes to accounts of hauntings, spirit visits or witchcraft. But out-of-body experiences are in a somewhat special category, with many ordinary people who have nothing to gain from embellishment or falsification, reporting most extraordinary occurrences that challenge the materialist-rationalist world view. It was after listening to an account of one from a close friend that Hugh undertook further research, becoming so immersed that he knew his next book had to be about this subject.

Nice one Hugh! It's all right for him, master of all he surveys, the world spread out at his feet. *In the Teeth of Hell* is behind him now and he's moved on to conquering more exalted peaks, free from any undertow of unfinished business. Oh, to be like him! Instead of being like me! Shall I do it now? Race up to the stage, draw the weapon and blast him into kingdom come? I know its lethality is only guaranteed from a range of under six feet, with a precise aim at vital organs, which leaves plenty of room for evasive action on his part. No…sit tight for the moment.

In turn, Kavener mentions Hugh's dazzlingly accurate depictions of army life and desert combat; of personality cults and messianic figures; of metempsychosis and other eschatological myths; and praises his bravura excursion into the field of apocalyptic science fiction. As ever, Hugh gives beautifully composed, sparklingly multifaceted answers, referencing all kinds of offbeat sources, showing off his aesthetic mastery of the English language and his intellectual might with every nuance of every phrase. I can positively sense the audience gasping with pleasure at the rich timbre of his posh baritone voice, the rhythm of its cadences getting inside us all, warming our beings from the core outwards.

But whilst the acquiescent fan side of me can share these sentiments, the stalker side is in full revolt, overcome with tedium and frustration. I don't want to be party to Hugh's latest ego trip, I want to have it out with him!

If only things could have worked out differently from the beginning. Why did he have to turn my love for him into the hard granite of bitterness and contempt? Why couldn't he have just accepted me as a human being on a level playing field rather than 'collect' me, as Frederick collected Miranda, and keep me locked up in a cellar, devoid of any rights, to be used as his literary canon fodder?

Yes, he could – should – have handled it all differently. He might have at least talked to me, man to man, rather than run away, as he did that day at the Victoria and Albert Museum. Had he done so, I might have better come to terms with the fact he thinks he's heterosexual and therefore couldn't properly reciprocate, before the whole thing got out of control and snowballed. Really he needs to take responsibility for the magnetic effect his personality has on the fans with whom he comes into contact. He shouldn't just whiz them up to Cloud Nine and leave them stranded there, unable to descend – and then exploit them into the bargain. After all, he started the whole thing – by giving me those sexy looks in Blackwells! Answer me this: if he's not gay or bi, then what the fuck is he playing at? It just doesn't add up!

In truth the worst excesses of capitalism are demonstrated in our 'relationship' – we're master and slave, with the rules configured so that he takes everything and leaves me with nothing. He's at the top of the food chain and devours everything below. Way back in another age, Al Jolson used to steal material from lesser entertainers and then get his lawyers to write letters accusing *them* of stealing from *him*! We haven't moved on much from those days. Why couldn't Helmut, as an anti-capitalist, see the terrible injustice in Hugh's larceny of my intellectual property? Never mind the Bicycle Thieves, what about the Novel Thieves?

As I'm thinking these thoughts, Hugh commences a reading from *The Elysian Fields*, and of course he chooses a beautiful, dramatic passage for that purpose. It starts with Captain Willoughby in the heat of battle and sees him perhaps fatally wounded by the strike on his tank, resulting in him floating beyond his body, seemingly still attached by a luminescent blue umbilical-like chord. He surveys the carnage of the fighting, but from an omniscient philosophical perspective where countless wars have happened and will always happen, and ultimately it matters very little. Next he carves his way up the tunnel of light, where the walls are rifled with furrows like a ploughed field, and the ultimate destination is a world of such sublime majesty that it's impossible to encompass or comprehend.

When Hugh finishes, the crowd breaks into rapturous applause and one man cheers, and then another. Three seats in front of me, someone stands up to continue clapping, and then another and another, till people are popping up all over and it seems like only the meanest spoilsport would refrain from joining them. Finally about sixty percent of the audience combine to give Hugh this standing ovation, and as he beams and waves his hand limply, like royalty, Kavener has to intervene to quieten things down so they can proceed.

In the course of this fiasco, my view becomes blocked, so I too have to stand to see what's going on, though naturally I refrain from clapping. With the rucksack in readiness at my feet, I decide that now has to be the time to act – take him out at the top, the climax of his performance. I know I can do it – I just don't *care* anymore what happens to me as a result! Yes, I'll be a kamikaze writer, sacrifice myself in the all-out attempt to kill Hugh and put everything to rights. I'll rush up onto the stage, force the gun to his middle section and let him have it – both barrels! If I spend the rest of my life in prison as a result, it'll be worth it!

As I'm wearing these emotions, trying them for size, the question-and-answer session is commencing. First off, a gaunt-faced blonde girl heaps effusive praise onto *In the Teeth of Hell* and asks Hugh what research he did into the techniques of Alfonso's baroque revenge attempts, particularly the mantrap. Huh! Maybe I should ask what research he did into the workings of Alfonso's brain, as I once considered doing when I discussed it with Helmut years back.

Still washing in the aftermath of my murderous intent, I visualise what it would be like if I had actually gone on stage and blasted Hugh. There would be chaos and mayhem, people would be screaming, rushing for the exits, and regarding me with horror, contempt and incomprehension – that above all. They would be thinking: Why would anyone want to murder this lovely man, this doyen of literature, this demigod of the written word, who has brought so much pleasure to millions of readers the world over? How would any of them even begin to understand my motivation? Whatever I say in my defence, however I try to demonstrate that I've been driven to it by an inexorable chain of circumstances, no one would want to listen or take any of that into account. They would just dismiss me as a nutter, a psycho, a pitiful human worm who's allowed rage and envy to swallow him whole.

And what about myself – how would I feel after I'd emptied two hundred BB shot into Hugh's guts and watched him die a horrible death? Would that have helped to resolve any of the issues surrounding his use of my letters without permission and offering me nothing in return? Whatever short-term catharsis the act may have afforded, soon afterwards it would wear off and I'd feel I'd gone too far – I'd be sorry for what I'd done. And all the king's horses and all the king's men couldn't put Hugh back together again, and I'd have to face the consequences of my actions – live the rest of my life as a captive hated pariah.

At the end of the day, he's a great big somebody and I'm a great big nobody. And I just can't do it, I can't rise up against him despite everything – if for no other reason than I won't get away with it! That's the lesson of tonight. But hang on, *The Facebook Murders* is supposed to end this way, and now it can't because it isn't working out. What's more, the scenario doesn't follow the plot of a horror or crime film – that's another thing to consider. *Yeah, yeah*…I know…

Well, this is truly a watershed moment – in the Watershed of all places! I think I'll have to think it out again. I, Nick Chatterton, cannot murder Hugh Canford-Eversleigh. The question is: can Jago Farrar?

19. Go Wild in the Country

I'm feeling at a loose end and in need of some company. A night out with Marcus would be a fine prospect now, followed by a bit of the other, but he's definitely with someone else. I could keep blaming it on my own insouciance, but I've asked around and several people say he's known as a flirty, flibbertigibbet type, highly fickle and unreliable. Perhaps I should try and pick up someone new, or go on Grindr again, but I want a meaningful connection! So instead I'll probably just head out to the Nova Scotia as usual nowadays and get sozzled with Patrick and the lads.

It's the day after the Watershed event with Hugh, and the anticlimax is catching up and weighing on me. I must get the novel back on track and decide where to go next. Jago is becoming restless; he's sick to death of hanging around in that shopping complex and he wants his orders! So, the original ending, where the Stalker shoots the Famous Writer at a literary event, is well and truly jettisoned, and another is needed, in keeping with the sweep of *The Facebook Murders* film theme. We've had *The Godfather Part II*, *Reservoir Dogs*, *Blue Velvet* and *The Wicker Man* – what now? I have a few vague ideas, but the answer lies with Hugh himself, and despite the inconclusiveness of the Watershed night, it was great seeing him again and I've become reinvigorated in that regard. Things have been stirred up at a fundamental level.

To paraphrase Ray Liotta in *Goodfellas*: *Hugh will never know how close he came to getting whacked!*

I might not have shot him, but the contact has made my stalker persona spring back fully into shape – it's like starting over again after all these years. Following the question-and-answer session, I considered going up and getting my copies of *The Elysian Fields* and *In the Teeth of Hell* signed, and perhaps making some pithy or caustic remark. Indeed the close-up interface of the signing would have afforded a better opportunity for an impromptu shotgun assassination, but I'd passed the point of being excited by such a prospect. The dictates of normal caution had overtaken gay abandon by now.

In the end I decided against joining the long signing queue, as I thought it best not to alert Hugh regarding my re-entry onto the scene. I'm playing high-stakes poker now, and I can't be bothered with the nickel-and-dime stuff. Best to keep him in the dark…for the while. On my way out, shouldering my rucksack, I took a last glance at the beaming faces of the queuing punters, all happy and expectant about meeting the great man, like children clustering outside Father Christmas's grotto. Well, I've been there, folks, and it's not all it's cracked up to be!

So, what now – the eternal question? Well, it's too early to eat and go to the pub, so instead I commence a surfing session, catching up on the latest about Hugh, with a particular aim forming in my mind. Soon I find the article I read a few months before, about Hugh's exponentially expanding wealth and property portfolio. As well as the Chelsea house, now valued in excess of ten million pounds, he has the villa in Tuscany (used as a set in *In the Teeth of Hell*), and in addition he's recently acquired a mansion in the Oxfordshire countryside, west of Oxford itself, but with a more precise location not specified. I try other searches, using different terms in an effort to gain this information, but within the pieces I dig up there is again nothing definite – no name of a small village, for example, that would narrow things down. He hasn't been there long enough for electoral roll details to be available, and he no doubt wants to keep this new address as secret as possible.

In trawling through recent interviews in search of clues, I find Hugh describing his new place as 'off the beaten track, and with enough space for large gatherings of extended family and friends'; and in another he says it's 'excellent for local walking'. A Cotswolds news site mentions Hugh in connection with an event in Burford, a small town in a beautiful setting that I visited years ago, but further searches including Hugh's name and 'Burford' yield no fruit.

After nearly a couple of hours, I have the feeling of going in circles, and I think I'm not going to find what I want. But then, on around the seventh or eighth results page of one search, I spy something different from the usual news and feature links. It's the blog of a dedicated Cotswolds rambler, and the page in question describes the route and events of one of his many walks. Making up a party with friends outside the King's Head in Dillisbury, he trekked west along a footpath and passed by Hugh Canford-Eversleigh's manor house on the way to Withy Wood.

It's definitely a 'eureka' moment, and very excited, I open a new tab and type in 'Dillisbury manor house'. Immediately a page full of great juicy links is staring back at me! On Zoopla, there are the details for Pokinghorn Manor, Dillisbury, Oxfordshire. It changed hands just under a year ago for eleven million, five hundred thousand pounds. And the estate agent's details are still online, including descriptions, a list of features, floor plans, maps of the grounds and copious photos. I'm in stalker's heaven! Next I put the postcode into Google Maps, and go to Earth view on full zoom. It's huge, with a tree-lined private drive, manicured lawns containing topiaries and statues, a tennis court, a swimming pool, several outhouses and the line of a footpath running nearby.

Upon a full perusal of the agent's brochure, I learn it has ten bedrooms, six receptions, seven bathrooms, a wine cellar, a gym, a stable with two flats, and three further separate cottages within the eighteen acres of grounds. This has to be Hugh's new place, as there are no other big houses in the vicinity that could fit the rambler's account. But just to make sure one hundred percent, I go back in the history to an interview with Hugh which features a photo of him standing in front of a distinctive curving staircase, with an ornate scrolled metalwork balustrade and highly polished wood handrail. It exactly matches the staircase in the brochure, right down to the bulbous upturned handrail end. Feeling most satisfied, I shut everything down and go out for a kebab and some cider.

When I wake the following morning, I ask myself what should I be doing – farting about writing and literary stalking or something else? The answer is clear: I should be looking for a flat with some urgency, as I will be hitting the buffers with this one in a month. Primed from yesterday in the area of property searching, I go online and see what there is in the field of Bristol studio flats to rent. First I try Gumtree, and it's the usual bedsits and rooms in shared houses masquerading as proper studios, and mostly in crappy areas such as Yate, Southmead and Avonmouth. 'A lovely studio in Horfield' – how oxymoronic is that? I knew this would depress me and it's doing that already.

I'm currently paying around four hundred and fifty a month for my half of this place, unfurnished, and that's a good rent for the flat and the area – Clifton. My chances of replicating such conditions on my own must be slim to non-existent. But I try Rightmove, and the search terms 'studios in Bristol' gives me two hundred and thirty hits. When I put in a rent cap of four hundred and fifty a month, it comes down to six – all rooms in shared houses. A cap of five hundred a month only takes it up to eight, with one proper self-contained studio in Eastville. When I enter the filter 'Clifton' with no price cap, the cheapest genuine studio is nearly seven hundred a month, way too much. No, I don't want a room in a shared house, bumping into the owner or the other tenants all the time, with their prurient interest in my activities. Not that again!

After many more searches, I eventually find something viable. A self-contained basement studio in Cotham, which is almost Clifton, at just over five hundred a month. I call up the owner on his mobile and have a good chat, with him saying it nearly went last night but the people haven't come back to him yet. So I ask if I can view the place, and he then starts asking probing questions. When it comes to employment I say I'm a freelance journalist, and he gives me the speech about wanting his tenants to prove solvency, so he won't have trouble collecting the rent. He says I can view the flat if I produce three years of accounts, showing I have a viable income stream. I say I'll get back to him.

That crestfallen feeling is overtaking me, but I slough it off long enough to return to the computer and type in something different: 'camping Dillisbury'. The search map reveals large caravan and camping sites near Chipping Norton and Burford, roughly north and south of Dillisbury, but both too far away from the small village itself for practical purposes. However, further down the search list, there's a dedicated campsite-finder website which provides a much denser map cluster, including smaller places. Borraton Farm Certificated Site looks ideal – basic facilities, tents accepted and only a mile from Dillisbury village. The three reviews are mostly upbeat, and one mentions it's within easy walking distance of the King's Head, where they serve good country grub and real ale.

I make a call and a woman tells me that this late in the year they'll be no problem – I can come whenever I want, so I tell her to expect me by late afternoon. More energised now, I compile a checklist of the things I'll need and begin packing. There's my high tech inflatable tent, last used at Glastonbury two years back, rucksack, hiking boots, cagoule – the old green one for good camouflage – sleeping bag, camping stove, lamps and torches, and mustn't forget the 20x magnification stalking binoculars. Shall I take the shotgun? I wonder. No, this is just a reconnaissance mission and I've had my fix of live-ammunition psychodrama at the Watershed, and that will do me for the moment! I'll leave it in the loft.

After locking up and putting everything in the car, I stop at Sainsbury's for basic food and drink supplies, and then pop into Ellis Brigham on Blackboy Hill for an OS Explorer map of the Cotswolds. Zooming up the M5, overtaking everything in the outside lane, it feels good to be getting away, and I start to sing along to tunes on the radio. When I'm heading east from Gloucester, passing ominously close to Coombe Monkdown, I'm reminded of Pippa and her remark, 'Go wild in the country', taken from the Bow Wow Wow '80s song, and I start humming that to myself too. In fact I saw the performance recently on an old *Top of the Pops*, with barefoot, Mohawk-haired singer Annabella going suitably wild on stage. Yes, the sun is shining, my spirits have lifted and it's a perfect day for a bit of country craziness.

*   *   *   *   *

The road running outside Pokinghorn Manor is just about wide enough for two cars to pass, if they take it easy, and there are grass verges where you can pull up. Close to the entrance, I slow the car right down and pass at around five miles per hour, glancing to my right, before stopping some distance away. I don't want my registration number to be recorded by some over zealous security camera leering out of the trees. High Cotswold stone walls surround the property, curving back to create a semi-circular space at the gate, with two tall elms either side. The gates themselves are of the sturdy wooden slatted variety, complete with an entry system and camera. Beyond them lies a gatekeeper's cottage, and when I drove past I could just make out a section of the main house front, lying at the end of the corridor of poplars that line the driveway. There is nothing to be gained from hanging about here, and I look forward to exploring the back of the estate on foot tomorrow.

Driving onto the campsite, which is no more than a medium-sized field at the farm entrance, my wheels momentarily stick on the mud track, and I think I really should have brought the 4x4 Land Rover. I meet the farmer's wife and then pitch my tent at the far corner, away from the fray but quite near the loos and showers. There are no other standalone tents here, just two caravans, four or five motorhomes, and a classic VW van.

After laying out my sleeping bag in the bedroom area, I sit down in the entrance and make myself a cup of tea on the stove. Then I consult the Explorer map, following the green-dotted lines of the footpaths around Dillisbury, snaking along to Pokinghorn Manor and down to Withy Wood and beyond. The estate itself is important enough to be named on the 1:25,000 large scale map, its grounds creating a discernable rectangle. I plan out some circular walks of four or five miles and longer, putting myself in the position of a fit middle-aged lord of the manor.

Before it starts to get dark, I don my cagoule and put the map, torch and phone in the pockets and head off to the pub. Dillisbury itself has a loose oval street formation, with the King's Head on the village square in the centre, a church and a school along one way and some shops and a post office along the other, with salubrious houses and cottages in between. When I arrive, there's a coach parked in the square and a party drinking in the pub, having visited a nearby stately home, so the barmaid tells me. Three old regulars are sat at the bar on stools, their beetroot cheeks and noses advertising them as chronic drinkers, the kind who live in pubs, familiar the world over. One of them gives me a friendly nod as I wait for my pint of locally-brewed real ale, and he asks me what I'm doing here. Birdwatching, I tell him, and fortunately he doesn't ask for further details.

As I'm eating a supper of Gloucester Old Spot sausages and mash, a trio come in whom I recognise from the campsite – two men and a woman in their late twenties, with northern European accents, perhaps Scandinavian. One of the men says hello, evidently remembering me too, and instantly that infallible sixth sense tells me he's gay. I return the greeting and give him a smile, not too strong, and carry on with the excellent meal, marshalling some onion gravy onto a piece of sausage on my fork. After I finish I get out my new anonymous phone and find Hugh's website. There's no particular need for secrecy here, but I may as well use up the data allowance on the SIM. Links to several new reviews of *The Elysian Fields* are posted, but I don't bother to read them. Instead I double-check Hugh has no more public appearances until the three scheduled next week, so he may well be taking a breather in the country…hopefully.

The next morning, striding along paths that will take me through several fields and eventually past Pokinghorn Manor, I have that old stalking sensation coursing through my veins – a combination of buoyancy and borderline mania. I'm hugely exited and my head is on the verge of exploding! Yes, I'm back on the job again, after all these years; it's like I've never been away. I remember the words of Tommy Leatherhead, my old cell mate when I did time nearly twenty years ago, and I reflect on how they've stayed with me, maintaining their relevance.

Tommy was a professional criminal who would do anything – burglary, drug dealing, credit card fraud, car jacking, you name it –

and he said he just loved living on the wrong side of the law. He told me it's all about the buzz, the risk that you undertake, and however much you plan there's always the unknown factor – chance or fate – that comes into play, and you never quite know how things will pan out. It was that element that kept him coming back, like a gambler or a dangerous sports fanatic – rolling the dice and testing the limits. Stalking is exactly the same.

On crossing a stile and emerging from a small copse into a field, the rear of Pokinghorn Manor comes into view, looking splendid in the weak sunlight. The main building has three gabled ends, bay windowed, with wings consisting of various adjoining structures spreading in both directions. There is a low-walled terrace and steps down to three levels of lawns, with immaculately pruned box trees and yew topiaries combining with Greco-Roman statuary and various lakes and fountains to give a positively royal palace gardens effect. As I walk further along the path, the tennis court and swimming pool become visible on the side boundary. Yes, this is certainly one up from a studio in Cotham!

The 'sweet spot' for viewing the house only extends for about fifty yards, and then the path dips down towards fields and woodland. If I was to remain stationary, out in the open and use the binoculars, I'd be conspicuous, so I look around for alternatives. Behind me, on rising ground, there's a fenced-off wood; if I could get inside, somewhere there would make a good concealed vantage point for observation. I bear it in mind and continue walking, with the manor becoming lost in yellowing autumnal trees as I lose height. There is an old high wrought iron fence running along the estate's bottom boundary, and I notice a gateway within its structure, secured by a large brass padlock. Could this be a means by which a resident might exit to commence a walk? Another thing to note.

Using the map to work out where I'm heading, I cross more fields and enter Withy Wood, hearing that familiar sound once again, but closer this time. Shotgun fire. This is prime pheasant and partridge country and the season is now underway. If I hadn't sawn off Pippa's Beretta, then perhaps I could join them, I think distractedly. At the far end of the wood, the path splits into two, with both directions affording possibilities of circular walks back towards the manor. I choose the shorter route, encounter rising ground and presently find interesting views in several directions. Over in an nearby field, a line of beaters are slowly on the move, flushing out the quarry and driving it toward the Guns, who continue to blast away. It's one of those timeless country sights, like looking at a moving painting.

Turning northwards, I see the rear of Pokinghorn Manor again, nearly a mile away from here, nestling in copper-tinged foliage like some English version of a Bavarian castle. I get out the binoculars and steady my elbows on a fence to lessen the shake. The stone-mullioned bay windows are reflecting the sun, their cornices sharply defined, but there's no visible human activity. I continue and make my way back to the street side of the manor, then go on to Dillisbury and get some sandwiches and a drink from the Co-op for lunch. Uneasily I detect the first signs of boredom creeping in – a common stalking problem.

In the afternoon, I return to the path at the manor's rear and this time I pick my way through the wood above its line, searching for a place to rest and view the house using the binoculars. It's heavy going amongst the undergrowth, and I take a fallen branch to help me thrash my way through. Presently I emerge by the barbed wire fence and find a perfect spot, behind a tree with a bough jutting out at head height, forming an ideal platform on which to rest the binoculars. I use the fallen branch to hack away some obstructing foliage, and from this greater height the panorama of Pokinghorn Manor is magnificent. As for myself, in my green cagoule and wide-brimmed hat I must be invisible to all intents and purposes. Now all I have to do is wait for something to happen.

But nothing does happen, and after exhausting the various binocular moves, scanning the multitude of windows for activity and doing surveys of the many features in the gardens, the old enemy boredom creeps back. What did I expect to happen? I wonder. Perhaps for Hugh to emerge onto the terrace and perform a naked yoga routine? Or Hugh with family and friends to run around the gardens naked, jump into the swimming pool and then have an extended orgy overlooked by Greek statues and chessmen topiaries? Actually the concepts in these fantasies are beginning to arouse me, and I slide my hand into my jeans and readjust my underwear for comfort. Country air definitely induces an aphrodisiac effect, and for a moment I consider having a wank, but then reflect I have reasonable grounds to save it for later.

Last night in the King's Head I got chatting to the woman and two men from the campsite, and it turns out they're from Amsterdam and doing a motorhome tour of rural southern England. After the Cotswolds, they're heading to Stonehenge, then Dartmoor, then Lands End, and eventually the Jurassic Coast on the way back to Harwich. Their names are Danique and Jan, a married couple, and Max – Danique's younger brother whom I'm certain is gay. The meaningful eye contact and signal exchanging got to be quite electrifying, but on the first night of their holiday Max could hardly make a big move in my direction. However we're all meeting up again in the pub tonight, and I think something might just materialise.

On top of this I'm recalling the amazing prison sex I had with Tommy Leatherhead, who sprang to mind this morning and now won't go away. Good old Tommy! As we were both youngsters, nineteen year olds, they gave us a cell together, and we became extremely good friends, bonding in a way that only people who've served time can comprehend. At our first meeting he asked me what I'd done to get put inside, and I told him.

'You glassed a guy in the face 'cause he called you a "poof"? Wicked, man!' Tommy regarded me with a mixture of admiration and curiosity. 'Well…are you?'

'What?'

'An iron hoof – poof?'

'I'm gay, if that's what you mean, but I'm no fucking fairy!'

'I hear you, man. I respect that.'

'What did you do?'

'Robbed a jewellery store, didn't I? A quarter mill in Rolexes,

Cartiers and diamond rings – and the old bill catches us 'cause some poxy do-gooder member of the public calls on his mobile and gives them our reg number.'

'Tough...'

'Yeah, tough alright, mate. Three fucking years tough! Anyhow... good to meet you.'

We shook hands and that night we had some really outré rough sex. Tommy was incredibly well built and strong, and he had a giant tube steak of a todger into the bargain. He passed for straight in the criminal world, but behind closed doors he was a gay boy through and through. Tommy is one of those guys who is highly intelligent but uneducated, and so looked up to me as a university dropout who had read plenty of books and knew the names of philosophers, artists and other prominent personages in history. Between bonking sessions, he'd ask me about Plato, Shakespeare, Freud, Da Vinci and Nietzsche, and then give his own philosophical take, threading together various weird conspiracy theories about who was really controlling what, some of it so crazy it had a striking surreal quality.

Tommy and I kept in contact after we'd left prison, exchanging Christmas cards, talking on the phone every few months, and meeting up for a beer in London when it was convenient. In the social media age, we became Facebook friends and emailed and messaged each other too, maintaining a long line in witty banter. He's always been a solid Facebook friend, consistently liking my posts and comments without the reserve of many of the writers I know. He's a really good bloke is Tommy, and of course he carried on in the world of crime and is now really successful...

Hello...here I am, daydreaming away about the past, and something is finally happening on the Pokinghorn front. I refocus the binoculars to catch Melody in a brown jumper coming onto the terrace with a wizened-looking guy in a cap, no doubt some kind of workman. As they walk down onto the lawns, she points out various things around the bushes and beds, and he nods in acknowledgement. They go out of sight near the bottom of the gardens and reappear on the far side, heading off towards the stable and cottages. So, activity at last! But what does it really amount to?

I wait around till early evening and nothing else transpires apart from another woman, some kind of domestic, coming out to put a bag of rubbish in the bin. Hugh probably has a whole army of servants living in the cottages and attic rooms, and he and Melody most likely act it up like Lord and Lady Grantham in *Downton Abbey*. I can imagine Hugh giving orders to a butler, and receiving non-judgemental obsequious respect whatever his wishes. 'Wipe my dick, Carson.' 'Of course, my lord! And shall I lick your arse for good measure?' Time to go to the pub.

Whilst I'm waiting for my meal, lasagne tonight, I do some more Hugh-related surfing and come across an interview he did for a Canadian magazine, which goes into much greater private-life detail than others I've seen. He says he got a place in the country because the children are more grown up now and away at school, and he became weary of the London scene, wanting an alternative – though he still goes up there regularly, but more for specific business purposes. What's most interesting is his description of his daily routine when at Pokinghorn. He likes to get up early, work out in his basement gym, and be at his desk before nine. The mornings are spent writing and dealing with any correspondence his secretary can't handle, and then it's a light lunch with Melody and whoever is staying over. In the afternoons, weather permitting, he likes to take a brisk walk and be back by teatime. Dinner is sometimes prepared by a chef who comes over specially from Oxford.

Unlike many, Hugh tends not to post personal stuff on social media, so nuggets of information such as these are valuable indeed. I mull this over as I eat my dinner, and then Danique, Jan and Max turn up and greet me like some long lost friend they haven't seen in years. They tell me about their visit to the nearby Elizabethan stately home and the walks around the extensive grounds. When asked, I tell them I did something similar – rambled around the estate of the writer Hugh Canford-Eversleigh, who lives not a mile away.

'No kidding!' says Max.

'Ever read any of his stuff?'

'No, but I have heard the name. He is popular in the Netherlands, I think.'

'He's popular everywhere.'

Walking back along the track to the campsite, torch beams showing the way, Max and I fall behind Danique and Jan, and Max leans in closer to me.

'Do you like to smoke…?' he says sensuously.

'What, you mean gear?'

'Yes, very good gear. Very trippy…and good for sex.' He laughs rumbustiously.

'You don't say? Yeah, I'll give it a go.'

'I could come to your tent and we could have a joint.' He points ahead. 'Give these two some time on their own.'

As Max sits cross-legged on my tent floor rolling the spliff – all grass, no tobacco – his long black hair waves in front of his face like a pair of curtains, almost getting tangled up with his gold nose ring. He really is a total hippy, a throwback to the '70s. I reach into my bag of supplies and pull out two cans of Grolsch, remarking that they're from his own country, and he laughs, rather too stridently. We crack the cans and he lights up, telling me to take it easy as it's very powerful stuff. I've never liked smoking, and as we pass the joint back and forth, I cough several times trying to hold the smoke down. Max is impressed and tells me I'm in for quite a surprise.

Soon all my extremities become hot and tingly and my head feels like it's flying, detached from my neck. Then I have an oddball moment of existential uncertainty, where I'm not sure who I am anymore. When I take a drink from the can to calm myself, I sense the lager travelling down my throat as a golden cascade, tracing the route of my oesophagus all the way to my stomach. After more time has passed, an idea comes to mind that I can see in the dark, and I leap up and go outside the tent to test this theory. Sure enough the whole camping field is glowing in purple paisley patterns, defining every nook, corner and gnarled convolution in the thicket of the surrounding hedge. Up above, the moonlit sky looks pyrotechnically enhanced, like it belongs to another planet. Max comes and joins me, putting a hand on my shoulder and reiterating that he told me it's amazing dope. He moves in and kisses me, and I reciprocate but break off presently.

'Can we do this later? I'm too high at the moment.' I wonder how high I'm going to get.

'Of course!'

Back in the tent, Max tells me all about the gay and drug scenes in Amsterdam, and it sounds really extreme. But my mind has jetted off to another galaxy, where the last couple of weeks with Hugh becomes reforged as an epic superhero movie, with me as the villain and both of us in tight spandex as we lock horns and do battle across huge tracts of aerial space, entering into multiple dimensions. Next I review the events of the day, which themselves have acquired an enchanted, comical, movie-like perspective – the squirearchal peram-bulations around Hugh's estate, the imagined *Carry On*-style sex antics, and the speculations about Hugh's *Downton Abbey* or *Upstairs, Downstairs* lordly activities. These images meld into a flickering montage of screen depictions of posh English country life, including parodies like the 'Ted and Ralph' *Fast Show* sketches and dramas such as *Brideshead Revisited* and *Gosford Park*...

Spontaneously, I get a formative idea for *The Facebook Murders* – another 'eureka' moment – and the earlier sense of heavy going on the project seems light years removed. *Yes, yes, yes!* I say to myself, and I want to reach for notebook and pen. But an impatient Max is now unzipping my jeans, and soon I'm hurtling into new fabulous realms, as I'm subject to the most incredible synaesthetic, poly-morphous, rainbow-coloured blowjob ever!

Danique, Jan and Max leave early the following morning without saying goodbye, making for Stonehenge. Perhaps some lucky person near Salisbury Plain will be receiving some psychedelic head tonight. I decide to give it one more day with Hugh, win or lose, and then go back to Bristol tomorrow. The weather is staying reasonably fine and the country atmosphere still inspires, and I'm in no hurry to return to boredom and disconsolate flat searching.

Making my way to the rear of Pokinghorn Manor, via the Co-op in Dillisbury, I still feel a bit stoned from the night before, together with a background accompaniment of mild paranoia and an increased sense of vulnerability. Progressively I develop an odd hallucinatory after-effect – impressions of Leopard within the texture of foliage on the trees, the arrangements of fallen leaves and horse chestnut shells on the ground, and also in the layout of distant hillsides, even reaching up into the cloud formations in the sky. The more I become aware of it, the more it comes on, and I feel hemmed in by unsettling phantoms, surreally congregating like Magritte bowler-hatted men. Drugs are weird, and I generally don't take them because I'm naturally weird enough already!

Yesterday I checked as best I could that the only ways into and out of the manor grounds are the main entrance and the padlocked gate at the bottom stretch of the fence. Therefore if Hugh goes for a walk, he would have to exit by one or the other. Since I can't be in two places at once, I resume my station in the woods, placing the binoculars on the bough and hoping for the best. Either he will come out of that gate, most likely in the early afternoon, or he won't. It's in the lap of the gods.

At around half past one, I eat a somewhat dry bacon, lettuce and tomato sandwich, munch a packet of Doritos and wash it down with a coke. A bit later, I consume a banana, and just as I'm stowing the skin inside the plastic sandwich wedge, I spy movement on the Pokinghorn terrace. Heart thrumming, I drop the wedge into the rucksack and peer through the binoculars. It's Hugh! He's wearing a Barbour jacket and brown cords, and he's talking to someone inside the entrance, finally waving goodbye. My body becomes totally rigid as I watch him descend the stairway onto the first lawn tier and carry on down. I have to act fast, and urgently I stuff the binoculars into the rucksack, shoulder it and start to move downhill myself.

I'm skipping through the undergrowth, heading towards the path, and through a gap in the trees I see Hugh outside the bottom gate, securing the padlock. He strides off along the path, and I carry on catching up, being careful not to make any telltale rustling noises. When I reach the path, I sight his back, seventy yards away, and it quickly disappears behind a bend. Putting on pace to get a little closer, I have a flash of déjà vu, taking me right back to the first time I followed Hugh from his Chelsea home to the Victoria and Albert Museum, and I recall thinking he was a fast walker back then.

Further along, threading our way through Withy Wood, I stay around forty yards back – close enough to keep tabs on him, but not close enough for him to become aware of my shadowing. So far he hasn't turned around and looked over his shoulder. By now I'm feeling brilliant, every cell in my body pulsating with life and the earlier paranoia forgotten. Here I am stalking Hugh again – right at the cutting edge! This is better than sex! Better than drugs! Suddenly he does turn around, and I quickly sidestep behind a wide tree trunk – I don't think he saw me.

Staying further back now for safety, I have a moment of panic when I reach the split in the path, and I can't see Hugh in either direction! Which way did he go? Then, directly ahead, I catch sight of some movement in the trees and realise he's taken a small grassy trail, not marked as a right of way. The bugger's gone off piste! This trail leads to an area of scrubland, and beyond that we find a wider track, taking us deep into another network of woods. Eventually we emerge into sunlit arable fields that belong to a large farm which has a sprawling redbrick farmhouse with an archway entrance. I let Hugh go ahead while I quickly consult the map, and I see what he's doing – he's extended the lower loop of the notional circular route into the big Canning Wood and will doubtless now continue on marked footpaths through the farm territory, back across fields and finally reach the main Dillisbury road and the front entrance of Pokinghorn Manor.

Hugh does precisely this, and I stay with him, but at a much greater distance because I know where he's going. On a long straight stretch through a sheep field, he does turn around and sees me, three times at least, as here there's nowhere for me to take cover. I wonder if he has any idea that the cagouled, hatted figure behind him is me, his old enemy, following in his footsteps, treating him as quarry and drawing up a blueprint for his demise? The notion is endlessly intriguing.

The cloud thickens, blocking out the sun, and presently drizzle fills the air. As we do the last stretch along the road in front of the manor, I expect Hugh to turn around one last time and look, but he doesn't. From about a hundred and twenty yards I watch him disappear from view, and when I pass the entrance myself I keep my face turned away, showing a disc of leather to any onlookers or prurient security cameras. So this is his usual circular walk, or one of them at any rate. It must be around seven miles and we've done it in a little over two hours. Returning to the campsite, more persistent raindrops plopping onto my hat, I feel an undeniable buoyancy – my mission has been a success and I've got what I need in order to complete *The Facebook Murders*.

20. The Art of Borrowing

Robin has sent me a text to say he's having a day off next Friday and will be coming over Thursday evening in order to stay and pack up his belongings in advance of permanently moving out. He wants me to be home on the Wednesday to receive a delivery of packing boxes from the removal firm. No 'please' or 'thank you', just an unembellished, epigrammatic message of the kind one would send to a servant or employee. And it's a text – once again he can't be bothered to phone and have a proper conversation. Robin – the mere idea of Robin – really brings me down lately, and I'll have to put up with him here on Thursday night and all of Friday, which is most disconcerting.

And the scenario makes me more aware that the buffers are getting closer regarding moving out myself. Since I returned from the Cotswolds, I've actually viewed two properties – a studio in St Werburgh's and another in Westbury On Trym – but they were both too small and grotty for me to make the leap and commit. I know I can't be fussy at this stage; my options are narrowing and crunch time is coming. This huge problem has been heaped upon me at the time I least need such a thing, and it's all the fault of that bastard Robin!

What I really want and need is peace and quiet to get on and finish my novel. I have been making notes, processing recent events, and designing a new structure for the final few chapters. The Cotswolds trip to see Hugh decisively did the trick and gave me what I was seeking. I now have something I didn't have before – a rationale for Jago to choose a shotgun rather than the Webley, and a plausible setting for him to enact his final murder. Bearing this in mind, I've been re-jigging many things – incorporating the events at the shooting school and the Pippa tryst, together with the Watershed psychodrama and its build-up, and of course my wild time in the country in the environs of Pokinghorn Manor. The next step is to write it all up within the draft.

But as a priority I've got to find somewhere to live, seal the deal, pack up and move – all in less than three weeks. Wearily I go to the computer again to trawl through property sites. I've registered with a few agencies now, but they only want to offer me the shitty end of their portfolios. Something acceptable will turn up soon, surely. As I do automatically every time I go online, I check for anything new on the Hugh front, and there is a breaking story. Eagerly I click on the link, and it looks really, really interesting: 'Hugh Canford-Eversleigh accused by memoir writer of using his ideas'.

Quickly I skim-read the piece, wanting to absorb the facts with minimum delay. I have the same buzz I had tracking Hugh through the woods and across the landscape – that sense of getting the upper hand at last. Calming down, I then reread the article slowly and carefully, nodding and smiling all the while. What has happened is that aficionados of out-of-body and near-death experiences have been devouring *The Elysian Fields* enthusiastically, as it's quite an event for an important novel to appear that's centred on such things. One of this group spotted 'remarkable similarities' between Hugh's celestial accounts and those contained in Jock Baltozer's 2001 memoir *The Infinities Beyond the Veil*, which is credited as a source at the back of *The Elysian Fields*. This guy then contacted Baltozer, who read *The Elysian Fields* and basically blew a gasket and went to the newspapers – doing exactly what I tried regarding *In the Teeth of Hell*, but finding himself in a much better position to achieve success. Nice one, Jock!

Baltozer, a respiratory consultant by profession, was involved in a near-fatal road traffic accident in the mid-'90s, when a lorry swerved in front of him on the M6, and he and five other car drivers collided in a multiple pile up. He was taken to hospital where staff fought to keep him alive for over an hour, and on finally regaining consciousness he recounted an outstandingly detailed and comprehensive near-death experience. As he was a doctor himself, he was taken more seriously, and he employed his medical knowledge to assert the unlikeliness of his experiences being internal, as he had virtually no brain function during several episodes of cardiac arrest. His memoir

The Infinities Beyond the Veil, which contains full clinical details as well as other-worldly ones, was well received amongst aficionados and believers in the afterlife.

The article then goes on to describe the many points of similarly between Baltozer's experiences and Captain Willoughby's, which include duplication of features within the heavenly landscapes, near-identical descriptions of the jewelled shimmering quality of the luminous beings, and strong congruence between the life reviews and prophetic visions in both. As Baltozer points out, not only did Hugh lift his descriptions almost verbatim, but also the whole narrative thread running through Baltozer's memoir was only minimally adapted to serve the middle part of Willoughby's story. Baltozer too underwent insights into the future, though his were more hazy and less definitive, and never elevated him to cult status. Most damning is Baltozer's final verdict after absorbing the content and implications of *The Elysian Fields*. He compares the experience to discovering that an expert cat burglar has gained entry to your home and taken something actually quite valuable, but has covered his tracks well and made it look like nothing much untoward has really taken place at all – just the same as my feelings after reading *In the Teeth of Hell*.

Well, that article really makes my day! I'm not alone, I feel, and I commence the boring chore of flat searching with greater resilience. At the end of the piece, Hugh exercised a brief right of reply, but only a day later a full defence of his position appears in another newspaper, practising damage limitation at breakneck speed. Hugh says that he credited Baltozer's memoir as a source, and he only used it to gain authentic factual details of an arcane area – much as one might use historical memoirs for period accuracy. Well, he would say that, wouldn't he? He denies copying Baltozer's work, but when you look at the side-by-side comparisons of Baltozer's passages and his, he could have done a copy-and-paste and just changed the odd word, and tinkered with the sentence structure. Hugh's whole attitude to the affair is arrogant and self-aggrandising, replete with a bloated sense of entitlement, making his needs as an author the paramount concern, overriding all others. He implies that because a work is factual – or 'reportage' – it shouldn't be accorded normal copyright protection, and anyone can plunder it for booty without offering anything in return apart from an acknowledgement – and I didn't even get that!

And the story runs and runs! Two days later a more in-depth feature appears, a thorough and ruthless evisceration of Hugh's entire oeuvre, entitled: 'Hugh Canford-Eversleigh and the Art of Borrowing'. It starts with a comparison of the two most nearly identical passages from Baltozer's memoir and Hugh's novel, wags a knowing finger, and then says that 'eyebrow-raising' similarities between Hugh's works and others are nothing new. Even his early short stories were sometimes uncannily like other stories – for example 'Wrecking Crew', about a suicidal Falklands veteran going loco, is a disguised reworking of J. D. Salinger's 'A Perfect Day for Bananafish'. And Hugh's celebrated first novel, *Thomas's Playroom*, though said to be a homage to *The Collector*, actually adapts many of its plot ideas. Yes, I always thought that, actually.

Moving on, the feature writer picks out many more of these similarities, where there is just too much closeness for comfort. Parts of *The Major Arcana* appear modelled on Dennis Wheatley's *The Devil Rides Out*, in particular the satanic rituals and practices of the cult, and their psychic control and manipulation of the girl acolyte. Regarding *Necropolitic*, the tone and style of its diary sections are compared unfavourably to Patrick Bateman's stream-of-consciousness narration in the Bret Easton Ellis shocker *American Psycho*, and elements of the creativity within the killings themselves recall the David Fincher film *Seven* (which incidentally has parallels to *Theatre of Blood*).

And the article gets better and better! When it comes to *In the Teeth of Hell*, it's dismissed as largely a *Fatal Attraction* retread, but actually gets praise for the verisimilitude of Alfonso's character, notwithstanding his bunny-boiler profile – well, what do you know? Concluding, the writer says that borrowing comes naturally to Hugh, and as an ardent researcher he probably forgets where the lines lie between his stuff and that of other authors. But as he's such a proficient wordsmith, and is able to stitch everything together with dazzling prose, he consistently looks good…perhaps better than he really is.

After reading that, I feel stunned, but in a good way. It absolutely crystallises everything I've thought about Hugh and his work since the traumatic experiences surrounding *In the Teeth of Hell*. I've been vindicated! And my case isn't isolated: this is what he does! Okay, Hugh is a terrific writer at the level of putting together a sentence, at creating vivid pictures and striking characters. But do the larger sweeps of his narratives have that same quality – what with so much derivation from outside sources and piggybacking on the work of others? I'm thinking more and more that the answer to that is: not really. Basically Hugh is a highly competent entertainer, a crowd-pleaser. He's always known how to press the right buttons and has become consummately successful in that regard. Indeed, he's the big man, with 2.3 million Facebook fans, 3.1 million Twitter followers and worldwide sales approaching a hundred million copies.

I think back to the recent Watershed event, and I laugh out loud. All those people in love with him, transfixed by his every word and giving him a standing ovation for reading out a passage that we now know is largely the work of another man, with Hugh's customary icing of gloss and sparkle on top. Yes, I was all starry-eyed like that audience once upon a time – I loved Hugh and his writing too, and he couldn't do anything wrong in my eyes. Every hair on his head and every beautifully wrought passage on the page were treasures to me back then. But now I see his feet of clay, I see the joins in his novels and the ugly clockwork behind the façade, making everything tick. He never really was all that special – it was all an illusion, smoke and mirrors, and now the mirrors are well and truly shattered!

It's Thursday afternoon and I'm trying to get on with some of *The Facebook Murders*, but progress is slowing, grinding to a standstill because my mind is elsewhere. Robin will be turning up at around half five or six, and I'm locked in the old syndrome of waiting for the grate of his key in the lock and whatever comes next. I actually haven't seen him in the flesh since he came around and made the announcement about the new salon, and that was weeks and weeks ago. Since then I've generated so much bile and anger regarding his behaviour, and I really don't know how it's going to play out. I only hope that he will get on with his packing and leave the interpersonal stuff alone, but I have a portentously sickly feeling in the stomach indicating that won't be the case.

At five o'clock I give up attempting to write and make a cup of tea in advance of watching *Pointless* on TV. Enduring a boring round about football – a subject in which I have zero interest – it occurs to me for the first time that Robin will be taking the TV with him when the removers come, and the leather sofa where I'm sitting and most of the other furniture too. I'll be left perched on a wooden crate, watching the walls. Just as my spirits sink further, there it is – the grate in the lock – and Robin comes in.

'Hello…how are you?' he says all singsong.

'Fine…'

'You don't sound fine.'

Lowering the TV volume, I look him up and down and see he's put wavy kinks in his long black hair, and he's wearing ultra-tight skinny jeans and a sequined black bolero jacket. He's at the height of fashion as usual.

'How's it going with you?' I ask as he sits down and drops his bag on the floor.

'Gre-aat! We've got the equipment in place for the new salon and we're having it fitted, ready for the opening soon. And the flat upstairs is pretty much sorted too –'

'You'll be taking the telly, and the sofa too…?'

'Well they are mine, Nick. Make us a cup of tea, will you?'

Without question, I go and make us both a cup of tea, thinking that things aren't actually working out as bad as anticipated. But when I return, Robin has that familiar evil cheeky grin on his face.

'So, where are you moving to, then?'

'I'm still looking…'

'*What...!* You haven't found somewhere yet?' He tosses back his hair and makes a goofy face at the ceiling. 'Jesus, we've got to be out of here in two weeks. You'd be lucky now to find somewhere that'd be vacant in a fortnight. What have you been *doing* all this time?'

'There's plenty of flea pits that are vacant right now...I've seen them.'

'Yeah...one of those'd suit you, Nick.' Robin chuckles mischievously. 'I'll tell you what you've been doing. Writing your masterpiece, isn't it? What's it called – *The Facebook Wankoff* or something?'

'Stop it, Robin.'

'All this time when you needed to get yourself fixed up with a new place, you've been sitting at that computer lost in cloud cuckoo land!'

'I have looked for places, but there's nothing satisfactory in my price range.'

'Well get yourself a job and earn some money! You're thirty-eight – that's a bit young for retirement, isn't it?'

'Cut it out, Robin! You're here to pack, not get on my fucking case!'

'Well, I suppose you could always live with that drunken oaf Patrick again. Or try the Sally Army. Not that it's anything to do with me anymore.'

'Exactly. So shut the fuck up!'

Before Robin can make another retort, I get up sharply and go to the kitchen. Putting both hands on the work surface, I steady myself and take some slow breaths, trying to stave off the onrush of more extreme anger. What's the guy playing at? He's spent two months pussyfooting around me, so as not to rouse my temper in the environment of the pending breakup; now he comes over to pack his stuff, and he tries his absolute best to wind me up like he used to! And would you believe it, he's coming into the kitchen to start again!

'Nick, I'm only trying to give you some advice –'

'I don't want advice from you, okay? I wouldn't be in this mess if it weren't for you! If I hadn't met you – or at least hadn't fallen into the trap of living with you – I'd still be over in my nice little place in Clifton Wood, free from hassle.'

'Yeah, yeah, but wherever you live, you'll still need money for rent. How much of your inheritance is left, Nick? Dwindling, is it? Going on the dole soon, housing benefit and all that? Is that your plan?'

'You're enjoying rubbing it in, aren't you? It's alright for you, with your new lover and business partner, moving on to your lovely idyllic life together, holding hands upstairs in the bedroom and downstairs in the salon.'

'I'm moving on because I've got a career and I'm developing it. You should be doing the same.'

'Well, I've almost finished my novel, if you want to know. I haven't been idle, far from it.'

Robin gives me that big sardonic grin again. 'You talk as if this novel is going to get you someplace. Same old Nick. When are you going to face reality and stop blaming others and outside factors for your own shortcomings?'

'Look, you came here to pack your stuff. *So go and fucking get on with it!*'

'Okay. Are you going to make us something to eat? A salad would be nice – cheese, egg, whatever. See you later.' He sashays away, his bum gyrating from side to side.

After he's gone, I find myself gritting my teeth, clenching my fists and involuntarily shaking up and down like a pneumatic drill. I want to smash plates, or put my hands around Robin's scrawny neck, half strangle him and then bash his head against the corner of the food cupboard. But instead I go to the fridge and peer inside. There's a bit of lettuce left and some tomatoes and cucumber, just over the sell-by dates but still useable. I also have plenty of cheese and four eggs, so the master's wishes can be gratified. As I put the eggs on to hard boil, I shake my fist again in the direction of Robin's room, where I can hear him opening drawers and shifting stuff around.

Following a timeless ritual, I place the lettuce onto two plates and get out the chopping board and the big Sabatier chef knife to thinly slice the tomatoes and cucumber, just as we like. In a weird way it's like nothing has changed between us, with domestic rituals acting as a salve. Next I cut off a chunk of mature cheddar and grate it into a bowl, and when the eggs have had ten minutes, I put them in cold water in the sink to cool. I wash four tomatoes, position one on the board and commence to carve it wafer thin, so each slice is limp and translucent and barely holding together. Sensing movement to my left, I turn and Robin comes up to the food cupboard and stands there, peering at me.

'You know, I've been thinking about you and this writing lark...' He smiles as I give him a hard stare. 'You've wasted all of your adult life on this dream, this delusion of becoming a proper writer, and –'

'Robin! For God's sake shut-your-fucking-gob! *Go away and pack!*'

'No! You need to hear this. Maybe it'll be the last thing I'll ever say to you to buck your ideas up...'

I reach for another tomato and cut one slice, and another, speeding up, utterly unbelieving that he's continuing to carry on like this.

'Get a proper job, Nick. Do something positive in the real world, before it's too late. Lets face it, this writing thing is pie in the sky. If you were going to succeed, you'd have done it by now. All you'll ever amount to is one of those small press, horror-wanker types of wri –'

Robin stops before he can complete the word 'writer'. The knife blade is two-thirds embedded into his chest – about seven inches of cold hard carbon steel is inside him. Just like with the glassing incident, it all happened impossibly quickly, and with a curious absence of any kind of thought, rational or otherwise. I must have been a swordfighter in a previous life – it was a classic lunge-and-thrust move, and typically I used far more force than I realised. Robin is trying to speak, but all that comes out are *puh...puh...* sounds and saliva.

'Sorry mate,' I say, and can't think of what to add.

Did I just do that...? It's utterly incredible!

I pull out the knife and an alarming quantity of blood fans out from the wound into the fabric of Robin's pale linen shirt. He puts his hand there, watches the palm fill with blood and gives me a sickly look of hopelessness and despair, finally sneering at me, as if he's always known this might happen and it's no great surprise. The wound swells with blood, which streams out much more profusely now, dripping onto the lino. I must have hit a major artery or nicked the heart – I'm no medical student, but it doesn't look good. Suddenly Robin's legs buckle, and I throw aside the knife and grip him by the shoulders to ease his fall to the floor. Once there, he assumes the foetal position, his body jerking spasmodically every few seconds. The blood is spreading out and pooling beneath him now. I consider phoning an ambulance, but I don't think there's much point.

My God! Real murder is so different to fictional murder! It's not *Bang! Bang! You're dead!* and you get on with the next thing – no, it's completely unlike that. You know that fear you sometimes get that you're going to do something dangerous – like jump off a cliff if you're standing too near the edge – and you won't be able to stop yourself? Well that's it. And I did it this time – I wasn't able to stop myself. After the event, it all seems so surreal, like it hasn't really happened and it's all some sort of trick – a glitch in the fabric of reality. I turn around and look at the half-prepared meal – the lettuce on the plates and the sliced tomatoes on the chopping board – and it seems like I'm viewing a tableau from a distant century.

My heart is beating very fast and everything is speeding up very nastily. I go into the lounge and sit down on the sofa, trying to take shallow breaths to calm myself down. *The One Show* is on the TV at low volume, with Alex Jones talking to camera in her happy-go-lucky way. What am I supposed to do now? I should do something urgently, but I don't know what, and my inability to decide is making me even more turbulent. My brain is so sluggish, and I feel weak and trembling, barely able to move. I try to force myself to think, but my thoughts are covered in treacle and won't budge forward. *Treacle?* What a strange word that is…

To make things worse, that old creepy sensation of watching

myself doing things has come back, like I'm not properly in my body but at a slight remove. It applies to mental processes too – I'm watching myself trying to make decisions and failing in that regard. And it's very scary, like I'm incrementally losing my grip on everything. Fearing I might seize up or crack up altogether if I continue sitting, I rise and go to the kitchen, and there is Robin, confirming my worst fears that it's not all a dream. He's absolutely motionless, with black eyes open and staring into infinity – he could be a dead Christ in a painting by Caravaggio or El Greco. It all seems utterly unreal, but I know it is real and that's horrifying. But I mustn't give in to the horror or I'm fucked.

I pour myself a large glass of water from the filter jug and top it up with some ice from the fridge, carefully avoiding the blood spillage. What will I get for this when they catch me? Murder on top of previous for GBH? At least fifteen years recommended in a life sentence. If I'm lucky I could be out by the age of fifty-three. I wonder what it's like to be a fifty-three-year-old ex con? And I'm in this mess because of the thing they always warned me about – poor impulse control. I drink deeply and almost laugh. It's like an old joke that Tommy Cooper or Bob Monkhouse might have told: *What do you get for poor impulse control? About twenty years!*

I go to the bathroom and take a long piss; then I refill my glass in the kitchen and return to the lounge and try to achieve stillness. The panic is coming in waves, and I have to ride out each one and somehow not drown in its wake. Perhaps I could cut up Robin's body and put the bits in his still flat-packed cardboard removal cases? I could then take them out and dump them somewhere. But what about the kitchen floor and cleaning off eight pints of blood, which has now assumed the quality of bitumen? Not an easy task…

Out of the ether I hear a phone ping – a familiar sound from the recent past, which somehow sucks me back towards the real world. Robin has just received a text. I fish his phone out of his shoulder bag, and what do you know, it's from Kevin!

Hi love, hows it going with the nutter, ha ha. Give us a call or text when u want. Kev xx

I look through the thread – umpteen little exchanges of love and more detailed business interchanges, going back months and months and eventually years. Like a detective finally unearthing incontrovertible evidence, I find the conversations from around the time Robin went off me, and I see just how he switched his affections away. I was right, absolutely right, all along. And they call me 'the nutter'? Well, who can argue with that?

Suddenly things don't seem quite so bad. Robin came over here expressly to pack and allowed a window of tonight, all tomorrow daytime and maybe tomorrow night in addition for the task. Therefore no one will have any claim on him for around thirty-six hours, till Saturday morning when he's due to start work again. Indeed, no one will note his absence and press any alarm bells for quite a reasonable stretch of time. That is no one except Kevin…

Again I peruse the message thread, getting the measure of the diction they use and their terms of endearment. I'm a writer, and replicating Robin should be no problem for a man of my talents. *Hi babe*, I begin. How nauseating! It conjures up images of Kevin (or Oliver Hardy) in the nude! *Nutter is a bit restless but I can handle him. Whew! Loads of work to do packing all my gear. Will call or text later. Hugs & Kisses Robby xx*

After I've sent the text, I go to Robin's room and drag his duvet off the bed. In the kitchen, I cover him over, saying sorry once again and goodbye. He was an annoying cunt, but he didn't deserve this. No, someone else fucking deserved this! The sense of having taken a giant step towards solving my problems comes over me, but I still feel very whizzy and spaced out. Treading on the corners of the duvet to avoid getting sticky blood on my shoes, I go to the fridge and unearth a two-litre flagon of Old Rosie, three-quarters full. I pour myself a pint and sip slowly, for medicinal purposes. Then I go to the medical drawer in the bathroom and rifle through packages of vitamin pills, plasters and pain killers, seeking something important. Yes, here it is – the Valium I was prescribed for my anxiety after Mum's death. There's four tablets left, so I take one and sip some more cider, and in half an hour I feel I can function again.

In fact I can do more than function – in my relief I give birth to a marvellous idea that extends itself like the links of a chain, onwards and upwards to some magical place, like a really good idea for a novel that's composed of many parts but comes to you all of a piece. The first step of the plan is to look in Robin's bag, and yes, here it is – his little pink spiral-bound notebook. Without that, all bets are off. Next I have to return to the body, and using the duvet to kneel upon, I get into his trouser pocket and take his wallet, containing all his plastic and eighty pounds in cash. He won't be needing it.

Now I go out for a walk in the crisp night air, tracing the usual head-clearing route past terraces of tall, basement-equipped million-pound houses, along by the Gothic, tobacco-coloured edifices of Clifton College, and then around Bristol Zoo, where some exotic animal exudes a plaintive burp-like cry. Life goes on and I need to adjust to its altered rhythms. I know I can pull it off if I keep my head…

Soon I reach the Downs, where joggers are still trotting around the boundary between the streetlamps, and I wander onto the grass, seeking seclusion in the cool light mist. Now I get out my burner phone and make a call from here, well away from the flat, so there's no possibility that in future it can be traced to that location and linked to the murder. I need advice and assistance regarding the feasibility of what I've got in mind. Then, all being well, I'll need to spend several hours online, putting things in place. And tomorrow – that's going to be a big day. Oh, how I adore understatement!

21. The Elysian Fields

I wake up properly at five-thirty, having had around three hours of patchy sleep with the aid of the rest of the Old Rosie and two more Valium. Yesterday comes rushing in, battering my consciousness like a tidal wave of mercury, but now I must do what I must do. The lump under the duvet in the kitchen is truly a part of reality now, and I've learnt to steer my way around its contours. Still, I feel absolutely terrible, barely human, as I go to the bathroom and splash warm water in my face and try to get myself together.

Kevin texted again around eleven o'clock last night, perturbed that Robin hadn't yet rung him. I texted back to say that 'I' had got bogged down in the packing and now had a headache and was having an early night. We exchanged goodnight sweet nothings and agreed that 'Robin' would call him today. That means I'll have to keep the tosser at bay and smooth his feathers again – as if I haven't got enough to do! – but I mustn't let him suspect anything is awry. On the plus side, Kevin is a little scared of me and passive in nature. As 'Robin', I told him not to ring himself because 'the nutter' might get angry if he overhears the two of them talking, and I'm sure Kevin won't disobey. That's my ace in the hole.

Finding a notepad, I make a checklist of everything I want to take with me, and then unearth suitable receptacles and tackle the chore of packing. Pity Robin hadn't confined himself to that! After coffee and a very sparse breakfast – I still have virtually no appetite – I go online again to check the fruits of my labours last night, and then I backup everything onto a portable hard drive. Hurrying now, I dismantle the tower with a screwdriver set and extract the computer hard drive – don't want any fucker analysing that! The cops might have found Jago's novel, *Social Media Avenger*, and broadcast its contents to the world, but I'm staying in control of *The Facebook Murders*.

Before I depart, I take a last forlorn look at the walls of shelves in my room, housing my thousands of beloved books and DVDs, all piled up to the ceiling – that was the thing I was most concerned about when looking for a new flat: adequate space for them. Goodbye, my children!

In Bristol centre, I park on a meter, allowing myself two hours to complete my various tasks. These involve visits to a number of banks and building societies in order to settle my affairs, another to Birds, the traditional tobacconists in nearby Baldwin Street – lovely sweet aroma inside – and finally I pop into Debenhams and purchase an equally traditional down-brim trilby hat with teardrop crown, which I will swop with my usual leather hat when the time is right. I look at my watch and see I've got time for a large coffee in Costas, to keep me going, and I even manage to eat a sweet Danish pastry to top up my calories.

It's after midday when I come off the M5 at Gloucester and take the A417, heading up Crickley Hill towards Burford. I'm starting to feel weird in the head again, a kind of spiralling anxious urgency, but I try to play it down. Kevin texted and I had to pull in at a service station to reply, which has lost me a valuable ten or fifteen minutes. He's worried that so much time has passed without Robin and himself speaking, and his clinginess has come out now and he really wants a heart-to-heart. I told him 'I' really understood and not to get flustered, and we'd definitely talk later in the day, but I really needed to get on, and my battery was low anyway, so I had to put the phone on charge. Lets hope that buys me a few more hours. Now I'm worrying that I won't get to the spot in time, and I put my foot down, thinking I should actually have skipped the coffee in Bristol.

All the while I've been telling myself that it's no big deal going back to Dillisbury, almost a side issue, as it's on the way to my principal destination anyway. But of course it is a big deal – the biggest deal going! It's not my intention to visit Dillisbury itself, or head to Pokinghorn Manor. After studying the Explorer map in bed last night, I picked out a small roadway or track that runs from the lower Dillisbury road to the bottom part of Canning Wood. My intention is to park at the junction, which will leave me a walk of just over a mile to get to the track within the wood that Hugh used on his circular walk on the day I stalked him. It is actually the remotest part of the route, almost the furthest point from Pokinghorn Manor, which makes it ideal for an encounter. I only hope I can get there in time!

When I find the roadway, I consider driving part way up, but it looks too rocky and muddy for an on-road vehicle, and I might get stuck and not be able to turn around. So I position the car unobtrusively on a verge, then I put on my hiking boots and my new trilby hat, and I get the rucksack out of the boot. Ready, I head off into the country again, and it's like I'm doing any old regular walk. The day is overcast and dull, with tall grey fluffy cumulus dominating the sky, but rain isn't forecast. Trying to be upbeat, I take in the network of sheep-dotted fields beyond the iron gates and dry-stone walls, and I breathe in the heady fresh air. Entering tree cover, I pass a derelict barn which partially houses an old bullnose lorry, completely rusted out, resting on tireless wheel rims and surrounded by assorted domestic junk. I smile, pretending I'm a sightseer.

But despite all this diversionary activity, I'm still extremely nervous and that sensation of 'watching myself' has returned. I haven't been feeling like 'me' at all, ever since Robin got knifed, and I'm having to cope with these bouts of depersonalisation and derealisation, if they're not two sides of the same coin, don't ask me. Yes, clearly I'm not myself, but I can function and that's the important thing. Being in the woods again, leaving behind the trappings of civilisation, is actually increasing the sense of unreality, which somehow registers as a positive. Actually things are turning a bit trippy, reminding me of the effects of the strong joints I had with Max on my last visit here.

Descending into Canning Wood, everything seems bright, unnaturally bright, and the whole environment is pulsing slightly in synch with my galloping heart. The autumn trees look like they've been taken into a salon and given copper, gold and caramel highlights...*Oh God, did I really stab Robin...?* Fallen leaves at my feet appear organised in their randomness, their curling edges like lathe-turned slivers of precious metals. *Yesterday I did the wrong murder, and today I'm doing the right murder…* Simple really…

Yes, the sheep-and-lamb logic seems unassailable, I think as I reach the chosen spot where Hugh should come along. The time is just after two o'clock, and I realise that if he started early I might have missed him. Of course he may not fancy a walk today, or he may have taken a different route, or he may be staying in working, or he may be in London or somewhere else. The other possibilities are numerous and the odds are stacked against me. Moreover, I only have a window of an hour at most, and then I'll have to get going otherwise I'll be in real trouble. Ultimately it all comes down to that random factor – chance or fate – as Tommy Leatherhead said. And at this late stage, I may as well hang for a famous writer as a gay hairdresser.

I stand off the track, behind the wide trunk of a mature oak and drop the rucksack. Unfastening the top, I draw Pippa's sawn-off Beretta, slip back the ornately decorated top lever and break it open. Then I pop in two of the heavy-load BB hunting cartridges, their shiny brassy ends flashing as I close the weapon. Feeling its weight, I consider it's more like a flintlock pirate pistol than ever today.

If and when I fire it, the shots may well be heard, but shotgun blasts in pheasant country in season are an ordinary occurrence. Also it could be down to a gamekeeper or farmer shooting vermin – foxes, weasels and the like. Moreover it's unlikely that anyone else will pass this way, or so I hope. It's off the marked rights of way, too far out for short-distance dog walkers and it's not en route to anywhere. And luckily I can hear no evidence of any organised shoots in progress. When Hugh and I did the walk the last time, we didn't pass another single person. Partially reassured that my intentions are sound, I straighten the brim of my trilby and squeeze the orange plugs into my ears.

Waiting for something to happen is so sick-making. I keep looking at my watch, oscillating between stony disappointment and queasy relief that so far nothing has taken place. By two-thirty I start to feel a little foolish that I ever thought this was a plan, and I look

208

forward to abandoning my post in another half hour. Then I see something, a quick flash of movement, and when I peer out further I discern the shape of a figure walking behind the foliage around the bend ahead. Instantaneously my heart beats so fast it's like my whole body is beating, and when the figure emerges, thirty feet away, I recognise Hugh, wearing the same outfit of Barbour jacket and brown cords as before. Everything starts to feel shuddery and time spreads out.

'THIS IS IT!' says a manic voice in my head, and when Hugh is about ten feet away, I jump out in front of him and brandish the gun in both hands, feeling a stampede of hooves gather in my stomach.

He stops dead in his tracks, his intensely blue eyes going wide, and he does a double take on the sawn-off barrels, but he gives the impression of remaining in control. 'You!' he shouts like he's referring to the lowest form of animal life. 'I saw you at the Watershed in the audience – and it was you following me around here the other week, wasn't it? Dammit! I knew something was up! Now put down that gun, please, and lets be sensible and talk this through.'

As Hugh is speaking, I'm thinking that I've got to act spontaneously otherwise he'll somehow gain the upper hand – and the reason I can hear him so well is my right earplug has fallen out – and if I don't follow through quickly I'll be serving life for Robin whilst he gets off scot-free again – I'm already past the point of no return! Those thoughts come to me in heavy staccato bursts, like railway carriages cannoning into the buffers of my brain, one after the other. *Clang! Clang! Clang!* I pull the trigger.

'Thou shalt not steal, Hugh. It's one of the Ten Commandments, but I forget which.'

My right ear, my head and indeed the whole wood is ringing with the blast, and I barely hear my own words. Vignetted by wisps of gun smoke, Hugh clutches his middle section and staggers and gives a big unearthly groan. Then he pulls open his jacket to reveal a nasty lurid crimson mess on his shirt, with some pepper marks circling, positioned a bit to my right of the centre of his stomach. Yes, this gun always fires to the right. Buckling now, he looks up at me, groans more extendedly and growls horribly.

'*Bastard!*' he says, putting all his energy into the expletive.

'No, no. Wrong line, Hugh. You're supposed to say: *God save the British Empire!*'

Hugh staggers some more and then sits down on the grass verge, bending over and grimacing. 'What are you talking about...?' he says, almost in a whisper. He sounds genuinely interested, as though he might use the information in his next novel.

'It's from *The Shooting Party* – the film your murder is based upon – Gordon Jackson gets shot by Edward Fox in the woods, don't you remember? I'm Lord Gilbert Hartlip, the Fox character, which is why I'm wearing this trilby hat.'

Hugh is staring up at me pityingly. 'You're mad...' he says in a weak but distantly satisfied voice, as if that conclusion makes the whole thing not so bad, nobody's fault really, neither mine nor his, but an act of God or nature.

'No, I'm not mad, Hugh, I'm a novelist. And we're in a novel – *The Facebook Murders*. You've done your version, now we're doing mine.'

I get out the packet of Tor cigarettes that I bought in Birds earlier and light one up. 'Here...have your last smoke.' I place it between Hugh's lips. 'It's damn fine tobacco, Turkish I shouldn't wonder...'

Hugh's lips quiver as I try to secure the cigarette in place, then he lets out another almighty groan and bellows several times like a farmyard animal. I notice the blood has spread, now soaking his entire midriff. As I catch the cigarette and stub it out, he looks at me with sleepy eyes. 'Have you got a mobile? You need to dial 999.'

'What – so you can live and I can go to jail? That doesn't seem right.'

Suddenly his eyes come alive with anger, and he tries to move against me, but the pain makes him wince and he falls back.

'Listen...Ni...N...N...' Hugh hiccups and a gob of thick blood ejects from the corner of his mouth and dribbles down his chin onto his shirt collar.

'The name's Jago – Jago Farrar!'

'What...?' His voice is now a barely audible whisper.

'You could have been my love, yet you chose to be my nemesis instead.'

Hugh looks at me with urgent quizzicality and tries to speak, but more blood gushes out of his mouth instead and I back off, fearing I may be sprayed.

A glance at my watch tells me time is getting short. I retrieve the orange earplug from the ground, rub it on my shirt to clean it, and stuff it properly into my right ear.

'You broke my heart,' I tell Hugh, 'and now I'm going to break yours.'

It still feels like it's not really me doing it, but then it isn't me... silly...it's someone else!

'Goodnight sweet prince...'

I raise the gun and holding it tight, I empty the second barrel into his chest from a distance of about fifteen inches, and then back away quickly in case of blood spray. His body jackknifes like a weightless oversized rag doll, and his eyes spin like billiard balls, going all skew-whiff. *Wow, I did it!* I think to myself, and instantaneously I'm flooded with a strange feeling, and I know exactly what it is. Closure. It was a tough thing to do, very tough, but I had the balls and the guts to carry it out, and now I feel proud of myself. He'd never have loved me back and never have admitted fault over using my letters, so this was the only way. Hugh had left me no choice.

Skipping through the woods back the way I came, conscious of the need to hurry as much as possible, the next part of that *Hamlet* quote comes to mind: *And flights of angels sing thee to thy rest!* I realise that Hugh attempted to ink in this scenario, as insurance against it happening in real life, and he failed! At the climax of *The Elysian Fields*, Willoughby confronts his final prophesy – that he will be murdered by a psychotic assassin, who thinks his death is necessary in order to save the world. Willoughby accepts that he cannot alter events in a pre-ordained universe, and after he's gunned down, the asteroid narrowly misses the Earth, so whichever way you look at it, the logic of 'crucifixion' obtains – Willoughby died so all of us can live – and his deification is inevitable.

Now I think of Hugh himself sailing out of his body and floating through the treetops on his own journey to the Elysian Fields, and I wonder if his angry spirit is tracking me, like in the movie *Ghost*. Maybe I am completely mad, I don't know, but whatever I can still function, and that's the important thing. My sense of derealisation is now so strong, it hardly matters what's real and what isn't anymore. The fifth and final Facebook murder is complete, and with Robin added to the tally that makes me a six-time killer – and I reflect once again that murder, like anything else, really does get easier with practice. I feel so high my head is in the stratosphere, and I can hardly sense my feet contacting the ground, but my reason somehow remains intact.

I've been lucky up till now, and I must consolidate on that good fortune. Remembering it from coming down, I find a copse of very dense trees and bushes, almost impenetrable. Taking the shotgun by the barrels, I lob it high into the treetops where it cartwheels over before dropping down somewhere in the middle. No one is going to find that in a hurry. I do the same thing with the remainder of the cartridges in their boxes, leaving myself clean in the event of a search. As an afterthought, I also stuff the Explorer map down between the foot of a gatepost and a wall. I won't be needing it and it links me to the general area.

But I retain the felt trilby hat, as it now has talismanic significance, and even Sherlock Holmes couldn't connect it to the murder scene by way of *The Shooting Party*! Yes, great film. I got the idea whilst stoned with Max, following my movie reverie and seeing the line of beaters earlier in the day. It's not a genre crime or horror piece, but it's still a marvellously telling movie about gun violence and its implications. The final long shot – where the party crosses the field and we get the roll call of those soon to be killed in the First World War – makes for a most memorable ending.

Getting back to the car without seeing another single soul, I feel

I'm home free, but then Robin's phone rings and the name 'Kevin' flashes up on the screen. I let it go to voicemail and then play the message back. Actually Robin received several other calls this morning and I handled them this way, all turning out to be hair-dressing enquiries. I listen to Kevin's anxious entreaties, delivered in his high reedy camp voice, sounding as if he's about fourteen years old. He can't believe Robin hasn't taken an opportunity to call him, and now with the phone going to voicemail he's convinced something is wrong.

Sorry Babe! I text back. *Left phone in the loo and still busy in the bedroom with the packing, really snowed under! Anyhow nick wants to have a big important conference about the future now, so tied up with that. Will ring soon, promise. Hugs & Kisses Robby xx*

I send the text, wondering what it will take for Kevin to go around to the flat, ring the bell, receive no answer and call the police. How long will the police leave it before breaking down the door? I try not to dwell on this as I zoom off down the road, leaving the outstanding natural beauty of the Cotswolds behind. My mood lifts as I hear no sirens, encounter no roadblocks and no armed police jumping out and pointing weapons at me, shouting: 'PUT YOUR HANDS WHERE I CAN SEE THEM!'

Heading east, I reach the busy town of Bicester and sit in a slow-moving queue, with rush hour traffic beginning to build. Cars coming from the big shopping village are adding to the congestion, and I feel exasperated at all the time I'm losing. Once I'm clear of the bottleneck, I go as fast as I can along the A41 to Aylesbury, then to Leighton Buzzard and finally Luton, following signs to the airport. I remember the estate agent's bumf for Pokinghorn Manor, saying it's well positioned for Luton Airport. Yes, very handy indeed!

I chose meet-and-greet parking for speed, and reaching the priority zone, I find I'm a bit tight for time but okay. At the check-in desk I hand over my documents and passport, and now comes the big test. It's doubtless too soon for a hue and cry to have developed for Nick Chatterton, but my flight to Malaga is nearly three hours, so by the time I arrive the Spanish authorities could well have been alerted and I'd be fucked. So I swapped identity once again. Holding the passport, the demure, heavily-made-up operative gives it a quick glance, scans it, and, smiling, she hands it back to me. I put my two big suitcases onto the conveyor belt and accept an excess baggage charge.

Queuing to get through security into departures, I again reflect that no one will be checking for Robin leaving the country, and to all intents and purposes I'm him. I may be a bit taller and brawnier than he is, but from a headshot photo we could almost be twins. We both have long black hair – a bit '70s – dark brown eyes and our face shapes are similar. Moreover, Robin's passport photo is eight years old and he had a short beard back then, so some latitude in appearance is acceptable. I've used his passport, I'm using his credit and switch cards and I also used his car, so the reg number and everything checks out. Today I am Robin as well as Jago Farrar! And as I'm still wearing the trilby hat, I also feel in character as Edward Fox in *The Shooting Party* – where does it end?

Sitting at the departure gate, waiting to board, I get a text from Kevin and my heart momentarily thrums. He's peeved that he still hasn't had a call, and he hopes Robin's having a good conference with 'nutter nick', and he's heading for the Tavern for a drink with friends. He's got the hump – excellent news! I look through the plate glass windows at the expanse of airfield, with its big skies now clear of clouds and lights twinkling in the consolidating dusk. Then I check for breaking news stories on Robin's phone. Nothing. I'm going to make it – I'm ready to cross the threshold and be reborn.

My new life stretches out before me like the yellow brick road at Dorothy's feet in *The Wizard of Oz*. Last night on the Downs I phoned Tommy Leatherhead, who now lives in Marbella and is a big cheese in the Costa del Crime scene. He's into all kinds of stuff – timeshare scams, money laundering, distributing ecstasy through the network of clubs in which he's a shareholder, and running cannabis and even cocaine from Morocco, just across the water. Tommy claims to be a multi-millionaire, and I don't doubt him. He's married with kids, but still 'goes both ways' when the fancy takes.

When I outlined my 'spot of bother', he said, 'No problemo, mate,' and told me to get my ass to Malaga Airport, where he'd meet me. He also owns many holiday properties, and at this time of the year I can have my pick of villas in which to hide out. I will get a new identity, and if I have money – which indeed I do – then I'll be sorted.

Yesterday, using Robin's cards and pink spiral-bound notebook, which contains all his pin numbers and passwords, I went through his bank accounts online and moved the funds to several current accounts, from which I withdrew cash this morning, along with my own savings – what's left of them. Sometimes acting as myself and sometimes posing as Robin, I asked for the maximum each bank would let me have, saying I needed it either for a car purchase or a long holiday. In this way, I accrued thirty-four thousand pounds, which I have about my person – in fresh fifty-pound notes and even fresher five-hundred Euro ones. But that's only around half of Robin's total nest egg, and the remainder I transferred internationally to some special accounts of Tommy's, doing it in segments so as not to raise red flags. I trust Tommy completely to pay me back. As for Robin, he had all that dough, more than I ever knew about, and he was so stingy all the time. Fuck him!

As I shuffle along the springy boarding bridge with my fellow passengers, I make uneasy eye contact with a bald, middle-aged man with a small moustache, and I realise it's Leopard, off duty and without his hat and coat, but still a potential menace. My heart starts to flutter again, and I try to stop being stupid and pull myself together. *He can't touch you – you're in the clear mate!* Looking through the bridge windows at the fuselage of our Easyjet plane, with its orange-and-white livery, I note that the vivid orange is exactly the same colour as that of my earplugs, and I get a nasty flash of Hugh lying dead with two bloody holes in his torso. Yet the cabin crew smile soothingly at me as I board and say their welcomes.

I might have done some bad things, but I was pushed into it, and it's not entirely my fault – and I'm not about to beat myself up about it, not right now. Because this is 'me' time, and I'm going to make the most of it and take my chance – my only chance – to be the person I always should have been. I identify my seat, a portside window one, and I have to ask two people to move so I can plant myself there. Once I'm buckled up, I have my last Valium, washed down with overpriced mineral water from the departure lounge. The plane gets away in good time, taxiing into position, and before I'm ready the thrust of takeoff is pushing me back into my seat, and the lights of Luton reveal themselves below. As we ascend and I yawn to make my ears pop, the whole dazzling encrustation of illuminated London manifests, and I start to get that old familiar, comforting dream feeling and relax a little.

Spontaneously I burst out laughing, and I have to contain myself as the passengers next to me give awkward looks. I'm thinking of Jago, poor old Jago, still stuck in that shopping mall on the M1 and doomed to wander around there forever, as though in some *Dawn of the Dead* limbo or netherworld – because I've taken his place and done his job for him! Have I really 'become' him? Considering this, I see it really doesn't matter who I am, whether I'm Nick Chatterton, Robin Frobisher, Edward Fox, Jago Farrar, Miles Hunniford, Damien Smithson, Archibald Wetherell, Donald Ponsonby, Aaron Slingsby or Ezekiel Fazackerley, and I bet there's someone above me and someone above him too, and so on to infinity in the outward direction as well. Essentially reality is what you want it to be.

Then in an amazing eruption of insight, which almost has me levitating from out of my seat, I see what's actually happened. My novel has flipped and turned into reality, like the two sides of a Möbius strip essentially being one! Yes, an unbelievable, unguessable twist has taken place! *The Facebook Murders* will no longer be about Jago, the murdering novelist, it will be about me *writing* about Jago, the murdering novelist! Yes, I think he's got it! The whole thing will be great, absolutely marvellous once I've changed all the names and properly fictionalised all the details – naturally I have the work in progress on that portable hard drive in my hand luggage.